To Brenda

Believe In Me

A TEEN MOM'S STORY

*So good to meet you —
can't wait to hear
what you think!*

JUDITH DICKERMAN-NELSON

Judith Dick Nel

Jefferson Park Press
Charlottesville, VA

Cover and Interior Design: Lisa Wayand
Typeface: Adobe Garamond Pro, Amethyst Script
Printer and Binder: RR Donnelley, Harrisonburg, VA

Dickerman-Nelson, Judith.
Believe in Me: A Teen Mom's Story / Judith Dickerman-Nelson.
ISBN-13:978-0-9849921-0-2
ISBN-10:0984992103

This is a work of fiction. Names, characters, places, and incidents are
either the product of the author's imagination or are used fictitiously,
and any resemblance to actual persons, living or dead, business
establishments, events, or locales is entirely coincidental.

Jefferson Park Press
Hilary Holladay, Editor and Publisher
2611 Jefferson Park Avenue
Charlottesville, VA 22903
hwholladay@gmail.com

With love and gratitude to my sons Matthew and Timothy and my husband William

Believe In Me

A TEEN MOM'S STORY

Things You Should Know

My mother abandoned me in 1963 when I was three months old. She didn't give me up at the hospital when I was born. She waited, giving herself some time. For ninety days she left me in foster care, and I like to believe she came to see me everyday, thinking she might take me back, that she wanted to find a way to keep me. Sometimes, I imagine her taking a bus to a triple-decker house downtown crowded with children. The foster mother lets her in, and my mother holds me, rocks me to stop my tears.

In my mind, I see how she turned away that last time, walking down the street in late January, cold wind lashing her face. She wipes away tears and stuffs her hands into her coat pockets, trying to forget, as if she could turn her heart into a cold, hard stone.

She gave me up through Catholic Charities in Boston, Massachusetts, and adoptions were closed then—there were no letters left in a file to give to a daughter when she grew up, no detailed description of why her parents gave her away like an unwanted present. The agency gave some information to new adoptive parents, and the story I heard was that my birthmother was Catholic, twenty and unmarried, and that my birthfather was the son of a Protestant minister. Their families probably hated that they were dating, and though I don't know the full story, I bet her parents made her leave. Then, when I was three months old, my young mother just turned and walked away, her arms empty.

I grew up in Greenfield, Massachusetts, in a quiet neighborhood. My parents reared my brother and me as Catholics, and our mom didn't work until we were older. Instead, she watched the kids, cooked the meals, cleaned the house, and did the laundry. I remember how she used to iron in the TV room at night while she watched the news, after she and my father had finished washing the dinner dishes. At bedtime she put me in warm pajamas, tucked me into bed, kissed me goodnight, and wished me a happy face in the morning. It was her bedtime blessing every night, a wish for bright days.

Growing up, I knew I was adopted because my parents read the book *The Chosen Baby* by Valentina P. Wasson to me. The cover was green, the book's spine tattered and worn from use. I loved this story of a man and woman who wanted children of their own but had to be patient and wait through the long process. When the lady from the adoption agency called with the amazing news that they could come to see the new baby, the parents in the story were excited and rushed to the office. The woman at the agency assured them that if the baby weren't just right for them, the agency would keep looking for another baby. I guess those parents could walk away too. It's a place in the story that makes me uneasy—even these parents who want a baby might turn and leave. Instead, they always picked the baby up and said, "This is our chosen baby."

So I always thought being adopted made me special. That is, until one day at elementary school when we got this assignment to create a family tree. I raised my hand and asked the teacher if it mattered that I was adopted. Mrs. Marshall told me to go ahead with the assignment and to use my parents' relatives. It made perfect sense to me—my family was the only family I knew.

But later at recess a boy named Bobby pointed his finger at me and shouted, "Judith's adopted, Judith's adopted!" He got his friends to come over, and they stood around laughing.

"Your mother didn't want you," someone said, and I felt like I'd been slapped in the face.

My mother loves me, I thought. But I was thinking of my adoptive mother, the only mother I knew. Somehow, I had forgotten there was some other woman who for one reason or another *hadn't* wanted me.

I felt small with them standing around taunting me. But I was angry and I screamed at Bobby to shut up. Mrs. Marshall, my third grade teacher, heard the commotion and blew her whistle.

"What's going on here?" she asked. Through my sniffles and tears I told her what had happened. Gathering the class together with me at her side, Mrs. Marshall explained what adoption meant and told how my parents got to choose me while other parents had to take what they got for babies. She told everyone to go back into the classroom. With her arm still draped over my shoulder, she leaned over and whispered in my ear, "You're special, dear. Don't you ever forget it."

8

I wanted to believe her. But at that point I wasn't sure what was true. If my birth mother had just given me away, she certainly didn't think I was special. For the first time in my life, being adopted felt like a strange mark that identified me as something less than, something without value.

Years later, when I was sixteen and pregnant, my mother told me she had been pregnant once. She and my dad were thrilled. But she had a miscarriage early on. We were smoking cigarettes together in the kitchen and drinking tea. With a baby growing inside me, it was hard to comprehend what that loss must have been like for her.

She became quiet. I thought about asking if my father held her when she lost the baby, if he was there that day. But I was afraid to ask. It was the first time she had even told me about her miscarriage. I imagined her bleeding into the toilet, her pregnancy ending in the bathroom.

I felt sad for my mother, but secretly there was a part of me that was glad. If she had brought that pregnancy to term, she and my father would have had no need to adopt me or my brother, who was four years older than me. And where would that have left us?

My baby's father came from a Catholic family too. But their family was bigger than ours with three boys and two girls. When I met Kevin in high school, his older brother was already married with a house of his own, and his younger brother attended Saint Joseph's Academy in my town, the same all-boys' Catholic school Kevin went to. His older sister lived in an apartment just outside Springfield, and his other sister, the youngest child, was only six and had just started school, the age when little girls made their First Communion.

In many ways my family was like his. My brother and I were baptized into the Catholic faith as babies, just as each child in the O'Brien family was. Later we made our first confession and then our First Communion. Every sacrament was a gift from God to help us live our lives in closer unity to Him. Our families helped us on our faith journey, and they took their role as Catholic parents seriously.

I made my First Communion at St. Agnes. Girls and boys lined up at the back of the church. The girls wore pretty white dresses and veils, like little brides, and the boys wore suits. We walked down the aisle with our hands pressed together in front of our chests, in prayer. We sat in the front pews, boys on one side and girls on the other.

We had been going to religious classes where we learned about the Eucharist. Jesus had died for our sins and the small white Host was His body, the wine His blood. We learned that God changed the bread and wine into the body of Christ and that the priest participated in this miracle, as if together God and the priest were special magicians. It was a lot to take in as a small child. But I understood that Jesus loved us all and so did the Father. They were always with us—Father, Son, and Holy Spirit. But Communion was special, a way for us to take Jesus into our own bodies.

We came before the priest one by one, and he held out the Host to each of us and said, "The body of Christ." We said "Amen," stuck out our tongues and received Communion for the first time. The dry Host sat on my tongue, and I was careful not to chew, letting it melt slowly instead. In this intimate act, I was a child of God, fully loved and accepted.

Outside on the church lawn family members gathered after the Mass. My parents snapped a picture of me with my friend Donna. We stood on the grass with our knee-high white socks and our pretty dresses and veils. With our hands at our sides, we posed, and the picture holds us in time, two first graders, both of us with red hair, smiling for the camera.

I didn't go to Catholic elementary school, since Barrows public school was right in our neighborhood. Each school day, my mother kissed my brother Paul and me goodbye and watched as we went up the street past the ranch houses and neat little capes. But when it came time for high school, I went to St. Anne's in Montague City, Massachusetts. It was a small Catholic high school for girls, and until I got my license my mother or someone else had to drive me to school.

Kevin's school, St. Joseph's, was in my hometown, but he came from Vermont, right over the state line. Until Kevin was old enough to drive, someone from his family took him back and forth too.

At St. Anne's, I tried out for the cheering team and made it, but I couldn't bring myself to cheer for girls' sports teams and quit after a few practices. I think the nuns and teachers always held that against me. But I loved cheering, so when St. Joseph's held tryouts, I went. I had been cheering many years for the Pop Warner football games, but I was still nervous about the tryout. When I made the team, I didn't know I would soon meet Kevin and my life would change forever.

Kevin played basketball and football for St. Joseph's, and I met him when he was on the junior varsity basketball team. He was a junior in high school and I was a sophomore. I was dating someone else from his school, and he was just an acquaintance. We rode on the same bus to basketball games, the cheerleaders in front and the boys in the back. We didn't have much time to get to know each other, then. But in his senior year, we used to bump into each other a lot at parties after games, and we started talking. Sometimes he'd ask me for advice about one of the cheerleaders he liked. We became good friends.

One fall day, a group of us cheerleaders met up at St. Joseph's with the football players we hung out with. The air was crisp, the October afternoon cool. Kevin was there, and we all gathered out on the football field. At games, the cheerleaders stood on the track in front of the bleachers while the guys played out on the field with its white lines marking out the yards. But that day, someone had a football, and we formed teams, with girls playing alongside the boys. Running around, we got warm and took off our jackets. It wasn't a serious game, and no one was tackling hard, but if you caught the ball, one of the guys from the other team would chase you, take you down.

On one side of the field, trees bordered the track, and when the sun came out from behind a cloud, it was as if God had struck a match and touched it to the treetops—they flamed yellow, orange, and red. Between plays, I glanced up at the sky and the trees and thought how beautiful everything was.

After a while we tired of our football game and decided to make a human pyramid. The largest guys got down on their hands and knees, close together. Kevin and his friend Trevor were on the bottom row because they both had strong, broad shoulders. The next level had girls and guys on top of them, and then another level after that. Finally, I was supposed to crawl up to the top, since I was the smallest and most experienced at climbing on top of other cheerleaders' shoulders. Just as I reached the top and was about to put my arms up in the air in a triumphant "ta da!" our pyramid collapsed. Laughing, we all fell down in a tangle of arms and legs.

I was still dating my boyfriend David then, but it seemed like we were always fighting. I longed for some easy laughter, and that day playing with Kevin and the others made me want that even more. I saw other boyfriends and girlfriends having fun, and they weren't jealous and possessive. I think that was the first day I looked at Kevin and found him attractive. He was six feet tall, lean and muscular from all of the sports he played, and he had big blue eyes that sparkled when he smiled. That day his light brown hair still had some summer-blond streaks.

I had only a twinge of attraction, though, because I knew I was taken, and he liked a fellow cheerleader, though she didn't seem to like him. We were just friends, but over the course of the year our friendship would grow until our conversations became easy and light.

It wasn't until spring, when the cherry tree blossomed in my backyard, that Kevin and I started dating. Prom season—the time of long gowns and tuxes, flowers and fancy dinners—that was when our friendship blossomed into a love affair. My first date with him was his senior prom. Then there was my junior prom. By the time his high school graduation rolled around, we were planning to spend the rest of our lives together.

Our plans didn't seem farfetched to me, and I'm glad I saved all of the letters he wrote, kept all the prom pictures, wrote in a daily diary, and kept a journal containing my poems and other reflections. They've helped me make sense of everything that happened beginning on that beautiful Saturday afternoon when Kevin and I were part of a human pyramid rising up and then collapsing in the crisp fall air. I've always loved writing, keeping track of events and how I feel. Even before Kevin, I wrote poetry—pages of verses that brought me comfort and a sense of peace. All of these things have helped me look back on my life, to search my past for clarity and truth. When I page through my diaries and poems, details come back to me. It is as if I'm holding kernels of understanding in my hands.

I guess I needed to look at that year to try and figure things out. Sometimes I think to myself *if only I did this, or if only I said that*. But you can fill a lifetime with regrets if you get stuck in 'if onlys.'

Looking closely at the pictures of Kevin and me, I marvel over the difference that lighting can make. In the nighttime photos, the camera's flash creates stark contrasts, and we look sharp-edged, a little stunned. In the bright light of day, we are brave and full of hope. At dusk, our faces are muted and mysterious, shadowed in the falling light.

In the end, that's what we're left with—all those variations of light, all those versions of ourselves. Yet we all want a chance to shake off the shadows and begin our next day bursting with hope and possibility. I know that's how it was for Kevin and for me. But I'm getting ahead of myself.

Our First Time

I'd known Kevin for a couple of years before we began dating. I started cheering for his school during my sophomore year, and we met at parties where we sipped beers and talked about the football game they'd lost that day or the basketball game they'd won—it depended on the season. Kevin played both sports, and I cheered, and we talked and we drank.

We became friends, and then I became his confidante, someone he trusted when he wanted to ask for advice about one of the cheerleaders he liked. That's how we started double dating. He'd been asking me about Lynn, who was on the squad, and I said I'd see what I could find out.

That winter, I went on five ski trips with Kevin. Lynn and my boyfriend David were there, too, of course, but it was one of the reasons Kevin and I got so serious so fast. We were already close.

After Kevin got his senior picture taken, he gave me one to keep in my wallet. On the back he'd written, "I don't know how to say what I want to say, so I'll just say thanks. Kevin."

I felt warm inside when I read his words, and he stood in front of me looking awkward, shuffling from one foot to the other. I stood on my tiptoes to kiss him on the cheek, and I swear he blushed.

When he smiled, it was like his whole face grinned, and his dimples deepened, and though I'd known him for quie a while now, it felt different that day standing with him in front of his school.

He asked me to his senior prom when he heard that David and I were breaking up, and I said yes. At first it seemed weird to go to a prom with a friend. But it turned out nice. It wasn't like I needed to learn how to laugh with him or feel comfortable in his presence—we were way beyond that.

We could sit in his car for hours, listening to Bruce Springsteen's *Born to Run* or *Darkness on the Edge of Town*, and when the music stopped we didn't need to fill the empty lull with conversation. We held hands, and sometimes it was like we knew what the other one was thinking without saying anything, as if we could reach into each other's souls and feel the meaning there.

On the night of his senior prom, we went to a post-prom party and then went parking afterwards. We didn't have sex, but when we kissed it felt like I could feel his heart beating, or mine, or both of ours beating together. It was powerful.

After that, we saw each other almost every day after school, and we talked on the phone every night. We couldn't get enough of each other's company, and already he was telling me that he loved me. I loved him too.

One Saturday evening, we played miniature golf. The second hole had a wooden windmill that was taller than me, and the blades went round and round blocking the space you were supposed to hit the ball through. When I tried, my ball bounced back and I had to do it again. Kevin and I laughed each time the yellow ball rolled back.

When it was his turn, his golf ball went right through the middle space, and he almost got a hole in one! He was much better than me, but we still had fun. We turned our clubs in at the little shack and sat on a bench. We held hands and watched the sky turn different colors as the sun set. It was like the night was putting on a show just for us—the clouds turned lavender and then a deeper purple before the dark settled in.

Later we drove to an industrial area where the parking lots sat empty during the weekend. We parked behind a building and listened to our favorite Springsteen tapes. We sang along to the melodies, the sad saxophone playing in the background. We kissed while the music continued.

"Let me show you how much I love you," Kevin said after we'd been kissing and touching for a long time. He tried to get me to lie down across the front seat.

"I don't think we should," I said. We both knew what he wanted, and I was afraid we were moving too fast, afraid we were crossing into something that would change the us we were becoming, taint the good that we had together by doing what we knew was wrong.

"But I love you. Please let me," he said, looking deep into my eyes. He gave me a long, lingering kiss that made my insides melt. I couldn't think straight and I wasn't sure I wanted to. He stopped and looked at me and smiled.

The whole world opened up when he smiled at me, and when he cupped his hand around my face, holding me gently in his hands, I wanted to be a part of the joy he was offering.

"I love you, Judith. I always have, and I always will."

"I love you too," I whispered.

We made love that night in the dark of his car with an outdoor light casting a faint glow over us.

We were already close—good friends who had become a couple—and we easily shared our hopes and dreams. But after making love, it felt like we had moved into a totally new and different place.

We began to see the future as something that we could share, and we began to talk about that future as a real place we would get to together. I think once we made love, we really did cross into something that changed us. We had given our whole selves to each other—body and soul, and there was no going back to a lighter, safer romance after that. When Kevin held me in his arms, hugging me close after making love, it felt like we'd never let go.

Getting Engaged

Kevin graduated and my school ended. Then summer stretched out before us with its long warm days ahead. It was a time filled with hope, a time when anything was possible. I had a part-time job at Foster's Supermarket, and I spent some of the money I made going to movies, buying ice cream, and shopping with friends. But most of the money went for gas or phone bills.

When we couldn't visit in person, we'd talk for hours on the phone. He spent a lot of time grounded because he kept breaking his curfew to visit me. But his parents didn't keep him away from the phone. When the phone bill came in that June, my portion was $106.29. I signed my entire week's paycheck over to my father to cover all my calls to Vermont.

When Kevin wasn't grounded, we were together constantly. We started to look at diamonds and dreamed about getting engaged. Sometimes he came to pick me up after work, and I'd find him sitting in his mom's red Comet, the radio blaring.

He picked me up one night wearing a light blue t-shirt. He'd gotten it on a family trip to Key Biscayne, and the color brought out the brilliance of his blue eyes. I got into the car and we took off. Kevin liked to sing along with the radio. That evening, he turned to me and sang me some lyrics. I loved listening to him, and he sang to me about love and trust, about knowing you could hold on to someone even when you were falling.

We made love often that summer, and it was like we were melding our souls together into one. I imagined that was how God intended lovemaking to be, a blending of two beings into one. When we were together like that, it was as if we were glimpsing the joys that God offered us in marriage. But in a way it was like we were cheating, looking too soon.

Because we were both Catholic, we knew a sexual relationship before marriage was not something God wanted for us. I think we would've gotten married that summer if our parents had let us. But I was only sixteen and he was only seventeen. Teen marriage was not what our parents had planned.

Even though we saw each other often and talked on the phone all summer, we wrote letters too. In those letters and on the phone we felt free to share our dreams. Kevin liked to outline his plans, let me know that he envisioned a future for us, and he liked to share the details. He told me he wanted to be with me for a long time, a lifetime.

He told me about a beautiful dream he'd had of us exchanging rings at an altar. He promised me that we would make those dreams come true.

When I was away from him, it was like being in the wilderness, alone. But his words on the page were manna floating down to me, feeding and strengthening my very being. He was the sustenance I needed, and his solemn words were promises I held onto. I gave him my promises too. I gave him everything I had to give. In return he had given me this vow—that we would spend the rest of our lives together. It was as if he were already my betrothed and we already belonged to each other.

But we needed an outward sign of our love, something that would show the rest of the world, and our parents, that we weren't just young kids playing at love. We were serious. Our pledge to one another was true and solid, like a diamond. So we started planning the type of diamond we might get.

"I think a small ring would look best," I said over the phone. "My hands are small and a big ring would look funny."

One night, we went to the shopping mall after work to look at rings. My mother worked at Jordan Marsh, and we stopped by to see her.

"Hey, you two," Mom said as she saw us coming up to the cash register in her section. She was a manager now, a recent promotion that put her in charge. "What brings you here tonight?"

"Oh, just shopping," I said, sounding silly and elusive. Kevin was holding my hand and with his finger, he drew little circles on my palm. Just this slight fluttering touch made it hard for me to concentrate. I looked at Kevin and smiled. He had a big grin on his face.

"Well," she said as she looked from me to him, "the two of you look positively giddy. What are you shopping for?"

"It's a surprise," Kevin said and impulsively kissed my mom on the cheek. I kissed her too.

"Bye, Mom. Gotta run!"

She knew something was up. I'd tell her soon enough. I couldn't keep secrets from her, and I didn't want to.

The jewelry section was around the corner from the cosmetics, and the smell of perfume and cologne was thick, overpowering. I didn't like the strong smells or the price of the rings. They started out at over five hundred dollars. Kevin didn't have that much money.

We went up and down the mall after that, in and out of jewelry stores.

"Can I help you?" a saleslady asked after we'd been looking at rings in a display case for a long time.

"Yes," Kevin said. "We'd like to look at some diamonds."

"Really?" she said. "How old are you?"

We left that store. I didn't want Kevin spending his money at a place that treated us like little kids.

We ended up driving down the street to Service Merchandise. They had many departments—furniture, bed and bath, stereo—but the most important one to us, the jewelry department, was just inside the front door.

The woman behind the display case was younger than the old ladies at the mall's jewelry stores. She was probably in her late twenties, and she came right over to us, smiling.

"What can I do for you this evening?" Her voice was warm and friendly.

"Well, my girlfriend and I want to see some rings," Kevin said.

She brought out some opals and sapphires.

"Those are pretty," he said. "But we want to see your diamonds. We're getting engaged, officially."

It was cute how he said that, and I blushed.

"How exciting," the woman said. She had her hair pulled tight in a short ponytail at the back of her neck and she wore small gold hoops in her ears. "Come on over here then." She directed us just around the corner.

She brought out one diamond at a time and let me try on each one. They were beautiful. The first couple she had me try on, though, seemed big on my finger. My fingers were thin, my hands small, and I didn't want a large diamond. That was lucky since Kevin had just under five hundred dollars in the bank.

We knew very little about diamonds. We hadn't even heard about flaws, cut, and quality. I knew the difference between shapes: a pear shape, a round shape, or an actual diamond-shaped stone. But when it came to grades of diamonds and stuff like that, we didn't know anything.

But it didn't really matter. We just wanted a small diamond that Kevin could afford. I tried on a round diamond set high on four prongs. It fit my hand perfectly.

"What do you think?" he asked, after the clerk placed it on my finger.

"It's beautiful," I said. I held my hand out to him and tilted it back and forth, so he could have a good look.

"It's kind of small," he said.

"Yes," I said, "but it's the right size for me."

"My delicate little Judith," he said and kissed my hand.

"We're not sure yet," I said to the saleslady.

"That's okay," she said. "We have plenty of round solitaires to choose from, no hurry. If you do buy it, you should know you can trade the ring back in later if you want to get a bigger diamond."

We thanked her and left the store. I couldn't imagine trading in a diamond that Kevin would give me. It didn't matter to me how small the rock was. The important thing was that it signified his eternal, undying love for me.

After picking out a diamond, we went and had a bite to eat at Brigham's in the mall. I had a grilled cheese and chips, and Kevin had a burger and fries. We walked around the mall some more afterwards, killing time until we had to pick up my mother from Jordan Marsh.

Back at my house we all sat down for a cup of tea. Dad was already sleeping. Mom went to bed around 11:30, and Kevin and I stayed in the living room talking. We talked about getting engaged, how Kevin would have to get the money out of his bank account. When we were together talking, the hours went by like minutes. It was 1:30 in the morning before we knew it.

"You better go," I said to Kevin when I realized what time it was.

"Yeah, you're right," But instead of leaving, he started kissing me. He pushed me down gently so my head was resting on the arm of the couch and his body was pressing against mine. I didn't want him to go. I wanted him to stay forever, right there, kissing me.

"No, really, you have to leave," I said pushing his shoulders up and off of me.

He lifted his weight off me and held himself up on one arm so he could look right into my eyes.

"You want me to go?"

"You know I don't want you to go, but you're going to get into trouble."

"What else is new?" he asked and kissed me on the forehead. He sat up, and then stood up to leave. I walked him to the door and he left.

The next day I had to work late at the supermarket. Feeling bored and wishing I could be with Kevin, I was at the cash register all night. When I finally got home and reached him on the phone, his voice sounded sad. I knew something was wrong and asked him what was the matter.

"I'm grounded," he said. "Again." His mother had caught him sneaking in late the night before.

"No!"

"Yeah, and she asked me where I'd been and if I knew what time it was. I told her we were looking at diamonds. She flipped out."

"What did she say?"

Kevin hesitated. "It was pretty mean."

"Go on, tell me."

"She said she hated you and that she knew you'd turn up pregnant."

That night was back in the summer, before we got engaged, before I got pregnant.

"You told her I wasn't, didn't you?"

"Yeah, but she was so mad it was like she couldn't hear me. I finally just went to bed."

It was my turn to be silent. Finally I asked him how long he was grounded.

"A week. My dad told me this morning. I really felt like working with him after that," Kevin said sarcastically. He worked for his family's landscaping business in the summer.

"That stinks," I said.

"I'm not waiting anymore."

"What do you mean?"

"To get engaged," he said.

"It's not like we have much of a choice," I said. "They're not going to let you take the car and come see me while you're grounded."

"I don't care! I'll mail you the money, and then you go buy it."

"I guess we could do that, but I'm not going to wear the ring until you can put it on my finger."

It was a long week without Kevin. But I talked with him every night for hours. He bought a money order at the bank and mailed it to me on Friday. It was funny because I ended up seeing him before the money order arrived.

I finished work on Saturday night, and he was there to pick me up.

"Did you get the money?" he asked as I jumped in the car.

"Not yet."

"But I want everyone to know I'm marrying you," he said and hugged me.

On Monday the money order arrived, and I cashed it and went to buy the diamond. I didn't like buying my own ring, but at least we had picked it out together.

He came to my house the next night and waited in the living room while I went upstairs for the ring. It was on my bureau in its brushed velvet box with the cover open. I came downstairs, into the living room, and sat down next to him.

Kevin took the ring box from me and got down on one knee. He took the ring from the box and reached for my hand. But he took the wrong hand and started to put the ring on my right ring finger.

"It goes on the other hand," I whispered and giggled. Then he slipped the ring on the correct finger and leaned up to kiss me.

"Marry me, Judith," he said.

To celebrate we walked to Friendly's for dinner and an ice cream. The night was warm, and we held hands on much of the mile-and-a-half walk. I felt like skipping. Over dessert, Kevin grabbed my left hand in his.

"You're all mine now," he said. And there wasn't anything else I wanted to be.

The Pregnancy Test

The summer sped by, and before I knew it cheering practice had started. But not my period. I was late, and I shouldn't have been surprised. Kevin and I had been having sex all summer long, talking about marriage, talking about babies, planning for our life together.

Then he had another fight with his parents. His mother told his father how Kevin had come home late again, and then the yelling started, and they grounded him again. He couldn't take it anymore, so he left. He told his father he was done working for him, and he hitchhiked from Vermont to see me in Greenfield.

I had cheering practice that morning, and when I got close to school, I saw Kevin walking toward me. He watched my practice and then we went back to my house. That's when he told me all about the fight and how he couldn't stay in a house where he didn't feel welcome, where his parents were always yelling and making him feel like he didn't belong, like he didn't have a home.

He was crying, and I held him in my arms and told him he was always welcome with me, that when he was with me he was home. He ended up staying at my house for nearly a week until his brother came and convinced Kevin that he should live with him.

School was starting soon for me, but Kevin wasn't sure what he was going to do. His parents had signed him up for a year of prep school so he would be a better student and stronger athlete when he applied to college the next year. But if I were pregnant, those plans didn't make sense anymore.

He talked with his sister-in-law, who was a nurse. Pam gave Kevin the name of a clinic where we could get a urine sample tested. She said this would be more accurate than the in-home pregnancy test kits sold at drugstores. So much depended on this test. With a positive result, Kevin might stay with me and not go to the prep school up in Vermont.

A few days later, we walked up to the counter at the clinic. I felt embarrassed standing there with the brown bag that held a jar of my urine. It seemed like everyone in the waiting room knew why we were there.

It turned out we couldn't get the sample tested without a doctor's order, so we went back to his brother's house and put the jar of urine in Kevin's room. No one was home and the late summer day was hot, so we went out for an ice cream at the Dairy Queen.

We sat on the hood of my mom's car. The metal was warm on the back of my legs, and I felt relaxed eating the melting ice cream. It was early September and Kevin was supposed to be at his new school. He was missing football practice and might not be eligible for the team even if he did decide to show up. It still felt like summer, though, and I wanted to believe he was going to stay with me.

When I dropped him off, Pam was home. With her dark brown hair pulled back in a ponytail, she didn't look much older than me. She said we could use her doctor's name for the pregnancy test.

On my way home, I went back to the clinic to try again with Pam's doctor's name. But the lady at the desk said my urine sample wasn't any good now because we hadn't refrigerated it. I felt childish and silly.

At school the next day, I couldn't concentrate. I wanted to get home and talk on the phone with Kevin, if only for a few minutes before cheering practice. I had to work in the evening and then I'd have homework to do.

The following day was Friday, and after school I went to work at Foster's. My days were filled morning to night, and I couldn't find time or a ride to the clinic.

After work I went to Kevin's brother's house to see Kevin. I helped Pam make a spaghetti dinner, and when her husband Richard came home, the four of us ate together, and I felt welcomed into their home life.

After dinner, Richard and Kevin went out to smoke pot on the porch while Pam and I cleaned up. It made me angry because we had told each other we weren't going to do that anymore, and there he was toking with his brother, breaking our promise.

Then Pam started on me in the kitchen, pouncing on me as soon as we were alone.

"Kevin needs to get to school, you know. You need to stop influencing him, stop holding him back."

"I'm not holding him back," I said. "He's not even sure he wants to go, especially if I *am* pregnant." I told her Kevin had applied for jobs while he was staying at my house. He could work during the day and go to college at night.

"You're going to ruin his life!" she screamed.

I stood there with my arms at my side, a dishtowel in my hand. I didn't know what to say. Just moments before, I'd felt like part of the family—sharing a meal, cleaning the kitchen. Suddenly, I was a threat that could *ruin* Kevin's future. It seemed Pam wanted to wipe me from his plans.

The guys heard the yelling and came into the kitchen. Richard stood about six foot, four, and looked every bit the football player he'd been in school. Kevin seemed small next to him. But he spoke up. "Hey, stop yelling at Judith!"

Then Pam turned on him too. "Don't tell me what to do in my own house," she said, and Richard came over to her side.

Lately it seemed like everyone was yelling and taking sides, as if there were separate teams and you could be loyal to only one.

Kevin took my hand and said, "Come on, let's get out of here."

I was glad he told Pam to stop yelling, but I wanted him to stand up for me even more, to ask what she was yelling about and set her straight. Instead, we were running out of the house like we'd done something wrong, like scared little children.

We drove to a deserted parking lot. I was crying, and Kevin looked sad.

"Well, we need to find out if you're pregnant or not," he said and kissed me. When he kissed me I couldn't think straight. He bit my ear and licked my neck.

"I know, I know," I said. "I'll go to a clinic tomorrow."

"Good," he said, and then we kissed for a while longer.

I pushed him away suddenly and asked, "Then what?"

Kevin looked at me, confused.

"If I'm pregnant. Or even if I'm not. What are you going to do?"

"I'm going to marry you. Pregnant or not. Isn't that why you're wearing that diamond?" He smiled.

We made love before I took him back to his brother's house. I felt so close to him when we were together like that. We both felt better when I dropped him off.

The next morning, I took my urine to a clinic near where I lived. But it was Saturday, and the place was closed. It seemed like I couldn't get a pregnancy test done, no matter how hard I tried. If timing was everything, then my timing was way off.

On Sunday, my parents dropped me off so I could spend the day with Kevin. We played touch football and backgammon and enjoyed a carefree day together. But when we talked about the baby, our conversation became strained because we weren't even sure I was pregnant. He still wasn't in school, and we were both in limbo. It felt like everything was up in the air. But when my parents picked us up and brought us home for a big Sunday dinner, the tension lifted and we talked and laughed.

Afterwards, he and I found a secluded spot in the woods and made love. It seemed like everything made sense then, like any questions we had were fully answered. I drove him home later and after he kissed me goodbye, he reminded me that I needed to trust him and believe in him.

I wanted so much to believe in him, and I did.

Since we were having no luck with clinics, I finally bought a drugstore pregnancy test. The next morning, I followed the instructions and used my first urine of the day.

I paced back and forth as I waited for the results. Kevin and I wanted a baby, but were we ready? Would he really marry me? He told me to trust him. I looked at the test when enough time had gone by.

Positive. My eyes widened. I *was* pregnant.

I stared at the test results. It was really true. I wanted to shout out loud. I was having Kevin's baby! I should have been scared: scared to tell my parents, scared to tell the nuns at school, scared to tell Kevin's family. But at that moment what I felt was joy, knowing I had life growing inside of me—life that Kevin and I had created together through our love.

Pregnant — My First Day Knowing

I dressed for school, putting on my plaid polyester skirt, zipping it up. It fit fine, but how long would I be able to wear this school uniform? How long before I started to show? I put on a white blouse and my maroon sweater. I looked the same but didn't feel the same.

All day long at school, I felt like I had a special secret inside. I couldn't wait to get home and call Kevin with the news.

"Guess what?" I asked when he answered.

"What?"

"I'm pregnant!" I exclaimed happily. During classes that day, I'd daydreamed about being parents together, holding and caring for our infant.

"I'm going home tonight," he said. "My parents want to talk."

It was as if he hadn't heard what I said, so I said it again.

"I'm pregnant."

"I know," he said. "I heard you."

"I was hoping you'd be happy. It's not like this is a mistake," I reminded him.

"Yeah, I know. I'm just confused."

I wanted him to be thrilled with the news, but he wasn't. We made plans to get together that night.

When I arrived at his parents' house, Kevin met me at the car and said his parents wanted him to stay home. Then, *I* was confused. I'd driven some distance to see him, and now he was saying I couldn't come in. He stood beside the car with his family's large brick colonial home behind him.

"I'm going to go to school," he said. "My parents said I could go even though we're still engaged."

"But I'm definitely pregnant," I said, wanting him to remember that he'd promised to marry me.

"Yeah, and I'm going to school."

I didn't understand. We'd been talking about what we were going to do for weeks. He'd been living at my house and then his brother's. He'd been out of his parents' house for three whole weeks. He'd applied for jobs. School had already started.

He'd said he didn't want to go. That he wanted to stay with me. He'd said he would go to college at night and work during the day. And now? Now that I was pregnant, he was leaving.

I started crying. Not just a little. A lot. I was totally shocked.

He held out two slips of paper.

"What's this?" I asked.

"They're names of counselors," he said. "Places where you can go to give a baby up for adoption. My dad got them."

"What are you talking about?"

My head was spinning. Adoption? He knew I was adopted. He knew I would never give our baby away. He knew that I didn't know who my birth parents were, and I'd told him how that made me feel like a part of me was missing.

He was still talking about what he and his parents had discussed, but I couldn't hear him. Suddenly, I felt like I was drowning and his words were swirling around me as if I were immersed in water.

"I still want to marry you," he said, and I heard that, like he had thrown a life preserver into the water.

"You do?"

"Yes, of course. But I don't think I can be a father right now." I didn't know what to say, and I couldn't talk if I'd wanted to because I was crying so much.

"Let's go for a walk," he said.

"I thought you couldn't see me," I managed to say.

"Yeah, well, a little walk won't hurt." He held out his hand.

I stepped out of the car and took his hand, and we walked around the neighborhood until we came to a big rock at the end of a road.

"I still love you," he said and tried to kiss me. I pulled away.

"Hey," he said. "I do." And he tried again. This time I let him. My face was wet from crying, and he'd been crying too. We stayed there hugging and talking for about a half an hour. I didn't want to let go because it felt like I was losing him.

When we went back to his house, I didn't want to leave. But again he didn't ask me to come inside. He kissed me goodbye, but I didn't know when I would see him again, and it hurt not knowing, like I had a weight on my chest.

On the drive home, I thought about how long it had taken to find out I was pregnant. Would it have made any difference if we'd found out the news while he was living at my house and looking for work? Would he have stayed with me then? The whole way home, I kept wiping my eyes with a napkin.

The next day I called him, and his mother answered. When I asked for Kevin, she said, "He's busy right now. But I'd like to speak with you. You thought you could trap Kevin by getting engaged. Well—"

"Wait a minute," I said, cutting her off. "Kevin wanted to get engaged."

"And then you used sex to manipulate him."

"It's not like I forced him!" I said, and it seemed like she was forgetting the arguments that had taken place at her own house that summer, forgetting why Kevin had left home. It was as if his family had another story about what had happened, and it was not the same story I was living. It seemed to me they were the ones who were doing the manipulating.

"He's leaving for school tomorrow, and you won't see him then," she said, and she sounded pleased, smug even.

Leaving for school? Tomorrow?

"Please let me talk to Kevin," I said, a whine rising in my voice.

I was left standing there, the dial tone sounding in my ear.

How was it that one evening we were making plans to get married and two days later, he was getting ready to leave for school? I felt dizzy. My world was spinning out of control, and I didn't know what to do. I hung up and just stood there.

Later that night the phone rang. When I heard Kevin's voice, I was glad. But as he spoke, my eyes welled with tears.

"I'm going to be there for you in the end," he said. "I love you." More than anything, I wanted to believe him. But he was leaving, and this late-night phone call was our quiet goodbye.

Runaway

One month and two weeks

Kevin was away at school, and I was pregnant. I told my mom right away but not my father. I just wasn't ready to face him. But then my mom said we needed to tell him, that he had a right to know. So at dinner one night I told him the news.

My father's long face turned red when he was angry, but I'd never seen him this mad—even his ears were red. He stood up from the dinner table and shouted, "You did it! You spread your legs!"

He pointed his finger at me, shaking it for emphasis, and then slammed his hands onto the table. The forks and knives rattled on the plates.

My mother and I sat there quietly, and she looked over at me, her steel blue eyes imploring me to hold my tongue. But I felt anger welling up inside, huge anger. How could he make it sound so ugly? I shoved my chair back.

"I'm not going to sit here and listen to you talk like that!" I shouted back and ran out of the kitchen, up the stairs, and into the bathroom. My dad yelled after me, but I had already locked the door behind me.

From there I could hear my parents' muffled voices. The yelling had stopped, and I sat on the floor with my knees pulled up to my chest. I was crying, more angry than sad. My mom's light steps came up the stairs and then she knocked.

"Judith, open the door," she said softly. "He didn't mean it."

But I was pretty sure he did, and it wasn't like I could forget my dad's voice. The awful words kept repeating in my head—*you did it … you did it!*

"Judith?" my mother pleaded. "Let me in."

I didn't answer, and after a few minutes she went back downstairs. I held my head, rubbing my temples. I could hear water running and knew my parents were washing the dishes—Mom washing and Dad drying as always. This ritual almost made it seem like any other night, except I was locked in the bathroom, feeling sick at heart.

I couldn't stay in the house anymore, not with my father thinking those thoughts about Kevin and me. I opened a window and quietly climbed onto our patio roof.

From there I could see our backyard and the next-door neighbor's. Beyond our yards, the brook ran and the woods stretched out. It was September and the setting sun filtered through the orange and yellow leaves.

I edged along the green fiberglass, trying to step on the wooden rafters beneath the roofing, placing my feet carefully so I wouldn't fall through. Our kitchen window was off to my right and looked out on the backyard. I was afraid my parents might see me, so I kept myself pressed tight against the house and moved away from where they were and toward the end of the patio roof. I had to keep looking down to make sure I wouldn't crash through.

For a second I looked back at the open window. Then I turned and jumped. It wasn't too far from the roof to the ground, ten feet or maybe twelve. But the jolt ran up my legs, and my knees buckled when I landed. I stood up, touched my still-flat stomach, and left the yard quickly.

I walked up Arcadia Avenue, past my neighbors' houses, the homes I'd played in as a child. When I was younger, I had to be home before the street-lights came on. Until then I could go up to the park for a kickball game or play cards at someone's house. But that was before boyfriends, before the pregnancy.

The streetlights were on, and I left our neighborhood, turning left onto East Street and then down Westford, past the school where Kevin had graduated in May. That seemed a lifetime ago, though it was only four months. The parking lot was full, and a light in the chapel shined through the stained-glass window, the red glow like a beacon.

How many times had I gone to that chapel Saturday mornings before football games? The cheerleaders sat in one row, players up front, and Father Tom told us how the game on the field was a prelude to how we would live our lives. He gave that sermon to encourage the players, but it was hard to listen, and we always fidgeted in the pews.

This season would be my last time cheering. I wouldn't be able to hide a fattening belly for long. I walked past the school and felt sad about quitting the team after football season. From there I went over the railroad tracks and headed toward the highway. I avoided the cracks in the sidewalk and thought of that old chant: *Don't step on a crack or you'll break your mother's back.* I used to sing that as a child, skipping over the broken places.

When I got to the highway ramp, I stayed as far to the right as I could. A sign read: *no pedestrians, no bicyclists.* On the highway, cars sped past me. I stayed in the breakdown lane where the pavement met grass. The air had turned cold, and I wished I'd worn a sweater.

Soon a sports car pulled up in front of me, and a man opened the passenger door. "Hey, want a ride?"

I wasn't supposed to get into cars with strangers, but then, I wasn't supposed to be out here in the first place. I was cold and didn't have a coat or a plan, so I jumped in.

"Where are you headed?"

"North."

"Yeah, well, that's the direction this highway's going." He laughed. "What are you doing out hitchhiking alone?"

"I wasn't hitchhiking." I paused and then added, "I had a fight with my parents."

"Ah, parents."

For a couple of minutes we sat in silence as his car whipped up the highway. I wished I'd put my seatbelt on, but thought it would look funny to do it now. We were going faster and faster, and though I couldn't see the speedometer, I knew we were speeding because we kept passing other cars.

"Don't mind if I smoke, do you?" Without waiting for an answer, he lit a joint and held it out to me.

I remembered smoking pot with Kevin and how good it felt to be stoned, how it felt like everything was okay, would always be okay. I wanted to feel that way again, but Kevin and I had promised each other we wouldn't hurt our bodies anymore. We'd gone on a Catholic retreat together and promised to treat our bodies the way God wanted us to.

"No, thank you. I don't smoke pot," I said.

"So what was the big fight about?"

"My fiancé."

"Your fiancé?" He chuckled and said, "You don't look old enough to have a boyfriend."

"I'm sixteen, and I'll be seventeen in November," I said with an edge of defiance in my voice.

"I guess that's old enough," he said and looked over at me, staring a little too long. It felt like he was staring at my breasts, which were already getting big.

I wished he'd just keep his eyes on the road. I thought it was funny that he didn't think I was old enough to have a boyfriend, like I was a kid or something. I guess he definitely wouldn't think I was old enough to be pregnant.

After ten or fifteen minutes, I was getting nervous. After all, this guy was a total stranger getting high while he drove north on Interstate 91. So, as we approached the next exit, I told him I needed to get out.

"Leaving so soon?" he said as he pulled across two lanes and into the breakdown lane.

"Thanks," I said. Then he reached over and flattened his hand against my breast before I could open the door. "Hey!" I yelled. I got out quickly, and he took off, pebbles and dust flying up from the tires.

I stood there shaking. I was lucky he hadn't taken me off somewhere and— my mind stopped at the thought of crimes too awful to imagine.

When I was little, adults said I acted like ten going on thirty. But right then, I felt like a little kid. Shivering in the dark, I just wished my mother would come and save me.

The side of the road was very dark. I stood there for a few minutes and then started walking. Crossing the bridge over the Connecticut River, I saw lights from cars driving along a road next to the water. Their lights reflected as they took a curve, and I stopped to look at the black river. I thought how easy it would be to jump over the railing. Crying, I stared at the river's velvety darkness. For a few moments I yearned to fall into it and slip away unnoticed.

But I wasn't made that way. Pushing away my frightening thoughts, I hurried over the bridge, knowing the road would go past the exit where Kevin lived. After that, I could push on to Middlebury Prep, his new school. His grades weren't good enough for any of the private colleges his parents wanted him to apply to, so he was living in a dormitory, trying to improve his record, and following their wishes.

I knew if I kept heading North I'd reach him, and, though I hadn't planned it when I jumped off the patio roof, I guess that's where I'd been heading all along. I wanted to be with him and tell him about the big fight with my father. I wasn't sure I could tell him about my terrifying car ride, but I knew whatever I said, he would hold me and make me feel safe.

It was his birthday, and I had planned to spend the next day with him anyway. My parents were letting me take the green Mustang for the whole day. I knew the drive would take more than two hours, but how long would it take me to walk there?

I still couldn't believe he'd gone away to this new school. He had almost stayed. When he was at my house in the summer and had gone looking for work, he almost got a job driving a truck. He'd driven a truck for his dad's landscaping business, and truck drivers made pretty good money. In the fall, we decided, he could go to night school.

It was a good plan, not at all crazy like the scheme he'd hatched early in the summer. Those warm nights, Kevin used to urge me to run away with him. Sitting outside my house, way past his curfew, we'd talk in hushed voices as he tried to persuade me to leave.

"Where would we go?" I asked.

"Anywhere," he said, nuzzling my neck. "It doesn't matter. We'll start our own life together."

I liked the sound of that, and we'd sit on his car talking about how we could do it, how we could both get jobs, rent a small apartment or just a room. We didn't need much. But then my adult-serious side would kick in.

"I need to finish high school."

"You could do that anywhere," he said and kissed me.

Part of me wanted to do it. Just go. But part of me was way too scared.

"I've got rope in my trunk," he said in a mock-threatening voice. "I could just take you."

As I walked up the highway that night, remembering summertime, I wished I'd done it, just gone with him. At least we'd be together.

A truck pulled up ahead of me. When I approached, a large man at the wheel rolled down the window and asked if I wanted a ride.

"No, thank you," I said, pulling back. I'd been lucky to get out of the sports car with my life, and now I was trembling, thinking how this truck driver could overpower me.

I must have looked terrified because he said, "okay, miss. But be careful." With one last glance at me, a worried look on his face, he drove away. I got the feeling he was harmless, but I couldn't risk finding out whether I was right or wrong.

The next exit led to Kevin's family home, and I thought about going there. But then I remembered the whole gang had gone to see Kevin for his birthday. His parents and brothers and sisters were probably finishing dessert at some fancy restaurant. Besides, it wasn't like I could just pop in to see them anyway, even if they were home. They were all mad at me.

Still, this was an area I knew. I trotted down the ramp and made my way to a pay phone in the town center. There was nothing else to do but call home, collect.

"Hi, Mom. It's me," I said, my voice shaking. My mother told the operator she'd accept the charges.

"Are you all right?" she asked, and I could hear the crying in her voice.

"I'm fine," I said. But I wasn't, and now I was crying too.

Birthday Celebration
One month, two weeks and one day

The next morning I was driving up the same highway, heading back to the man I loved, a picnic basket beside me. I'd meant to leave early, but the fight with my father and the odyssey beginning with my flight off the patio had exhausted me. Or maybe it was the tiny cells dividing and growing inside me, using all my strength to grow strong—maybe that's why I was tired.

Whatever the cause, I was running late with more than two hours of driving ahead of me. I turned the radio on and half-listened to the singers pledging fidelity to their lovers. I pushed the accelerator on the green Mustang and began to speed. I didn't want a ticket, but I wanted to get to Kevin as fast as I could.

Driving alone to see him for his birthday, I had time to think about my pregnancy. Part of me was scared, part excited. We'd dreamed about having children together, and now it was happening. I smiled thinking about how happy we could be.

On the prep school campus, big brick buildings lined the street like sleeping giants. It was ten a.m. on a Saturday, and most of the students were still sound asleep. I passed the main buildings and followed the directions I'd scribbled down. Down a side road, I spotted Kevin's brick dormitory, a beautiful old building.

The door opened and Kevin, grinning so wide his dimples showed, bounded down the steps. He grabbed the Mustang's front bumper and pushed it up and down, laughing as he horsed around.

"I didn't think you were coming," he said as he pulled me out and into his arms.

"I was up early baking muffins and packing a picnic lunch!" I put my head on his chest and breathed in the smell of him mingled with Coast soap. That mixture of scents was my favorite in the world. He lifted my chin and kissed me for a long time.

Then he let me go and swept his arm towards the dorm and the school beyond.

"This is my jail," he said. "But I'll show you my cell later. Let's go for a walk."

He took my hand, and we set off across the street to some trails by a stream.

"Hey, slow down," I said. His legs were much longer than mine and it was hard to keep up. He let go of my hand and climbed up on a wooden fence and bounced on it.

"What are you doing?" I laughed because he looked like a little kid.

"I can't help it," he said. "I've been up and waiting for you for hours. I've got all of this energy inside and I have to get it out." He jumped off of the fence and ran down the trail and back to me. It was like his sprints in football, and he did it again, just to show me what his practices were like.

We walked around, and Kevin told me more about his new team, how he was number 58 and how at first he was really nervous, especially since he'd missed the August practices and some in September too. When we got engaged, his parents told him they wouldn't pay for his prep school. That's why he moved in with my family and missed the beginning of football season. They finally gave in when they realized he wouldn't back down.

"So I'm afraid the coach might not think I'm good enough."

"Hmm," I said. The conversation made me sad. He was feeling insecure about football, while I worried about our life together. His worst fear was falling short at a game, and mine was not being good enough to keep him by my side.

I didn't want the sad feeling to overtake me, so I set my doubts aside. On the way back to his dorm, I tried to reassure him.

"I bet you're one of the best players on the team," I said and squeezed his hand. He smiled. "Remember when I used to call out your name?" I let go of his hand and started the cheer. "Kevin O'Brien, he fights, he fights for the green and the white!" I jumped into the air and shook my fists, as if I were holding pompoms.

He laughed for a second, but then looked serious.

"Do you think it's okay to be jumping around like that? It won't hurt the baby, will it?"

"No, the baby's fine," I said. "He's safe and warm in here." I took his hand and touched it to my stomach.

Then we walked back to his dorm holding hands. On the way, I told Kevin about my trip up the highway the night before. I told him about the guy in the sports car, but I left out how he groped me and how terrified I was. And I didn't tell him how it felt like I was heading nowhere, how when I called my mother collect, I felt empty and scared. I'd tried so hard to run away from home and come to him, but I only ended up right back where I started. I kept that inside because I didn't want to ruin our day.

Still, I'd said a lot. He dropped my hand and turned to look at me, the smile gone from his face.

"What?' I asked.

"Oh, I don't know," he said sarcastically. "Trying to get yourself killed or something? What were you thinking?"

"I wasn't, I guess. But I just couldn't stay."

He put his hand on my stomach and said, "Yeah, well, you have to think more now, you know."

Holding hands again, we walked back to his dorm without saying any more. He opened the door, and we went down a long hall to his room at the opposite end. Inside, there were bunk beds against the wall, two bureaus and two desks, both covered with books and papers. On one desk was a picture of a girl with long blond hair.

"Who's this?" I asked, picking up the framed photo.

"It's Brian's girlfriend, Terry."

Kevin had told me about his roommate from New York. The two of them had hit it off, and I was glad Brian had a girlfriend back home too. I figured he and Kevin wouldn't be picking up girls at parties after games. But thinking of Kevin at parties without me made my throat feel tight.

"Where is Brian anyway?" I asked, looking around. "And where's my picture?" I knew he had a picture of me in his wallet, the one from my junior prom, but I thought he'd have one on his desk too.

"Ahh," Kevin said and turned around waving his hand toward the empty room. "I asked Brian last night to crash at someone else's room." He grabbed my hand and pulled me over to the bottom bunk. Taped on the wall right near his pillow were three pictures of me. He told me I was the first thing he saw every morning when he woke up and the last thing he looked at when he went to sleep at night. "Then every night I dream about us."

"You are so smart." I was feeling like my old self again.

We sat on the edge of his bed, kissing. At first we kept our eyes open, and looking in his eyes, I felt like I was looking into a sea of warmth. Then I closed my eyes and let myself slip into that warm feeling. When we kissed, I couldn't stop myself from going further. The desire was too powerful, even if I knew having premarital sex was a sin.

He pushed me gently down onto his bed and undressed me. We made love, and if kissing was slipping into a sea of warmth, then joining ourselves together as one was sailing off onto that sea and to places we could only go together.

"Happy birthday," I murmured as we lay entangled on the narrow bed.

"Best present." He lifted my chin with his finger and kissed the tip of my nose. Then he took a strand of my red hair and twirled it between his fingers.

After lounging around for a while and eating some of the muffins I'd made, we drove up to the mountains and spent the day hiking. The day was crisp with fall breezes, and I was glad for my sweater. I had skipped out of cheering for his old high school so I could spend the day with him.

It all felt strange. I had cheered every fall Saturday for years—from Pop Warner when I was in fourth grade all the way until now, and I never missed a game. Fall and football went hand in hand, and I was still cheering this year, even though I was pregnant. I'd start to show soon, though, and I wouldn't be cheering for the basketball or the hockey teams come winter. I probably wouldn't have the chance to cheer for a college team. I might not even make it to college, after all. But that afternoon on the mountain, I tried not to think about such things.

After walking for a while we spread our picnic lunch on a blanket at the edge of the trail, near the trees. We were tired from the hike and lay down to rest. It seemed we owned the mountain—we hadn't seen anyone else all day— and it felt like the day's beauty was just for us. Kevin bent over my face and touched his lips to mine. With the sunshine streaming behind him, he made love to me again, under the blanket and beneath that brilliant sky.

Into that scene came a sudden high-pitched voice.

"This is a hiking trail, and that's how we got our little friend!" The woman was with a man carrying their toddler on his back. I buried my head in Kevin's shoulder, embarrassed. When I was pretty sure they were gone, I looked at Kevin, who was wearing a wicked smile.

"This is a hiking trail," he mimicked, "and that's how we got our little friend!" He laughed and I giggled. "Besides," he said, "it's too late to worry about that now."

Kevin and I finally talked about our future over lunch. He said he would finish his year at prep school, and then we'd get married after the baby was born. He'd work and go to college part time to build a better future for us. I'd snuck wine and plastic glasses into the picnic basket that morning, and now was the time to toast our life together. With the diamond on my left hand sparkling and the knowledge of our child growing inside, I didn't doubt for a moment that our plans would come true.

What Will They Say?
Two months

r. Mason stood at the front of the room, droning on about some histori-cal event that meant little to most of my classmates and even less to me. He was one of only two male teachers in the school, and I swear he was afraid of all us girls. He was new that year and so nervous you could see sweat on his brow. How would he feel about my passing a note? Would he be a hawk who swooped down on it?

I was nervous too. The class was half over, and I hadn't heard a thing. But I was sitting there scribbling, pretending to pay attention. I ripped a page from my notebook, folded it into a small square, and slipped it to Sandy, one of my best friends. It reminded me of those fancy folded squares—little origami for-tune-tellers that you held in your hands, opening and closing—a game to play with friends. You'd choose a number and then that's how many times they'd open and close the paper. Then you unfolded a piece of the square to reveal a message underneath, as if the message you got held some deep meaning.

But my note *did* hold deep meaning. It held the secret I'd been keeping and an important question about my future. I glanced over as Sandy read the note, and her eyebrows went up slightly.

Sometimes when we were all being silly, we'd sit on the wall outside the caf-eteria after lunch and practice "eyebrow ballet." My cheerleader friends Amy and Sally liked to try, but Sandy did it best, lifting one eyebrow and then the other, moving them up and down, making them dance.

When she read my note, though, it was just a subtle lifting of one brow.

The note was brief, but I'd re-written it a few times during class. Basically it read: *I just found out I'm pregnant. Do you think they're going to kick me out of school?*

Sandy was the first friend I'd told. I was afraid the nuns were going to throw me out as soon as they learned my news. I didn't want to leave. This was my senior year, and I planned on finishing, especially now that Kevin was off at prep school. It didn't seem right for him to continue and for me to get thrown out. I looked over at Sandy. She was busy writing, and it only took a few minutes. But it seemed longer as I waited for her answer.

She handed me her reply. I carefully unfolded the paper, hoping she wouldn't judge me, hoping her message would give me some glimmer of hope. She'd written: *If you want to stay in school and finish, then that's what you should do! They can't make you leave.*

I smiled at my friend. Inside my heart I felt a bit of light coming in.

Later that week I told Karen. She was quiet and smart and hung around with Betty and Sarah—some of the nerdier kids at school. I had friends in many circles: jocks and cheerleaders, other popular kids, and the nerdy kids. There were others, like the ones who hung out back smoking on their break. I got along with them too. Some kids were into drugs, but nothing too heavy. Karen wasn't into any of the party scenes, and we mostly talked about religion and writing. We both wrote, and we both believed in Jesus.

So when I told her I was pregnant, she was surprised. Certainly, the Bible disapproved of premarital sex, and it wasn't as if I didn't know that. I did. I knew Kevin and I had been sinning, but it seemed like we just couldn't help ourselves. It was as if we were magnets drawn together, and when he told me he loved me and pulled me close, I couldn't say no. I hoped Jesus could forgive me, forgive us. I hoped He understood how much Kevin and I loved each other.

"Maybe you should tell Ms. Maxwell," Karen suggested.

"I don't know. What if they have to throw me out?" I asked. Then I added, "If they don't know I'm pregnant, they can't throw me out."

"True," Karen said and pushed her glasses up. "But they are going to find out eventually. I think Ms. Maxwell will know what to do." Ms. Maxwell was our English teacher, and Karen and I trusted her. We had shared our writing with her, and sometimes she shared hers with the class. I decided to go ahead and approach her, even though the prospect made me nervous.

I went by her classroom at the end of the school day. She listened quietly. When I told her I was afraid they would kick me out of school, she spoke up.

"No one is going to make you leave school, I'm sure of it," she said.

But I couldn't figure out how she could be so sure. She told me the school would stand behind me, that they would want me to have the baby. I felt relieved I wasn't going to get thrown out.

We went to talk with Sister Claudia, the principal, whose office was behind the secretary's desk in the main office. I'd never been in that office, not in three years. To me, going to the principal's office was a sure sign of trouble. And I guess I was in trouble.

Walking in with Ms. Maxwell made me feel a little more secure. Large and round, she reminded me of one of my aunts who liked to cook big meals. But seeing Sister Claudia seated behind her desk took away my sense of security. What in the world was I going to say to her, a nun?

Ms. Maxwell started the conversation. "Judith has some very important information to tell you, Sister. It's rather surprising news. As you know, Judith has been a stellar student over the past three years."

Before I even started, I felt like a failure—*has been a stellar student*, as if those days were behind me, as if I'd thrown everything away.

"So," Ms. Maxwell continued, "I'm sure you will be able to help guide her."

I hadn't even told Sister I was pregnant yet, but I started to think that maybe they had some code words between them because when I looked at Sister Claudia, her face was full of concern, as if she already knew the truth about my problem.

"Well," I started to say and then cleared my throat. Words weren't coming very easily.

"It's okay, dear, you can tell me," Sister said, peering at me over her glasses.

I started to feel as if I were in a confessional, telling my sins, but this time I had an audience I could see instead of a priest hidden behind a curtained divider. Maybe this was a way to begin confessing, by telling my sins to a nun.

"I'm pregnant," I said. "And engaged." I showed her the diamond on my left hand, as if somehow that would make the magnitude of my sin less.

"Hmmm," she said. And then there was silence as she thought this over. She drummed her fingers on her desk softly.

Finally, she started talking again, and what came out of her mouth wasn't anything I would have ever expected to hear from a nun.

"I can imagine on a warm summer's night when the moon was full, that two young lovers could find themselves together wanting to express their love. The depth of such love knows few limits, and this love can be hard to deny."

For a minute, it seemed like none of the rest of us were in the room, as

Sister waxed poetic about young love. Her voice took on a sweeter tone than the students were accustomed to hearing. Had *she* ever known these feelings of love?

"I think it would be best if we kept this from the other students for as long as possible, until it can't be hidden anymore," she said.

"I've already told a couple of my friends."

"Yes, well, I'm sure you'll need to talk with your friends, but try to keep it limited to a chosen few."

I said I would. Our meeting ended after she had assured me the school would give me every kind of support necessary. She suggested I have my mother call later.

I left the office feeling almost jubilant. It was as if I were already forgiven, already washed clean. I was going to finish my senior year after all. I would graduate with all my friends. Maybe I'd even make it to college one day. I allowed myself to think about that, allowed myself to imagine going off to college. I held the thought like a dream in my hands.

I had driven to school that day, and as I pulled out of the parking lot, I could see the metal cross on top of our classroom building. The cross was black against the sky, and that afternoon it looked strong and hopeful, a sign that I wouldn't ever be alone.

When Words Are Lies

Two months and one week

I talked with Kevin on the phone one night, and he was miserable. He'd gotten a letter from his mother that made him hurt inside.

"What did she say?"

"It was harsh," he said. "She wants us to get an abortion."

It hung in the air: *abortion*. The ugliness of that word was huge. How could his mother think I could have the baby cut out of me and go on like nothing had changed? How could she even suggest such a thing? I was shocked and disgusted. There was a long silence between Kevin and me.

"Tell me what she said." I wanted to know how she could justify my having an abortion. Both of our families were Catholic. We weren't supposed to *believe* in abortions.

"I'll mail the letter to you."

"Can't you give me some idea now?" I asked. "I mean abortion? Come on, what is she thinking?" Kevin and I had spent a weekend together at a Catholic retreat the previous summer. It blew my mind that she would suggest we consider abortion.

"I can't explain it to you. You have to read it."

Four days later, the letter arrived along with one from Kevin. I read his first. He told me about a football game and how he ended up getting thrown out because he yelled at the referee. He wanted me to come and see him play in his next game.

His letter was four pages long, the front and back of two pages filled. I loved getting letters from him, and when I read them it was almost like hearing his voice. I kept every one he sent and stored them in order by the postmark date. When I felt lonely, I'd take them out and re-read his words, listening for the sound of his love.

His letter was long, but his mother's was even longer. It filled six pages of cream-colored stationery, and she had folded the paper into thirds. She wrote in black ink, in careful cursive letters, and when I read her letter, I heard her voice too. But hers was angry and terse. She pointed out the obvious—Kevin faced some major decisions right now and he was at an important point in his life. I was at an important point in my life too, but I don't think she had expected me to read the letter, and she didn't care about me.

She said she and Kevin's father were sorry I was pregnant. As the letter went on, she blamed me, like somehow it was all my fault. She made it sound like Kevin knew what was right, while I was a whore who'd forced her son to do things he would never choose to do.

I stopped reading for a minute. Her words made me angry and reminded me of when she accused me on the phone of manipulating Kevin. Did she think he had been an unwilling participant? Like I tied him up and forced him to have sex? I continued reading.

She explained how the news was hard on everyone. Then she told Kevin to stop seeing me since he didn't plan to marry me.

But what was she talking about? What did she mean saying he didn't want to marry me? He'd given me a diamond! I was shocked, and she hadn't even got to the part where she pushed for abortion. It seemed like she was just warming up, trying to prepare Kevin for her main point.

She talked about my parents and explained how a baby would be a financial burden on them. It was like she didn't think her son or her family would have anything to do with our baby, financially or otherwise. When she got to the part about the abortion, though, I felt sick to my stomach. Somehow she had convinced herself that God would want us to have an abortion since that was really all we could afford. Kevin had worked all summer, but after buying the diamond and spending so much time with me, he was broke.

She talked about God and how He would want us to be responsible, that an abortion was the obvious solution to our problem. So there it was. God *wanted* me to have an abortion. If it weren't so crazy, it would almost be funny. God wanted us to have an abortion? Well, of course! Why hadn't I thought of that?

I tossed the letter onto my bed. I knew I had to finish it, but the insanity of her logic was almost too much for me. She was suggesting we abort her first grandchild.

I paced back and forth. How dare she bring my parents into this? I doubted she knew I was adopted or that my mom had lost a pregnancy. How could she think she knew how my parents would feel about our baby? I went into my brother's room to use his phone. He was out, and I sat on his bed and dialed Kevin's dorm. Some kid picked up on the second ring.

"Can I speak with Kevin O'Brien, please?" My voice was loud, but I still managed to say please.

"He's at practice," he said. I should have known that. I just wanted to tell him how ridiculous I thought his mother sounded. And what was that part about him not wanting to marry me? I hung up and stared at my brother's black walls—he'd painted them without my parent's permission, and they were angry when they saw the dark room.

I went back to my bedroom, took out my journal, and plopped onto my bed. I wrote a poem fast and furiously:

> They wanted me to kill you,
> but that wasn't in my heart.
> You were already life within me.
> You were living from the start.
> But they couldn't see this
> and can't accept you now—
> or for that matter me—
> and there's nothing we can do.

I felt a little better, a little stronger even. Writing always helped me sort out my thoughts. I picked up the terrible letter and read the rest of it.

In her mind, it seemed, ending this pregnancy would solve all our problems. Or was it her problem that she wanted solved? Maybe she thought a baby would be embarrassing for her and her family. Maybe an abortion was less evil than people knowing her son had sinned, that maybe they weren't the perfect Catholic family after all.

Mrs. O'Brien had five children, and she'd sent all of them to Catholic schools. How could she reconcile her thoughts with the teachings of our Church? Every Sunday during our Profession of Faith, we said out loud what our faith meant. Toward the end of the Profession, we said:

He will come again in glory to judge the living and the dead,
and his kingdom will have no end.
We believe in the Holy Spirit, the Lord, the giver of life,
who proceeds from the Father and the Son.

The giver of life. The Lord was the giver of all lives, not just those that we decided were convenient.

The small life inside my womb was a gift from God. It didn't matter that the tiny cells dividing inside me were still just a blurry mass. It didn't matter that we had conceived this baby in a sinful act. Nothing mattered but the baby growing inside, a living gift from God. This was not something to be scraped from my uterus and tossed away.

I couldn't figure out Mrs. O'Brien, and her argument made no sense to me. Her words were like lies. At least Mr. O'Brien had given Kevin slips of paper with contact information about adoption. At least he didn't want me to kill the baby.

My birth mother gave me up when I was three months old, but if she had chosen to have an abortion, I wouldn't be alive. I knew my parents thought my brother and I were special, that we were gifts. I had been given life by God and by a woman who gave me away.

Now, God had given me a growing life. To Mrs. O'Brien, this meant I was given a choice. But I didn't see it that way at all. I was carrying her son's child, and this little life was the product of our love. I wasn't going to kill our baby, and I wasn't going to give him away.

That night when I wrote in my diary, I cried thinking about how the O'Briens didn't want me to keep my baby. It was pretty clear they didn't want me in their lives or their son's, either. For a long time I stared at the green flowers on my wallpaper, feeling terrible. Finally, I put my diary away and tried to sleep.

Letters In The Mail

Two months and two weeks

The postmarks read October 17, October 18, and October 19. Three days in a row, Kevin had written to me. I loved getting these envelopes, and when I opened them the smell of Coast soap came out. He rubbed the soap on his letters so I would think of him, but I was always thinking of him. He didn't have to worry.

I went up to my room, sat on my bed, and opened the first letter. He talked about an upcoming home game and asked me to come see him play. He said if my parents wouldn't let me use the car, I should ask his parents. I hadn't seen Kevin since his birthday a month ago, but I wasn't about to call his parents. How could I? How could I ride for over two hours with them, one wanting me to abort the baby and the other wanting me to give the baby away?

I finished the first letter and went on to the next. His second letter talked about an algebra test he'd taken, and how well he'd done. He said he liked working hard for me and our baby, and he wanted me to know how much he loved me. That made me smile.

But the third letter shocked me. We'd talked on the phone after I read the letter from his mom, and I'd asked him to write and tell me what he wanted. This was that letter. He said he thought it would be easier on us if I got an abortion. My heart nearly stopped when I read his words.

I had a hard time concentrating, and the green flowered wallpaper looked blurry through my tears. We'd talked about making a baby together, and he'd said if we were having a baby, it would be hard for his parents to stop us from being engaged and spending the rest of our lives together. He made it sound like he wanted me to get pregnant, and every time we made love, it seemed like we were trying—so we could stay together, so his parents couldn't keep us apart.

His letter continued and he talked about wanting to finish school and how he didn't think we would know how to raise a child. His words made it clear he was more concerned about making things easy for himself than he was about helping our baby come into the world and grow up. I remembered how in the summer he'd told me how he'd prayed to be the father of my children, about how we should *grow wildflowers* together—our secret code for making a baby and getting married.

His letter said he'd stay with me if I decided to have our baby and that he would never leave me. He told me he did want to marry me after the school year. At least he still wanted to marry me. He ended with plans:

> I want to see you for your birthday and I think that's probably the earliest I can get down there to see you.
>
> I don't want you to misunderstand this letter. I think it is important for us to spend some time with each other. It'll be better for us to talk in person. Can you come up for my game this Saturday?
>
> Love, Kevin
> Believe In Me!

He said I could send the letter to his mother. But why would I do that? So she could see that he was telling me to have an abortion? To let her know he still wanted to marry me? I wasn't sure, but I didn't mail it to her. Instead, I kept the letter with all of his others.

So, this was it. He wanted me to have an abortion. But he still wanted to marry me, maybe after this year of school if I didn't have an abortion.

I put my head down on the pillow and cried. If Kevin didn't want our baby, I figured he didn't want me, either. But how could that be? He was still talking about when he would marry me, not if. My head hurt, and my pillowcase was getting wet. Should I consider an abortion? Thinking about it made me feel sick.

How could he want me to take our baby out? Whenever we'd dreamed about making a baby together, it felt as if that reality would be the ultimate manifestation of our love, something—*someone* the whole world would see. Then everyone would know the magnitude of what we felt for each other.

I sat up and wiped my eyes on my sleeve. I wanted Kevin to know how wrong I thought abortion was. I wanted him to know that I couldn't understand how he suddenly felt that abortion was okay. I know he said in the letter that these were his decisions, but he was using some of the same wording his mother used. For both of them, it all came down to finances in the end.

I wrote an angry letter full of sarcasm and hurtful words. I lashed out at Kevin, letting angry words flow as my pain fill the pages. My mother used to warn me about putting things in writing—she said you had to be careful. But I wasn't careful. I said what I thought needed to be said and mailed the letter off while I was still mad.

When I heard my mother at the front door later that evening, I remembered that Kevin had asked me to come to his game on Saturday. I was still angry about his supposed decisions, but I wanted to see him. I wanted to know if he could hold me and still want me to throw our baby away.

I ran downstairs and said, "Mom, Kevin wants me to go see his game this Saturday. Can I go? Can I take the car?"

"No, Judith. I don't think so," she said wearily and ran her fingers through her short, silvery hair.

"Please, Mom. I really want to see Kevin. I miss him so much."

"Judith, at least let me get in the door!" She took off her raincoat, and I went back upstairs, thinking I might have a better chance if I gave her some space.

At supper I started again. "Mom, have you thought about the game on Saturday?"

"What's this about?" my dad asked through his food, chewing with his mouth open as he always did. His dad had died when he was only eleven years old and table manners didn't rate very high then—being the oldest, he had to get a newspaper route to help his mom.

"Judith wants to go up to Kevin's school to see a football game," my mom told him. "I've told her I don't think it's a good idea."

Well, that about sealed the decision. If my mother told my dad that she didn't want me going, there wasn't much use in arguing.

"But Mom," I started in anyway, "I have to see him. Can't you understand?" She couldn't or wouldn't. I'd have to skip another day of cheering, but I didn't think that was the problem. I'd have to use their car, but they didn't have plans. It seemed they were just trying to keep Kevin and me apart. I started to think everyone wanted that.

Before cheering that Saturday, I drove Mom to work in silence. She knew I was angry when she leaned over to give me a kiss goodbye, and I turned away.

"Don't be so upset, Judith, it's just a game. There'll be others," she said as she got out of the car.

Just a game? Was she crazy? She wasn't pregnant. She didn't have to worry about Kevin walking out—seeing him was the most important thing to me. How could she act like it didn't matter? Parents could be so stupid!

After dropping Mom off, I picked up Sally, and we put her megaphone and pompoms in the backseat with mine and drove to Amy's for our traditional pre-game breakfast. We filled up on eggs and bacon, sausage and toast, orange juice and coffee. It almost felt like a regular fall football Saturday.

"I'm stuffed," I said as we headed over to Mass in the school's chapel. The football players sat in the front pews as usual, and we sat further back. Every week we prayed for a win, but we lost most games anyway—it was a season of losing. I didn't listen to the priest's talk that morning. Instead, I was quietly praying for Kevin and me, and for our baby.

Later, the team lost again. But the day was beautiful with the sun shining and the stands full. We cheered for the guys who couldn't seem to get a touchdown. The leaves on the trees were brilliant, the air crisp, while we yelled out our cheers. It was a perfect autumn day, but I had more on my mind than the outcome of a high school football game.

At halftime, while we were eating hotdogs, I shared my secret with Amy and Sally. I thought they were going to choke.

After the game, I went home and napped. The pregnancy left me exhausted. Later, when the mailman came, I received two letters from Kevin—a bonanza that normally would have lifted my spirits. But his words of love felt false. He said he'd written every day but hadn't received any letters back from me. That meant he hadn't read my angry letter yet.

He invited me to an away game that was coming up, and I hoped my parents would let me to go. He reminded me to put perfume on my letters and wished me a nice time in Kentucky. On Sunday, I was going on the senior retreat. At first I hadn't planned to go when I thought I might not graduate, but after I told the principal about the pregnancy, she encouraged me to go. Kevin said he was afraid I didn't want to see him anymore after reading his mother's letter.

I hoped the postman had lost my letter because my words were so mean. Kevin signed his letter the way he usually did—Love Kevin, and then scrawled at the bottom three words: *Believe in Me!* I wanted to believe in him, more than anything. But that evening as I packed for the retreat, I wasn't sure what to believe anymore.

Senior Retreat
Two months and three weeks

*P*arents stood on the sidewalk in front of the school while we boarded the bus. Some girls were giggling, and we sat in our seats waiting while the teachers made sure we were all accounted for.

I could see my mom and dad standing there like all the other parents. But they looked different. My mother's lips were pinched, and my father's shoulders slumped—like they were both worn down. It was early morning and perhaps we were all a little tired, but they had a secret the other parents didn't, and its weight was like an anchor dragging them down.

The bus's engine was running, and the fumes made a few parents on the sidewalk cough, and some started back to their cars. When we pulled away from the curb, my parents were still there, and I waved from my window seat. They smiled up at me, and my mom blew me a kiss. I touched my fingertips to my lips and returned the gesture.

October and the morning was cool. I was glad I'd worn a turtleneck under my sweater. There were more than forty girls on the trip, over two-thirds of the senior class, and most of us had dressed alike in blue jeans, turtlenecks and sweaters. Sunday, and we didn't have to wear uniforms like weekdays at school, but in a way we still did. Our preppy sweaters looked nearly the same, as did our carefully blow-dried hair feathered back or pinned with barrettes. We felt liberated from our school uniforms, but we were still the privileged parochial-school girls conforming to our own dress code.

Before leaving the school, a priest said Mass in the auditorium, and we all ate the Host. Parents and teachers listened to the words of blessing, and they prayed for our safety and for the Holy Spirit to touch us on our retreat. We girls fidgeted in our chairs, finding it hard to concentrate, knowing we were leaving with our friends, leaving our homes and our families behind for a week. Afterwards, we had coffee, hot cocoa, and doughnuts.

On the bus, the doughnut sat heavily in my stomach, and I started to feel queasy. I often got carsick on long trips, and I wasn't sure if it were that or morning sickness. Karen, my friend who'd encouraged me to go see Ms. Maxwell, was sitting with me.

"I don't feel very good," I whispered to her when we were riding through town, not yet on the highway. "I think I'm going to puke." She shifted so I could get by her. I went to the back of the bus and into the tiny bathroom. Sitting on the toilet, I ran water in the sink and let it pour over my hand. Then, I stood and splashed some on my face. I didn't get sick after all and went back to my seat.

"You okay?" Karen asked.

"Yeah, I guess." I put my seat back and closed my eyes, but I couldn't sleep. The giddy voices of forty teenaged girls kept me awake.

We arrived at Spaulding College in Kentucky late at night and didn't have time to do anything except unpack and go to bed. The next day was filled with inspirational presentations. With titles such as "Let the Holy Spirit Lead You," "Faith is the Answer," and "Jesus Lives in You," these talks were meant to fire us up. Some students tuned out as soon as someone at the podium began to speak, but others listened intently, trying to hear how they might get the Lord more deeply into their lives.

I was one of those who listened. I liked retreats and the way they could spark your passion for God. When Kevin and I had gone on a retreat the previous summer, we'd packed enough clothes to run away together after it ended. I wasn't even pregnant yet, but we wanted to take off and live our own lives. Kevin was tired of the arguments with his parents and hoped we could live without fighting and love each other every day. Instead, we got cold feet and went home, afraid to hurt our parents and unsure where we would have gone if we had left.

Sitting with my senior class this time, with Kevin so far away and our child inside me, I felt strange. I felt distant and separate from most of my friends, because my life was branching off in a different direction than theirs. But I felt closer to God.

In my heart, I knew that by continuing my pregnancy, I was doing what God would want me to do. But I also sensed that my choice would affect my life in ways I couldn't yet imagine. It was as if I were standing at the edge of a cliff with my feet on slippery stones. I could fall off at any moment, but I found solace knowing my Lord would always be there for me, ready to catch me.

The day's events ended with a prayer service. We sat in a large circle and passed a lit candle. Ms Maxwell started and held the candle in her hands. She sat quietly at first and then spoke in a low voice. She was talking to God, praying out loud, but you had to listen carefully, as her voice was only slightly above a whisper.

Then she passed the candle to a girl who passed it on to the next. Each one of us held the candle and looked at the flickering flame. We were supposed to offer a prayer to our Lord, following the leader's example. Most everyone just sat there with the candle in front of them and said nothing. They held it for a few minutes, a length of time that seemed to lend itself to quiet prayer, light from the flame illuminating each face.

Karen sat next to me, and when she got the candle she spoke in a soft voice.

"Jesus," she said, "be with each of us on our journey. Some journeys will be more difficult than others. Some people have bigger problems than others. Please bless us on our way."

I felt like she was talking about me, and for a minute I was afraid she was going to say something like "help my pregnant friend here as she struggles." I held my breath while Karen kept talking. She liked poetry, like me, and her prayer was laced with metaphor. When she finished, she handed me the candle. She hadn't told my secret, but she'd given enough away so that people knew someone was in some kind of trouble.

I looked into the jar that held the candle. The wax had melted and the flame was reflected in this pool. I stared at the wick burning red at the tip. The bottom of the flame was blue, and the center was an ever-moving darkness with orange above and around this darkness. I felt like I was in the center of the candle, in the darkness feeling lost.

I didn't have anything I wanted to say out loud, but I prayed in my head. I prayed for Kevin and our baby. I prayed for my family, and I prayed for his. I prayed that his family would accept me and the baby. I prayed for the strength I would need in the months ahead. And I prayed the Lord would lead me out of the emptiness and darkness that sometimes enveloped me.

I was lost in prayer and thought. It was as if I were no longer in the group with all of my classmates around me. Instead, I was deep into my conversation with God. Karen nudged me after I'd held onto the candle beyond what seemed normal. I passed it to the next girl.

The prayer service reminded me of the time Ms. Maxwell took us to a room, lit a candle, and read a poem she'd written. She cried when she read it, and my classmates and I didn't know what to do. We just listened as she spoke about dragons and having to slay the dragons. It seemed she was reading it more for herself than us. Her crying made us nervous and her poem hadn't made a lot of sense. But I thought I understood what she'd been talking about—fear and how it could stop you from moving forward, from doing what was the good and right thing to do. I thought about this while we were sitting in a circle at our prayer service, and though I'd already passed the candle on, I prayed for the courage to conquer my own fears.

When the service ended, the group leaders handed out letters for each of us to read back in our rooms. They suggested we spend some time in prayerful thanksgiving before dinner.

In my room, I opened a letter from my neighbor back home, Mrs. Z. She told me she'd given up desserts for me and that she knew I'd understand what a sacrifice that was for her. I did. Desserts were her favorite, and doing without and praying for me meant a lot.

My other letter was from my mom:

> Dearest Judith,
>
> It seems strange sitting here tonight writing to you while you are sleeping upstairs. We have always talked and talked about anything and everything and I for one am glad we could do this since I am not one to put much in writing—you're the writer in this family. You will be miles away when you open this letter and we wanted you to know we will miss you and our loving thoughts and prayers are with you.
>
> We are so proud of you and all of your accomplishments. You have always been and always will be our bright and shining star. I don't know if you will be reading this letter in private or if it is part of the schedule and you have to share it with others. Some things cannot be written but we want you to know we admire your courage and strength to stick to your convictions. You have helped Dad and me to find peace within ourselves. Our marriage is a good one and we have a deep love for both of our children. Their happiness means our happiness—their hurts are our hurts too.
>
> We are glad you decided to go on the retreat—new places to visit and friends to meet. We hope you enjoy every minute of it. We will be waiting your safe return with open arms.
>
> Love,
> Mom and Dad

The letter was written on beige notepaper with a matching envelope. My mom's handwriting was neat and pretty, a cursive script that filled three small pages. She spaced her lines neatly, like double spacing with a typewriter. She must have worried over that letter and wondered whether I might have to read it aloud. So her references were cryptic—any parent could say they admired a child's strength to stick by her convictions. Who would know my mother was referring to my continuing a pregnancy so many wanted me to abort?

I got teary eyed when I read the letter. My dad had been so angry with me when he found out, and my mom so disappointed. The fact that she said I would always be their bright and shining star made me happy. Certainly, I felt like I'd lost all luster in their eyes. And to have in writing that they loved me still, accepted me, and were even proud of me, was the boost I needed. I knew God was on my side, and now I knew my parents were too.

Of Nuns and Wildflowers
Two months, three weeks and one day

Sister Linda didn't look like any nun I'd ever seen before. She was young, probably in her late twenties, about the same age as Kevin's oldest brother. She didn't wear a habit like most nuns, who reminded me of penguins, their black and white outfits billowing in the wind when they walked across our school campus. Sister Linda didn't hide her hair underneath a veil, and when she walked down the staircase at Spaulding College one evening to greet us and assist in the tour, she might have passed for a student.

I couldn't focus on the tour. We walked around campus and in and out of buildings. The classrooms with their desks looked much like any other classroom. But I was pretty sure I wouldn't be going to college, and seeing these rooms made me sad. I'd always done well in school and had once planned on applying to Harvard, Brandeis, and other fine colleges. I thought about that as Sister Linda talked about different programs and popular professors. I looked out the window and thought about how this time next year my friends would be off to college, starting new lives. What would my own life look like then?

Someone was asking Sister Linda about applications and SAT scores, stuff that no longer pertained to me. The scene outside—students rushing off to dinner or the library—blurred as tears filled my eyes. I didn't want anyone to know I was crying, so I stared out the window and tried to think of something else.

"Judith?" Sister Linda said. "Are you coming?"

Everyone was filing out the door, moving on to some other place, and for now, I was supposed to pretend it was somewhere I could go as well. I followed.

Later, when the tour was over, we went to a meeting room set up for dinner. The round tables were covered with white tablecloths, the napkins folded like open fans and placed at each setting. The water glasses were already filled and waiting for us. At the front of the room was a podium with a microphone and at the back were banquet tables covered with food.

We sat down, and Father Tim, a priest at the college, led us in a prayer thanking God for the food we were about to eat and for bringing us safely to Kentucky. He asked God to continue to bless us and guide us as we finished out our retreat.

We all said "amen" and made the sign of the cross, touching our forehead with our finger tips—*in the name of the Father*, then touching the middle of our chest—*and of the Son*, then touching our left shoulder—*and of the Holy*, and finally our right shoulder—*Spirit*.

The simple prayer and blessing lifted my spirits, and when I got in line with the other girls to spoon lasagna and salad onto my plate, I felt like one of them again. We sat and ate and laughed and talked. At least for the moment, I still belonged.

After dinner we listened to a presentation about the college and the value of an education at a Catholic college. We were coming from our own small private Catholic high school, and many parents valued that sort of education. But a pep talk about college, Catholic or not, didn't have much to do with where my life was going.

We gathered in the grand foyer to find out where we would be staying the night. My friends were going to experience dorm living. In pairs, they were going to spend the night with a college student. The plans for me were different, however.

I was paired with Karen, but we were kept back until all of the other girls had left. We were going with Sister Linda in her tan sedan, and we put our bags in the trunk. The three of us sat in the front seat together, so neither Karen nor I would have to sit in the backseat alone.

"So, how are you feeling, Judith?" Sister Linda asked as we pulled away from the campus.

"I'm fine," I answered, startled. I guess I knew the nuns at my school would talk, share my secret, but here I was with a nun I'd just met, and she already knew.

"I suppose you both must be wondering where we're going. We didn't want to make it obvious in front of the other girls, Judith, so that's why

Karen's here too."

I was glad they'd thought of ways to help keep my secret. I didn't feel ready for the whole senior class to know about my pregnancy.

"We're going to spend the night at a home for pregnant teens. It's where I work and live," Sister continued.

We weren't on the road long. But it was already late when we pulled into a driveway. The place looked like an elementary school—a one-story brick building. Most of the lights were out except for a few at one end. That part of the building was attached by a short enclosed walkway to a big Victorian house. We pulled up in front of the house.

Inside there was a reception desk, and I was surprised to see a woman waiting to greet us.

"Hi, Sister," Sister Linda said to the woman behind the desk. "This is Karen and Judith. They'll be staying with us tonight."

"Nice to meet you," the woman said and held out her hand.

We followed Sister Linda up two flights of stairs and down a long hallway. Finally arriving at a door, Sister took out a key. Inside her apartment, there was a small kitchen that opened onto an equally small living room with two armchairs and a coffee table. Off to the side was the bedroom with a twin bed against one wall and a full bed on the other side.

"Do either of you want anything to drink?" Sister asked.

"I'd love a cup of tea, if you have it," I said, and Karen said she'd have one too.

Sister poured water in a teakettle and turned on the stove. We sat in the living room, but it was like we were still in the kitchen because Sister was only a few feet away. When the kettle whistled, Sister asked us to make our tea the way we liked it.

Sipping tea made me think of my mom back in Massachusetts. She and I often drank tea after cleaning the dinner dishes. We'd take our cups into the TV room to watch a show together, or if nothing was on that we wanted to see, we'd just sit and talk.

I was feeling a bit homesick, but sitting with Sister Linda was comfortable. She made us feel welcome and at home in her little apartment.

"So tell me about the baby," Sister said after Karen and I settled into the armchairs. She grabbed a folding chair leaning against the wall and sat in that. She smiled at me, warm and friendly.

"Well, I'm a couple of months pregnant, I think."

"Do you know when the baby is due?" she asked.

"No. I haven't gone to the doctor yet." Then I told her about Kevin and me.

"What are you going to do?"

"Well, I'm going to finish out this school year, and Kevin's going to finish his year at prep school. The baby will be here by then, and we'll get married after that. We'll probably have a summer wedding. It's kind of confusing, though. His parents aren't very happy about any of this. Kevin sent me a letter his mother wrote to him. It was pretty upsetting."

I wasn't sure I wanted to tell Sister that his mom wanted me to get an abortion and now Kevin said he felt the same way.

"Are they upset about the wedding plans?" she asked.

"I'm not sure they know about the wedding plans. Kevin wanted me to send the letter he wrote about our plans to his mother, but I didn't. His mother wants me to get an abortion," I confessed.

"Oh no!" Sister said and her hand flew to her mouth.

"It's true. Even Kevin said he thought it would be better for us if I have an abortion." I stopped there because as soon as I said that Kevin wanted me to abort our child, my eyes started filling up and my throat started to ache.

Karen fished in her purse for a tissue, but she couldn't find one. Sister was up and back with a box of tissues that she set on the coffee table between our mugs of tea. It was hard for me to go on. I wiped my eyes and tried again.

"It's just that it doesn't make any sense to me. We talked about growing wildflowers, it was our dream."

"Wildflowers?" Sister asked. "What do you mean?'

"Oh, it's kind of silly," I said. But I explained. "Kevin got grounded a lot last spring and through the summer. We kept breaking his curfew. By the time he'd drive home to Vermont after visiting with me, he was always late. So one time his parents let him go out for a walk, and he told me that he stopped and prayed that we'd get married and have children. He saw these beautiful wildflowers that grow in the spring but then stay around for a long time. They're tiny white flowers, or white with little bits of purple in them with orange-yellow centers. Have you ever seen them?"

Sister Linda shook her head no.

"I think I've seen them," Karen said, "at the side of the highway sometimes, right?"

"That's right. They grow in big patches along the highway. So when Kevin was out walking, he picked three: one for me, one for him, and one for our baby. But this was way before there was a baby. It was a wildflower for each of us." I laughed lightly. "After that, we'd always talk about growing wildflowers together. It meant getting married and having a baby."

"That's sweet," Sister Linda said. "The part about the wildflowers," she added.

"Yeah, it was," I said. "But now that I actually am pregnant, it seems like everything has changed."

"What do you mean?" Sister asked.

"Well, suddenly everyone wants me to get an abortion. I don't know. I just feel so confused."

I didn't want to talk about all the sad things. I didn't want to talk about how afraid I was that Kevin wasn't going to stay with me. So instead, I shifted the conversation to more positive things about our relationship.

"Kevin loves to ski," I told Sister and Karen. "Actually, before I was even dating him, we went on a ski trip together. We went to Stratton Mountain and spent the whole day together."

"Isn't that like a date?" Karen asked.

"Well it would've been. Except he brought a girl named Lynn and I was with my old boyfriend, David."

"Oh, that's right," Karen said. "You weren't seeing Kevin last winter."

"No, I wasn't, but I hung out with him a lot. We were good friends. And that day on the mountain, we had so much fun. Lynn and David skied together most of the day, and I got to spend it with Kevin."

Sister Linda said, "That's funny, but wasn't your boyfriend mad?"

"No. Like I said, he spent the day with Lynn. Kevin and I had a great time," I said. "It really was like we were already boyfriend and girlfriend. There was this one run where I fell down. Kevin was way ahead of me, and at first he didn't know I'd fallen." I paused for a minute thinking back on that day. "He climbed back up to get me, to see if I was all right."

And as I told the story, I could see Kevin in my mind, coming up over the crest of that hill, digging the edges of his skis into the snow just to reach me. He was away at school now, but I hoped he would keep coming back for me—the way he did that afternoon on the mountain.

Against a Stiff Black Habit
Two months, three weeks and two days

She wanted us to call her Linda. It seemed a little odd since she was a nun. But after staying up late and talking with her about Kevin, it was as if she were a big sister rather than a nun. Someone I could confide in, someone I could share some of my fears with.

Linda woke us early and the smell of coffee already filled her small apartment. Karen and I had slept together in the full bed, side by side, the way I imagined I would one day sleep with Kevin, waking in the morning to the weight of his body next to mine. Linda was in the twin bed. Choosing the life she had, Linda would always sleep without a man. Resting in bed, thinking of Kevin, I hoped I would not be alone.

Sitting up I pushed that thought out of my mind and dangled my legs over the side of the bed. I did that most mornings since the pregnancy, trying to gauge whether I needed to make a run for the bathroom right away. I didn't feel queasy, so I put my feet down and joined Linda, who stood at the kitchen counter pouring coffee. She wore a lavender bathrobe, silky and pretty, and her blond hair was already combed neatly. I smiled, thinking again how she just didn't look like any nuns I knew. But then again, I'd never awakened in the same room as a nun before.

"Coffee?" she asked.

"Mmm, yes, please," I said. My voice came out scratchy, morning-groggy.

Karen was already up as well. "Are you supposed to be having coffee now?" she asked. Her large round glasses on her round face made me think of an owl.

She looked so serious.

"I don't know. I always drink coffee in the morning."

Linda poured a mug for me. "How do you take it?"

"Cream and sugar, please," I said. She made my coffee while I leaned against the counter. We joined Karen in the living room.

"What would you two like for breakfast?" Linda asked.

"I don't eat breakfast," I said.

Karen looked at me. "Don't you think you need to start eating breakfast now?" she asked, her tone slightly sarcastic.

"Probably, but it just makes me sick," I said.

"Well, that feeling will usually only last for the first few months," Linda said. "You'll have a better appetite soon." She offered me some saltines. "These might settle your stomach."

It seemed she knew more about pregnancy than even my mom. But since I was adopted and my brother, too, my mother had never carried a baby to term. She'd had just the one pregnancy when she and my dad were trying to have their own baby. "I lost the baby early on," she'd told me. But then she brightened up and said, "I might not have had you or your brother if that hadn't happened. God works in mysterious ways." That was my mom, always looking for the silver lining.

I nibbled a cracker and sipped my coffee.

"Well," Linda said, "we have a nine o'clock appointment over at the nursery. So we need to get ready soon."

We took turns in the small bathroom. It had a shower stall but no tub. I washed up and got dressed. My stomach didn't look pregnant, but already my breasts were changing. Normally, I had a small chest, but now my breasts were getting rounder and fuller. My bra felt tight, and I thought how a new bra would probably be my first pregnancy purchase.

In the hall outside Linda's apartment a young girl walked by. I thought she looked even younger than me. Her dark hair was in a pixie cut, but what I really noticed was her big belly. She was huge. Not just your average round belly, basketball-stomach big, but huge. It was like her whole body was consumed with being pregnant. Even her face looked swollen. The girl waddled more than walked, and her belly bulged out on both sides of her body. Was that going to happen to me? Would my body change so much that it wouldn't even feel like it was mine anymore?

"Good morning, Felicia," Linda said. "This is Judith and Karen. They've come to look at our home."

"Hi," Felicia said and looked at Karen and then me. I wondered if she was trying to figure out who was pregnant. Maybe she thought we both were. I thought that was pretty funny. Karen had never even had a boyfriend. I wasn't even sure she liked boys. I don't mean she liked girls, except as friends—just that I'd never heard her discuss boys the way my other friends did. Boys were a major topic for most of my friends. But not for Karen.

Karen said, "Hi," and I stood there dumbstruck. Felicia gave a little wave and disappeared into a room off the hallway.

Linda saw the shocked look on my face and said, "Twins. She's having twins. That's why she's so big."

I relaxed a little and felt relieved and hopeful my body wouldn't look like that. We went downstairs past the reception desk and then down a long corridor and through an enclosed walkway. It reminded me of the connection between Saint John's Hall and Saint Mary's Hall back at school—two buildings attached with a similar walkway, like an umbilical cord.

Linda led us to a door and said, "This is the nursery." We went in. It was the size of a large classroom. On the back wall a chalkboard hung, unused.

More than one baby was crying. An older nun dressed in the traditional black and white habit held one of the babies. With a cloth diaper draped over her shoulder, she was rubbing the baby's back, but the child kept crying. Another nun sat in a rocking chair with a baby in her arms.

"Sister Catherine," Linda said. "Let me give you a hand." She scooped up one of the screaming infants, held the baby in her arms, and swayed side to side, her body rocking slightly. The gentle movement soothed the babe, and the crying stopped.

I saw babies in bassinets around the room, plus the three held by Sister Catherine, Linda and the other nun. Along one wall, there were dressing tables and baby swings waiting to be used and a couple of empty playpens. The smell of baby powder filled the room.

"Where's Jane?" Linda asked.

"Oh, she just stepped out to the bathroom," Sister Catherine said.

A minute later, Jane returned. She was older than Linda but younger than Sister Catherine. She wore a black skirt and a white blouse, but no veil. I assumed she was a Sister too.

"Jane, can you grab Latoya?" Sister Catherine asked. "I think she needs a diaper change."

Jane took the tiny baby to one of the changing tables. I watched as she took the diaper off, held the little feet in one hand, and lifted the little girl high enough to wipe her bottom. She spoke to us as she worked, and I was amazed she could do both with so little effort.

"So who do we have here?" Jane asked.

"Judith and Karen. They're here on a senior trip from Saint Anne's Academy."

"Welcome," Jane said. She had finished with Latoya and put the baby back in a bassinet. She washed her hands before coming over to shake our hands.

I was beginning to wonder where the mothers were. I hadn't seen any teens besides Felicia.

"Which one of you is thinking of coming here?" Jane asked.

The question surprised me. What did she mean? Suddenly, I imagined my parents wanting me to go far away during my pregnancy, wanting to discard me the way my birth mother had discarded me so many years before. Maybe Mom and Dad were so embarrassed by my pregnancy, like the O'Briens, that they planned to hide me away as I got bigger. Maybe Mom had talked with Kevin's mom and they'd agreed on this so I wouldn't humiliate them. I was feeling paranoid, like there was a conspiracy to send me away.

Linda's voice broke in on my anxious thoughts. "No, no, neither of them! They're here for their senior retreat, and their principal thought they might like to visit. They're at the retreat center through the weekend."

But I kept thinking. Why did they bring me here? I remembered my mother's beautiful letter and realized she wouldn't do this to me. It had to be my principal and the other nuns from school who wanted to make sure I weighed all my options.

"Where are all the mothers?" I asked.

"They've gone home," Sister Catherine answered.

I didn't get it yet.

"Why aren't they here taking care of their babies?" I asked.

The Sisters looked at each other. Then Linda came over to me. She still had the baby in her arms. "They're not keeping their babies," she said. "They've given them up for adoption."

I remembered the slips of paper Kevin had handed to me before he went away to school, how his father had scribbled the names of local Catholic agencies that took babies from mothers who couldn't keep their children for one reason or another. And here I was at such a home, only far away in Kentucky. I imagined how happy the O'Brien family would be if I came here.

"All of these babies are going to be adopted?" I asked.

"Yes," Sister Catherine said.

It hit me hard. The idea that all of these little ones were being given away, that not one of their parents wanted them enough to keep them and love them hurt me. I was sure I would start crying if we didn't leave.

"Would you like to hold one of the babies?" Sister Linda asked.

I didn't. I just wanted to get out of there. The sight of the babies lined up in bassinets, the changing tables on the wall, the institutional feel of the room—it was all too much for me.

"Can we go now?" I asked Linda quietly.

"Certainly, sweetie," she said and handed the baby to Jane.

Karen hadn't said much of anything. We left the nursery and went back to Linda's apartment. I didn't want to talk and told Linda I needed to lie down.

"That's fine, Judith," Linda said. "But we do have to get back to the retreat soon. They'll be starting again. In fact, we're going to be a little late already. Is half an hour long enough?"

I went into the bedroom and plopped down on the bed. Then I rolled over and buried my face into the pillow and cried. I was crying for the little babies in the nursery, so shiny and new, so perfectly formed. I was crying for the mothers who'd given those babies up, like things you could discard, like an old blanket you could just throw away. And I was crying for myself.

There was a heaviness in my chest weighing me down. I felt close to those babies, even connected in a way. My birth mother had given me up through Catholic Charities when I was an infant. Maybe I spent time in a home like this, some nun holding me against her stiff black habit.

I was fearful when I saw that girl in the hallway—so young, so pregnant, and so alone. I was afraid of being like her, of being that alone. And I was afraid because a chasm seemed to be opening up in front of me, wide and gaping, and I was afraid it would swallow me whole.

Rumors and Betrayals
Two months, three weeks and three days

*A*s the retreat continued, I felt more and more distant from all the other girls. We went to Churchill Downs, the racetrack where the Kentucky Derby takes place. Without crowds and galloping horses, it was nothing more than a large, empty stadium. The starting gates were just cages of metal. All of the emptiness reminded me of my own feelings of desolation.

I couldn't work up much interest in anything, and I kept thinking about that mean letter I'd sent to Kevin, the one where I told him why I thought abortion was wrong. It felt like I hadn't spoken to him for forever. What was he thinking and feeling when he went to classes or played football? What was happening in his mind and heart?

I couldn't concentrate on much that was happening around me. Instead, I kept thinking about the things I'd written, the things I'd said and done. What if my angry words drove Kevin away? What if my refusing to have an abortion made him leave me?

"Hey, Judith? Isn't this place wonderful?" Karen asked.

I looked at Karen, and she was smiling. "Oh, yeah, great."

"Are you okay?"

"I'm all right."

"Are you sure?" She touched my arm and let her hand linger there for a minute.

I shook her off and said, "Fine, I'm fine."

Her hand dropped to her side, and she looked down. I could tell she was hurt, but I didn't have anything to say right there in the middle of the race-track. With the rest of our senior class hanging around, I couldn't tell her how I really felt.

That evening we had pizza at the retreat center. A number of our teachers were oddly missing. I didn't feel like hanging out with Karen and her inquisitive, sorrowful looks. She was concerned about me, but I couldn't bear to talk to her anymore. So I sat with a different group of friends: Sally, Amy, Sandy, and Barbara. Amy and Sally were cheerleaders like me. I'd known Sally since kindergarten, and we'd been close since junior high. She was friends with Karen too, but they didn't share interests like writing and God, the way Karen and I did. Sally kept a lot of things to herself, especially now that she'd been seeing Eric for about a year. She probably shared everything with him, the way I did with Kevin.

I could talk about Kevin with Sally, and I felt like she understood. Kevin and Eric had graduated together, and I had pictures of the four of us from that day. Sally knew how lost I was feeling since Kevin went away to school because Eric was off at college, and they were trying to hold their relationship together during the transition.

Sally, Amy, and Sandy knew I was pregnant, but not Barbara. Barbara was going out with my ex-boyfriend David, and I didn't want her to know yet.

"So how's Kevin doing?" Amy asked as we ate our pepperoni pizza.

"He's okay," I said. "He's trying to get used to the school. His team has a game next weekend, and he wants me to come see him."

Amy glanced at Sally and asked, "It's not going to interfere with our game, is it?" She was co-captain of our cheerleading squad.

"No, it's on Sunday," I said. I didn't feel as committed to cheering anymore. How could that take priority over a chance to see my fiancé, my baby's father?

"Hey, what about Eric?" I asked Sally.

"He's going to come to our game on Saturday," she said and tucked a long strand of brown hair behind her ear.

"Do you think he'll come to the party later?" Amy asked.

"I don't know," Sally said. "I want him to, but he's got a project for school."

We had a party after every game, win or lose. It would take place at some-one's house—a cheerleader's, a player's, or even some other student who liked us and liked to party. Usually, the parties would take place in a basement or backyard. Since my brother Paul was old enough to buy alcohol, he'd get me some if it didn't interfere with his plans. We always found a way to get beer and wine. The parents left us alone if they were around, but it was more fun if they were out. Sometimes we got rowdy, especially if we'd won. But the parties didn't seem as important to me this year, and I wasn't drinking anymore.

"David should be there," Barbara said. She was a dancer and had dirty blond hair like Kevin's.

It still felt awkward to hear her talk about David. I'd gone out with him for over a year, and we both thought we'd last forever. But we fought a lot—and I mean all the time. It was hard to remember why we thought we were good together. Sally never thought so. She liked David, and we'd double-dated with her and Eric, but David and I usually ended up in some stupid argument and ruined the night for everyone.

"How's David?" Sally asked Barbara.

"Yeah, how *is* David?" I asked. I didn't mean it to, but a slight sarcasm crept into my voice. He wasn't my boyfriend anymore, and I was engaged to Kevin. Still, when I thought of David with Barbara, with her pretty dancer's body, it made me jealous and aggravated. Suddenly, our warm pizza party had cooled, and Sally frowned at me.

I lightened my tone and asked nicely, "Is he planning on playing hockey this year?"

Everyone relaxed. Barbara answered, "He hasn't decided yet. He doesn't want to play JV his senior year, and he doesn't think he'd make varsity."

"Kevin felt the same way about basketball," I said. "He did winter track instead."

It was funny sitting with this group of friends talking about boyfriends and sports. As cheerleaders we were part of a jock crowd. But our school was small, so you could be friends with more than one group. The lines weren't as rigidly drawn as at some schools. Our girls' school had jocks—the star basketball players, the field hockey players too. These girls often played more than one sport, and they were a little tough, some a little butch. There were even rumors that one of the athletes had a thing with another player. But there were always rumors, and they didn't matter much. You could still sit in the school cafeteria with the sports nuts, or the cheerleaders, or the studious nerds. Probably some people would think my pregnancy was another rumor. Only when I started to show would they know for sure.

After dinner we went back to our rooms. There were no more scheduled events until the next morning when we would have our closing ceremony. We were going to meet in Sally and Barbara's room after washing up—a little pajama party on our last night.

I was brushing my teeth when I heard doors slamming and raised voices.

"What's going on?" I asked Karen who was coming down the hall when I came out of the bathroom.

"I don't know," she said. "Amy's saying someone went through her stuff!"

Suddenly the hallway was filled with girls.

"I'm telling you, my things aren't how I left them," Amy was saying to Barbara. "Go check your things."

People went back to their rooms but left their doors open.

"Hey, me too!" Sally yelled from her room.

"My blow dryer's not where I left it," someone else called out.

Voices filled the hall, and kids yelled from their rooms about what was different. I went into my room to see if any of my things was missing. I was worried because I'd purchased a pair of yellow knitted booties at the retreat's gift shop, and I didn't want anyone finding them and wondering why I would need yellow booties. My suitcase was open on the chair where I'd left it. It looked the same to me. But I knew I'd tucked the booties in a suitcase pocket, and that's not where they were now. Instead, they were placed on top of my things, right out in the open. I knew someone had gone through my suitcase.

I walked over to Sally's room. "Someone definitely went into my things," I said and told her how someone moved the booties.

"That's weird. My things were gone through too," she said. "Nothing's missing, though." After everyone had a chance to verify that nothing had been taken, we all met in our class president's room.

People were talking over each other. Some girls were really angry. I was worried that my secret was out.

"If nothing is missing, then it wasn't about stealing," I said.

The statement didn't make anyone feel better. Someone had gone through our things while we'd been eating pizza and we didn't know why.

Amy spoke up. "Well, my cigarettes are gone."

We weren't supposed to have cigarettes on the trip, but the smokers had managed to sneak one or two late at night in the bathroom with the fan on and the window cracked. I'd had a couple drags the night before with Sally and Amy.

"Mine are gone too," Barbara said.

I didn't think any of this was about baby booties in my suitcase anymore. While we were still trying to figure out what was going on, some of our teachers appeared at the doorway.

There stood Ms. Maxwell the English teacher, Miss Olsen the algebra teacher, and Sister Claudia our principal. "We need to see Amy, Barbara, and..." Sister Claudia rattled off a few more names, and then they all went off with the girls they'd come for.

The rest of us waited. A sense of unease weighed heavy in our silence. Why would anyone go through our things?

When the girls came back, they were angry. Seems the teachers had rifled through our stuff while we were at dinner. Miss Olsen said they had reason to believe someone had drugs and therefore felt obligated to make a search.

It was true that some of us smoked pot at parties, but none of us bought or sold pot, and no one was stupid enough to bring drugs on a senior trip. Cigarettes? Yes. But drugs? No. All the teachers had found were a few cigarette packages.

"What's going to happen?" Sally asked.

"After-school detention," Barbara said.

"How long?" I asked.

"A week," Amy said.

"That's crazy," I said. "For God's sake, they give us a smoking area out back by the cafeteria, and juniors and seniors are allowed to smoke. What's the big deal?"

"They say it's because we hid it and smoked where we weren't supposed to," Amy said. "Remember, it was one of the rules for the trip, no smoking."

I couldn't believe the teachers had gone through our things. I imagined them rifling through our stuff and then hoping we wouldn't notice. But they planned to punish the kids found with cigarettes, so clearly we were going to hear about what they'd done. Our senior trip was supposed to be about building relationships. We were supposed to trust our teachers, especially the nuns. Weren't they, of all people, supposed to be honest and truthful?

In the time it took for the teachers to sneak into our rooms and go through our bags, they'd undone any progress made during the retreat, and our trust was now broken.

I was raving to Karen later that night about the teachers, going on about how I couldn't believe what they'd done. "Hey, are you listening to me?" I asked. She seemed distracted.

"Judith, I have to tell you something," she said. "I told Betty and Sarah that you're pregnant."

"You what?" I asked, incredulous. It was bad enough that the teachers had betrayed us, but Karen was my friend. I was looking at her hard, waiting for her to say something.

"Over pizza," she said.

Like it mattered what they were eating.

"Why did you tell them?" I thought about how I'd hidden the yellow booties so carefully, how the principal had asked me not to let other students know, and how it wouldn't be long, now, before everyone knew.

"I don't know," she said. "You seemed so sad, earlier. I wanted to get their opinion on what I could do to help."

"Their opinion?" I asked, my voice rising. "None of you even has a boyfriend! What do any of you know about how I might be feeling? Where do you get off?"

"I'm sorry."

But right then I didn't care about her apology. With nothing left to say to her, I went to bed. The day had been full enough with broken trusts. I just wanted to go to sleep, and then go home.

Up Against the O'Briens
Nearly three months

We finished our retreat the next day and then the bus drove through the night. When we arrived back at my high school, parents were already there, waiting in their cars. The bus pulled up to the curb, and the adults got out and waited on the sidewalk. I didn't see my mom and dad at first. Did they forget what time to pick me up? Then I saw them standing side by side, my dad a good six inches taller than my mom.

We filed off the bus, tired and stiff, and I stretched my arms up over my head. My mom saw me and pointed, and she and Dad came over. Mom wrapped her arms around me in a big hug and stroked my hair. Dad patted my back with a little too much force.

"Hey, that hurts," I said.

"Is that the first thing you have to say to us?" Mom said holding me back, her hands on my shoulder. She kissed me on the lips. "We missed you."

"I missed you too," I said, and it was true, especially after I'd read the lovely letter she wrote. I gave her another hug, glad for her love, and I gave my dad a kiss too.

"So, any letters from Kevin? Phone calls?" I asked.

"Now, Judith," my mom answered, her tone a bit stern. "Why would he call? He knew you were away."

"Right. But letters?"

"I think there might be one."

There might be one? She sounded so nonchalant, like it didn't matter whether there was one letter, two, three, or none at all. Maddening.

At home, I found his letter on the counter and lifted it to my nose. I could smell the Coast soap, and I imagined Kevin taking the time to glide the bar across the sealed envelope. I took the letter up to my room.

I plopped down on my bed and held the envelope to my chest. It felt like I was holding him, this piece of him sent through the mail, his soft smell coming back to me. Before I even opened the letter, I had tears in my eyes. I could feel the filmy soap on the outside of the envelope and under my fingertips when I put my finger under the sealed flap. When I opened the letter and unfolded the pages, I could feel the soap there too.

> Dear Judith,
>
> When I got your letter I knew you were mad as soon as I opened it. I couldn't smell your pretty perfume and your angry words were all I had to greet me. I wish you weren't so mad.
>
> I think we need to see each other so we can talk. I do love you and we will get married. I just thought it would be easier without a baby. You need to have a little more faith. I have a game at Deerfield Academy the weekend after you come back. Please come. My family's going to be there, and I want you there too.
>
> Love, Kevin

At the bottom he'd scribbled *Believe in me!* with a pretty swirly line underneath. It had become his motto, one he repeated over and over. *Believe! Believe in me.* And I wanted to. More than anything, I really wanted to.

I stayed on my bed with the letter resting on my chest. I felt good that he wanted to marry me, still. He was saying he planned to stay with me. I needed him to stand by me, and the fact that he wanted me at the game with his family was a good sign.

My parents agreed to let me drive to Kevin's football game. Mom planned to make a big Sunday dinner afterwards, and Kevin was going to join us. It was going to be the big day when Kevin told my parents his intentions. I thought it was sweet and funny. I mean, I already had the diamond he'd given me and a baby growing inside. It seemed to me his intentions were clear.

I got lost going to the game, so by the time I got the car parked and walked to the stands, the team was already on the field. I stood by the bleachers, feeling a little awkward. The O'Brien family sat together, and I couldn't decide whether to go up and join them or sit by myself. It felt like a huge decision. I decided to sit away from them but where they could see me.

I looked out at the field for Kevin and spotted his number 58 as his team lined up for the play.

"Hey, Judith," I heard Joanna, Kevin's older sister, calling out to me. "Come sit with us," she said, patting the spot next to her. Her hair was dirty blond like Kevin's, and she kept it neat in a short bob. She was tall like her brothers.

We had gone to see her over the summer in Springfield, and it was fun driving with Kevin, sitting close to him in the family pickup truck, his arm draped across my shoulder. He made me feel safe and warm. At Joanna's apartment we'd had a light dinner with good conversation. Joanna had finished college and was all grown up, living on her own. That day, it felt like Kevin and I were grownups too.

I climbed the stands toward the O'Brien family. Kevin's parents and his brother Richard and Richard's wife Pam were there. So were Kevin's younger brother Randy and their little sister Julie. Randy was two years younger than Kevin, and he played on St. Joseph's football team. He reminded me of Kevin, and sometimes after cheering practice, I'd chat with him. But right now, Randy was on the other side of his parents, not looking at me, like we were strangers.

"Hi," I said and waved to everyone as I sat down.

Mrs. O'Brien smiled, but it was a fake, plastered-on smile. Like the one she had on the day of Kevin's high school graduation. I had taken a picture of her and Mr. O'Brien with Kevin and Randy and Julie. Kevin was the only one in that picture who looked genuinely happy. He had on his quirky smile—one side of his mouth slightly higher than the other. That should have been a happy day for all, but his family didn't seem too thrilled with me, even then.

"So how have you been?" Joanna asked.

"Fine," I said. "Busy with school and cheering." I wondered if anyone had told her about the pregnancy. I figured she must know.

"You're still cheering this year?"

So she did know. "For now," I said.

"Hmm."

Hmm what? I thought. But I didn't say anything. Her response didn't seem to call for one from me. We turned our attention to the game. Kevin's team was marching down the field, about to score. They did and we stood and screamed. It seemed to me like Kevin was looking over at us, but I couldn't really tell. I waved in case he could see me.

During the last quarter, Mrs. O'Brien came over and sat next to me. Pam did too. With Joanna right next to me, I was surrounded by O'Brien women. The guys instinctively moved away from us. I didn't know what to think.

Mrs. O'Brien jumped in first. "You're running out of time," she said.

"That's right," Pam followed up. "You need to schedule an abortion right away. You only have until the end of the first trimester." Since she was a nurse, I guess she knew what she was talking about.

"Sometimes, under certain circumstances, it can be done later, but it's a much more difficult procedure," she continued.

I thought about my unborn baby, swimming like a little fish in my womb, but with tiny hands growing, with a heart and a brain. My life certainly would be easier if I had an abortion. But I couldn't do that to my baby.

Joanna spoke next. "It's probably for the best," she said a little doubtfully.

Well, at least one of them seemed to be questioning the idea. I mean, they were all Catholics! None of them should've been thinking about abortion.

They leaned in, and Mrs. O'Brien continued, "When are you going to make that appointment? There's no time to waste." Her fake smile was gone now, and her features were set in a scowl. Her eyebrows were low and knitted together, a crease forming in the space between her brows.

I chewed the corner of my thumb, grabbing a bit of skin between my teeth, and didn't answer right away. The whole conversation felt surreal.

"Never," I finally managed to spit out. "I am never having an abortion!" I said this emphatically, a little louder than I intended. But I wanted them to know this was not a topic up for debate. There was nothing they, or anyone, could say to change my mind.

They looked around, clearly hoping no one heard what I'd said. Some people glanced over at us, and Mrs. O'Brien seemed horrified that others might know I was pregnant. They stopped talking to me then, as if my announcement swept away all need for communication.

The game had ended while they were badgering me, and the guys got up and stretched their legs. I got up too and walked some distance away from the O'Brien clan. I waited on the track that surrounded the football field and then walked onto the edge of the field. Kevin and his fellow players were filing past the opposing team, shaking hands with each player as they went by.

I was watching Kevin. I couldn't wait to touch him and reassure myself that he was really mine. I wanted to tell him what his family had been saying to me, but they were all right there. When he finished the last handshake, he started looking around.

Then he saw me, and I saw a smile spread across his face, a big wide grin.

He strode across the field toward me. His family had started walking over to him, but he went right past them. He didn't even acknowledge them at first. Instead, he came to me, dropped his helmet, put his arms around me, and scooped me up into the air. He spun around, in a little dance-twirl. In his football uniform with the shoulder padding, he seemed larger than life. And when he stopped spinning he still held me high.

I felt like a trophy, something he could carry triumphantly off the field. Something he would want to keep forever. He lowered me so my face was even with his, and he kissed me. Right there in front of his family, in front of his coach and his friends. He kissed me, once, twice, three times. And on the third kiss, he left his lips on mine. His eyes were open, his big, beautiful blue eyes looking deep into mine.

He placed me down, gently. "Hi," he said.

"Hi." I felt a little shy right there in that field, with his family looking on. I knew they were mad. I could almost feel their eyes drilling into my back.

"Did you see your family's here?" I suggested he go and greet them.

"Oh yeah," he smiled at me, an impish smile. "I hadn't really noticed."

"Nice game," Mr. O'Brien said and slapped his son on the back.

Richard was right there too, and he gave Kevin a pat on the back. The women were there, and Mrs. O'Brien came over and kissed him on the cheek. Then Pam and Joanna kissed him too.

"We've planned dinner at that Italian restaurant you like out on Route 2," Mrs. O'Brien said to him. "We've made reservations for eight." Eight. The number didn't include me. I knew it, and it hurt. But maybe they didn't know I'd be there. Kevin and I were supposed to have dinner at my house. My mother was making a roast.

Kevin still had a smile on his face. He wasn't seeing the problem. I tugged at his sleeve, got up on my tippy toes and whispered in his ear. "Mom's expecting us for dinner, remember."

Kevin loved my mom. Everyone did. My brother's close friends even called her Mom. Kevin had started to as well, and it was like he was already part of my family.

"Oh, right," he said. "I forgot." He stopped smiling and turned to his parents. "We're supposed to be eating at Judith's house tonight," he said. "She brought her car and they're expecting us."

Good, I thought. Because I couldn't imagine telling my mom we wouldn't be there after all.

"But we made reservations," Mrs. O'Brien retorted, and then added, "Judith can go home and have dinner with her family. You can come with us."

So this was it. The lines were drawn. His family. Mine. And she was making it pretty clear I wasn't welcome in theirs.

"Yes, Kevin," Mr. O'Brien said. "We already have reservations and everyone came down for your game."

Kevin turned to me. "Do you think your mom will mind too much if we go to dinner with my family instead?" he asked. "They did come all the way down to see me."

"She's probably got everything all ready. Besides," I said, turning closer to him and adding in a whisper, "your parents don't want me to come to dinner with you."

"Don't be crazy," he said. "Of course they want you to come to dinner. I'm not going without you."

He was still holding my hand and he squeezed it reassuringly. I looked at his family standing in a tight little huddle. They didn't look like they wanted me at all.

"Okay, so it's settled," Kevin said with conviction. "We'll see you there." He walked me to my car. "I'll take a quick shower and meet you right here." He kissed me again before jogging off to the locker room.

The O'Briens were piling into the family Cadillac. If Kevin had gone with them, they would've been packed in like sardines. But Julie sat in the back seat on her big brother Richard's lap, and there was still room for one more squeezed in tight. Not me, though. There definitely wasn't any room for me. Not in their car and not in their hearts.

Around a Crowded Table
Three months

We arrived at the restaurant, and the parking lot was packed. I let Kevin drive because I liked being his passenger, his co-pilot. Next to him, in my parents' green Mustang, it was like we were partners, but he was the one steering and in control.

"Look," I said. "There's a space towards the back. Hurry before someone else gets it." But when we got closer, the spot seemed small.

"I don't think we can fit," I said.

"Sure we can." He liked to see the possibilities where others might not. He guided the car slowly between the lines. "Just watch your door when you get out."

Hand in hand, we walked into the restaurant.

"I need to call home before we sit down," I said, spotting a pay phone just inside the main door. I dug some quarters out of my purse and dialed. Kevin opened the door to go inside without me.

"Hey, wait for me!"

Standing close to me, he took a few strands of my hair between his fingers and fiddled with it. Then he bent over and nuzzled my head.

"Cut it out." I could hear the phone ringing at home. "Hi, Mom?"

"Judith, where are you?" she asked. "Dinner's on the table, and we've been waiting."

"I know. I'm sorry. Listen, I'm at Carmello's here in Greenfield. The O'Briens had reservations."

"So did we," my mother said, testily.

"I know," I said, drawing out the word. "I'm sorry."

"Mmmm," she said.

Kevin tapped me on my shoulder. *Come on*, he was mouthing. "Hurry up," he said. I put my finger to my lips, shushing him.

"We'll come by after. Save us some dessert," I said.

"Right," my mom said tersely.

"Ooh, she's mad," I said after hanging up the phone. "Really mad."

"Come on, let's go." It was as if Kevin hadn't even heard me. "My family's waiting."

The host took us to the back of the restaurant, where the O'Briens were gathered around two tables that had been pushed together. When they looked up at us, I felt awkward and out of place.

Kevin sat down, forgetting about me or so it seemed. I just stood there.

Then he got up. "Here," he said, pulling out a chair, "sit here." I sat down with Julie and Randy, the youngest siblings. His mother was at the other end with his dad.

I longed to be at home. But here I was with Kevin's family in a fancy restaurant where I felt completely unwelcome, especially after sitting in the stands with the O'Brien women telling me to have an abortion.

I didn't think I'd ever understand them.

Sitting at the children's wing of the table reminded me of the time we'd had a summer barbeque at his family home. Everyone was there except Richard and Pam. It was a beautiful day, and we played Wiffle ball in the front yard and then took a swim in their pool. His mother had steak on the grill and corn on the cob wrapped in foil. When it was time to eat, there were two tables. Kevin, Randy, Julie and I were sent to one while everyone else sat at the other. We'd been relegated to the children's table that day, and now here we were again, our status no different even though we were soon to be the parents of the O'Briens' first grandchild.

"You made it!" Joanna said warmly. She sounded welcoming, and I relaxed a little.

Richard jumped in. "That was some game, Kevin. The coach played you almost the whole time!"

Kevin beamed. "Yeah, I wasn't sure how it was going to go this season, getting there late and all. But when he saw how good I was at practices, well, he's been playing me a lot."

"Hey, maybe you can get a scholarship for next year." his father said. "If you keep playing like you did today."

"Who knows," he said. "Anything's possible."

"Have you applied to any schools yet?" Pam asked.

"No, not yet. I've been too busy focusing on school work."

"You do need to get those grades up," Mrs. O'Brien reminded him.

"I know, Mom."

This conversation about college and scholarships seemed like a dream world beyond my reach. Part of me might have wanted these good things for Kevin before the pregnancy, but not now, not when our plans were so different. I didn't know what to think about the talk swirling around me.

Everyone was talking about college, college. While they talked, I just sat there and thought. Why wasn't Kevin telling his family what he'd told me? I wanted to interrupt and say something like, "Oh wait, remember Kevin, you're not going to college next year. We're having a *baby!*" But it didn't seem like the time or the place to bring that up, especially with little Julie sitting there. But when would be the right time?

A waiter came over and poured water for Kevin and me. Another waiter was already serving salads.

"We already ordered," Mrs. O'Brien said. "We didn't know what she would want." It was as if she couldn't bring herself to address me. "Kevin, they're bringing you lasagna, your favorite. That's what we ordered for her too. The food's going to be here any minute."

I was feeling left out, like I was in some kind of bubble that kept me separated from everyone. It was a bubble that kept me hidden enough so that all the O'Briens felt like they didn't need to talk to me. But it didn't make me invisible. They could see me sitting there, but I think they wished they could make me go away, take a pin and pop the bubble so I would just disappear.

While Kevin's family continued to talk about his future, the food arrived. "You're going to have a lot of fun at college," Joanna was saying.

I didn't want to hear any more about his college plans for next fall. I picked up my fork and tried to concentrate on the meal. The lasagna looked great, but I was having a hard time getting a single bite past the lump in my throat.

In a Warmer Place
Still three months

On the way back to my mother's house, I was quiet for most of the ride.
"What's wrong?" Kevin asked. "You hardly ate anything."

"Nothing. I'm fine."

"Okay," he said. "Suit yourself."

But I had my arms crossed over my chest, with my chin down, and I was anything but fine. After about twenty minutes of driving, I broached the subject I'd been afraid to bring up.

"So," I started. "We're going over to my parents to talk about what we're planning to do, right?"

"Right."

"But after that dinner with your family, I don't even know what we're planning to do."

"Nothing's changed," he said. "What are you talking about? You've still got that diamond on your finger, don't you?" He reached over and took my hand. "Ah yes, there it is," he said, moving my hand this way and that. "See how it glimmers?"

He smiled at me and I smiled back. He had a way of making me forget my worries when I was with him. It was like he could take an eraser and with one sweep, clear away all my concerns, wipe the slate clean.

"Do you think Mom saved us any of her famous apple pie?" he asked suddenly.

"Maybe. If she didn't throw it out to spite us for missing Sunday dinner."

But she hadn't. We went inside and she put her arms around Kevin, gave him a big hug and kiss. Then she went in the kitchen to make coffee and warm up the apple pie. Kevin took off his school jacket with the number 58 on the sleeve and helped me take off my coat.

Mom filled the creamer with half-and-half. "Here," she said to Kevin, "take these into the dining room." She handed him the creamer and sugar. Then she turned to me and said, "How was dinner?"

I scrunched up my nose like a rabbit, pursed my lips, and then leaned over and whispered, "Pretty bad. I'll tell you later."

Dad came down the stairs and joined us. "Oh, they finally made it," he said to my mother. Was everyone going to talk about us as if we weren't there?

Kevin went over and put out his hand. "Good to see you, sir," he said. Kevin called my mother "Mom," but Dad was "sir." I guess some things were going to take time.

"Yes, well, we've got a few things to ask you," my dad said.

"John," Mom said sternly. "Not now. Can we at least have out dessert first?"

It wasn't a question that needed an answer. As usual, when my mother said something, she meant it and that was pretty much it. Between my mother and father she clearly had the upper hand. If Dad said no to a request, my brother and I could always go to Mom and plead our case. But if Mom said no first, there was no court of appeals.

Mom and I dished the apple pie onto the Sunday plates, not the fine china, but not our everyday dishes, either. These were the plates she displayed on the dining room hutch. The china with its hand-painted flowers stayed hidden in cabinets except on holidays. But these dishes with their deep purples and greens came out every Sunday when my mother served dinner in the dining room.

"Get the vanilla ice cream from the freezer, honey," Mom said. I scooped the ice cream on top of the pie slices and brought the plates into the dining room two at a time. The cups and saucers were already out, and Mom poured coffee for all of us.

Dad sat at the head of table as he always did, and Mom sat at the other end by the window that looked out at the backyard. Kevin and I sat next to each other. My brother was out with his friends.

"Mom, this is delicious!" Kevin exclaimed.

He was right. Sitting in the dining room with my mom and dad and Kevin, I felt so safe and loved. Compared to how cold everything was with the

O'Briens, this whole scene was delicious.

When we finished our pie and had sipped enough coffee, Mom and I cleared the table while Kevin and Dad went into the living room. We left the dishes in the sink and joined them.

I sat with Kevin on the couch, and Mom sat in the matching armchair with its pale rose pattern. Dad had pulled his chair in from the dining room. There were two blue wing chairs on either side of the fireplace, but it seemed Dad wanted to be closer to everyone than either of these chairs would allow. This was an important meeting, the first time since finding out I was pregnant that we'd all sat down together to discuss the future.

My father started things off. "What are your intentions for our daughter, Kevin?"

He looked completely serious with his long arms crossed across his chest.

"Well, sir," Kevin began, speaking with unusual formality. It was as if he needed to recognize the seriousness of this event too. "I'm going to finish out this year of school first. I started it, and I plan to finish it. I'm working hard, and I want to show everyone that I can do a good job. Then, after I graduate, and after Judith graduates," he said, taking my hand before continuing, "and after our baby is born, I'm going to marry her. If you'll let us, we'll probably live here for a while. Just until we can get on our own feet."

"Are you sure about this, Kevin?" my mother asked. "We don't want you rushing into anything you're not ready for."

I couldn't believe what she was saying to him. Didn't she want us to get married?

"I've never been more sure of anything in my life," he said. He put his arm around my shoulders and pulled me closer to him. "I love Judith."

I could feel tears welling up in my eyes. I felt so happy hearing him tell my parents that he loved me and was sure he wanted to marry me. It was all I could ask for.

My dad stood up and Kevin stood up too. Dad took Kevin's hand in his— the two most important men in my life clasping their big hands together— and Dad said, "Welcome to the family, then."

Mom came over and kissed Kevin right on the lips. She kissed me too.

"I only hope you two will be happy," she said.

Coming Home
Three months and one week

Kevin had slipped the diamond ring on my finger in August. The big talk with my parents took place at the end of October. Then, in early November, Kevin was planning on coming to my house for the whole weekend, for my birthday. The visit was his birthday present to me.

I'd wanted to go up to his school on Friday night and stay over. Kevin thought that would be fine, that none of the administrators at his school would notice one girl sleeping over. He could sneak me in, no problem.

But my parents were having none of that. I thought they were being unreasonable. We were already engaged, already pregnant with our child. What difference did it make if I stayed in the same room with him?

My parents wouldn't even let me borrow the car to go get him. And since he didn't have a car, I had no idea how he'd be here in time for the game where I was supposed to be cheering.

I called one of the cheerleader co-captains on Friday night.

"Hey Amy, it's Judith," I said. "I'm not riding up on the bus tomorrow." For away games, the Wildcats took the school bus. The cheerleaders sat in the front rows with the cheering advisor, Mr. King. The football players sat behind us.

"What do you mean? Why not?"

"Remember, Kevin's coming down for my birthday." I was sure I had talked about Kevin's upcoming visit at our cheering practices. For the past week, it was all I could think about, all I could talk about.

"Yeah, I know. But I don't see what that has to do with our game," Amy said, her exasperation clear.

"I'm not sure what time he's going to get to my house," I said. "And I'm going to be here for him."

"Guess we'll see you at the game," she said. She didn't waste any time getting off the phone, no gossipy conversations tonight.

I called Sally.

"I think Amy's mad," I said. "About tomorrow." Sally knew I wasn't riding up on the bus, and she understood. If Eric were coming home from school, she would wait for him, maybe even miss a game.

"Yeah. She mentioned it at practice today, when you'd already left," Sally said.

"She acted like she didn't even know what I was talking about when I talked to her a few minutes ago."

"Well, she knew. She's just giving you a hard time. Maybe she'd understand better if *she* had a boyfriend. She's probably just jealous."

"Maybe." I wondered if anyone would be jealous of my current situation. Pregnant at sixteen in an all-girls Catholic high school? I wasn't sure it was something to envy. But talking with Sally made me feel better, and some days I did feel lucky. Like when I got letters from Kevin, or when I looked at the ring on my finger. But other days I felt a darkness settling over me, like heavy clouds before a thunderstorm, and then I was scared.

Saturday morning, I woke up late. It was already nine o'clock. My shades were down and my room was dark, when light should've been coming through the blinds. I could hear heavy rain coming down. My cat lay curled at the end of my bed, and when I threw my covers off, he stood up, stretched, and yawned.

As I dressed, I discovered my favorite jeans were tight. I left the top snap undone and found a long shirt to wear over them. I looked out the window at the rain pouring down in a steady stream. It didn't look like there'd be a game today after all.

"Judith," my mother was calling upstairs, "telephone."

I thought it might be Kevin calling to cancel.

"Judith," my mom called again.

"Coming," I yelled as I walked slowly down the stairs, not wanting bad news. Mom saw my long face and said, "It's Amy."

I looked up and smiled thankfully. Amy had called to say the game was postponed until tomorrow. I took the call in the kitchen, sitting down in my mom's chair next to the refrigerator.

"Do you want any breakfast?" she asked after I hung up. She was pouring herself a cup of coffee at the counter.

"No, thanks. But I'd love a cup of coffee." She poured it for me, adding the cream and sugar that I liked and then brought both cups to the table. I moved over to my seat and she took her usual place.

"So what time is Kevin coming?"

Not an offensive question, but I snapped, "I don't know. Whatever time he gets here."

She took a sip of her steaming black coffee and didn't say anything. I don't know how she didn't burn her lips each morning. Dad had to put an ice cube in his coffee every day before he could drink it. He was upstairs getting dressed, and his empty cup sat on the table with the *Boston Globe* next to it.

Mom and I sat there in silence for a few moments.

"I'm sorry," I said. I knew my tone had been harsh, and it wasn't how I wanted to start the day. "I'm just worried he's not going to make it down."

"He'll be here." A woman of faith, she believed people kept their word.

After finishing my coffee, I brought my cup to the sink and looked out into our backyard. The blue curtains were tied back neatly and a basket of plastic red tomatoes hung from the top of the window frame. The rain was heavy, puddling on our back porch.

I went into the living room and sat down to wait. Every twenty minutes or so I'd get up and look out the front window.

"Looking out that window every five minutes isn't going to make him get here any faster," my dad said to me when he saw me gazing out the window.

"Really?" I asked, my sarcastic reply sharp like an arrow.

"Good morning to you too." He went into the kitchen to have coffee with Mom and sit and read the paper the way they did every Saturday and Sunday.

I was not a pleasant person in the mornings anymore. I woke up tired, groggy, and sometimes a little nauseated.

"John, leave her alone, she's a little beside herself this morning," I heard my mother say. She was always pleading my case or my brother's one way or another. She had the patience in this family.

When Paul or I got into arguments with Dad, it was Mom who would try to stop the argument from escalating. One time Paul rolled the family car, a silver-gray Monte Carlo. The car was huge, and he totaled it. Even the roof was crushed in. Looking at the pictures of the wrecked car, I couldn't imagine how he and his friends crawled out alive.

My father raged when he heard the news. "What the hell were you think-ing?" he said, getting right up in Paul's face, as if he'd wanted to roll the car, had turned the wheel sharp at a corner, and pushed it up on two side wheels on purpose. Paul didn't even bother answering and tried to push by, but Dad stood his ground. Paul's brown eyes flashed with anger, and his lips were a tight thin line across his face.

We were in the kitchen and I thought Paul might hit him if he didn't move. My brother had big, muscular arms with a scar above his elbow from when he fell off a dirt bike, and he was stronger than my father.

My mom yelled, "John! Enough!" and with just a couple of words, she had defused the situation. He let Paul pass by and storm upstairs to his room.

Other times, Mom didn't say anything. She just touched my father's arm or looked at him with a glare strong enough to stop him mid-sentence. My father was a hard-working man who liked a beer or two after a long day, and my mother was the one who watched the kids, cleaned the house, and took care of all the meals. She had a paying job now, but even when she was a fulltime homemaker, she was in charge.

Sometimes I thought about how much of a disappointment I must be to them. My brother had given them some problems over the years with trips to the emergency room, fights in school, smashed cars, run-ins with the law, troubles with drinking and drugs. But I had been the golden child—a good student loved by teachers, a cheerleader. I was popular and pretty. But now, I was like a bad cliché, the cheerleader pregnant by her football-player boy-friend.

Right around noontime I finally heard steps on the front porch. I hadn't seen him walking down the street, so I wasn't sure it would be Kevin. I opened the door just as the bell rang.

Kevin stood there, dripping. His hair was dark with water plastered to his head. He had a duffel bag in his hand.

"Kevin," I said almost in a whisper and let him in.

I went to put my arms around his neck, but he pushed me away. "I'm wet," he grumbled.

My mother came out from the kitchen. She'd been browning hamburger at the stove for spaghetti sauce and was wearing an apron.

"Oh, Kevin, let me help you with your things." Ever the caretaker, she took his duffel bag and tucked it in the corner. "Judith, get him a towel for his hair."

It seemed kind of funny that she was so concerned. If she'd just let me go up to his school last night, or even early that morning, he wouldn't have been standing there looking like a drowned rat.

He had on a blue and white plaid flannel shirt. With its thick gray lining, it was more like a coat than a shirt, and it was heavy with water.

"Here, let me take your shirt," I said to Kevin as I handed him the towel.

"Why don't you go upstairs and change into some dry clothes," my mother said. "I can toss the wet ones in the dryer."

Kevin hadn't kissed me yet, hadn't even let me hug him. His mouth was set in an angry line. He took some clothes from the duffel bag and started upstairs. My mom stopped him and took his wet face in her hands and kissed him. "It's good to see you," she said warmly.

I smiled, though I was feeling a little jealous that she got Kevin's first kiss. His face softened a little after that, and I was glad for her soothing ways.

I put the kettle on for some tea while he changed clothes.

"Do you want some tea?" I asked Mom. Dad had taken the car and gone out. It was good they'd canceled the game, since we'd counted on borrowing the car to get there.

"No, thank you. Why don't you two sit in the living room and have some privacy. I'm sure you have catching up to do without me. Just make sure you put the coasters out." She was worried we might leave white rings on the end tables.

When Kevin was dried and warm, he was more like his old self. My mom ended up going over to a neighbor's house, so we were alone—except for Paul, who was still asleep in his room. Kevin pulled me to him, finally, and started kissing me.

"I was beginning to think you didn't want me anymore," I said in between some long kisses.

"That's a stupid thing to say," he said, sounding a little pissed. "I hitchhiked all the way down here in the rain to be with you on your birthday. Do you know how long it took me to get here?"

I didn't.

"I left at seven o'clock this morning, and I've been on the road for five hours," he said. He sounded really irritated.

"Thank you," I said. "Now, let's make sure I make it worth your trip." I pushed him down on the couch and started kissing him. When I lifted his shirt and ran my fingertips over his skin, he smiled.

Kevin and I stayed on the couch kissing and touching until I heard my brother moving around upstairs. Paul came downstairs, and with a brown mustache coming in and a stubby beard he looked like he hadn't shaved in days. I asked him to take us to the mall and was happy when he said yes. After Paul totaled the Monte Carlo, my parents bought him a used Fiat.

In the little sports car, I sat on Kevin's lap on the way to the mall. I'd taken my whole birthday weekend off from work to spend with him.

Kevin and I went to McDonald's. I loved sitting there with him, eating fries and laughing over unimportant things. It was great to have him back by my side, and we walked around the mall holding hands after lunch.

"What do you want for your birthday?" he asked.

"You!" I said and laughed.

We went in and out of stores, and I really didn't want anything but Kevin.

The rain had stopped while we were wandering around, so we walked home. My mother and father had left a note saying they'd gone out for the evening. They'd left us alone, and I thought how sometimes it seemed like they had blinders on. They had no idea what went on in their house when they were out.

I made dinner for Kevin and me, and we sat at the table eating corn, chicken, and mashed potatoes. Afterwards, we did the dishes together. I washed and he dried, and it reminded me of my parents and their routines. It felt like Kevin and I were creating our own.

"Judith," Paul said coming into the kitchen. "I'm having a party tonight. Can you put snacks out on the patio?" He was being nice because he wanted me to do something. "Hey, Kevin, how's it going?" he added for good measure.

"Do Mom and Dad know you're having a party?" I asked.

Paul rolled his eyes and said, "I told them I was having a few friends over."

Kevin helped me put chips and pretzels into bowls, and we placed some in the garage and some on the patio. Paul cranked the stereo, and rock music blared from its speakers as his friends pulled up. Their cars lined our street, and they hung out in the garage, the patio, and the kitchen. They even spilled into the backyard.

Kevin and I slipped upstairs to my bedroom where no one would notice us. We talked and kissed, laughed and joked, and then we went into the bathroom, and I turned on the bathtub faucet. Sounds from the party floated upstairs, but with the door shut, it was as if we were ensconced in our own world. Kevin washed my hair, pouring warm water from a cup to rinse out the shampoo. Afterwards, we went back into my room where we quietly dried each other off. He kissed my neck and shoulders, and we made love on my bed. No one knew where we were. No one cared.

Later when the party was winding down, we hung out in the kitchen with Paul and a couple of his friends. My mom and dad came home and joined us—they never knew the true size of Paul's party. I sipped soda while Mom had wine, though she already seemed buzzed and her cheeks were flushed. The guys drank beer, and we laughed late into the night.

I made up the couch for Kevin with sheets and blankets Mom brought to me before she and my dad headed up to bed. Paul's friends left, and after everyone was asleep, Kevin and I stayed up talking. I didn't want to go up to my room and would have stayed there all night, but I was afraid my parents would be angry if they came downstairs in the morning and found me there with Kevin.

"Don't go," he whispered.

I snuggled down with Kevin and we talked until early in the morning.

At five o'clock I finally kissed him good night and went up to my room to sleep, if only for a few hours. I was so excited to have him home, right downstairs in my living room. It was hard to sleep alone in my room when I knew he was so close and I could be holding him in my arms.

Safe in His Hands
Three months, one week and one day

The next day, I woke up early and went downstairs. I sat on the edge of the couch next to Kevin and looked at him. He was still sleeping, but I kissed him on his full lips. He opened his eyes and looked into mine and then pulled me down into a hug.

After basking in the warmth of his arms, I went to make coffee. Dad was in the kitchen getting ready to make Sunday breakfast as usual.

"Good morning," he said. I went over and kissed him on the cheek. Then I got the coffee and went back in to sit with Kevin. After setting down the cups, I took two cigarettes from Kevin's pack and lit one for me and one for him.

"Aren't you supposed to quit smoking?" he asked.

"Of course," I said. "But it's hard."

He took the cigarette out of my hand and put it out in an ashtray.

"Hey!"

"Well, you have to stop sometime," he said. He took another drag off his cigarette and then put it out. "Maybe I'll quit too."

"I'm going to get ready for the game. I'll see you in a few minutes," I said and kissed him before going upstairs.

I took out my skirt for cheerleading. It was dark green with two big pleats in front, and the inside of the pleats were white. It wasn't the skirt I'd been wearing since September. That one was too tight, and one day before a game, I had to trade skirts. It took a lot of switching with other cheerleaders before each of us had one that fit. I zipped up the skirt on the side and put on a white turtleneck. A sweater with the Wildcats' big cat sewn on the front went over the turtleneck. I grabbed my green and white pompoms and my megaphone.

"Don't you look cute," Kevin said when I came downstairs. He was smiling.

"Why, thank you."

"Judith, see if Mommy wants her breakfast in bed," Dad said from the kitchen.

Their bedroom was at the top of the staircase, and the door was open a crack. Mom was reading the Sunday paper in bed.

"Do you want your breakfast up there?" I yelled from the bottom of the stairs.

"I could have done that," Dad pointed out.

"No, honey, I'll be right down," Mom said.

Paul never made it down for Sunday breakfasts—out for late nights, he slept late too. He didn't join us for dinner most nights, either, and my mom would bring a dish to his room when he was at home.

Kevin and I went into the kitchen and sat down. Then Mom joined us, and Dad served. He made my favorite, bull's eyes. He'd take juice glasses and cut round pieces out from the center of bread. Then, he'd melt butter in a pan, put the bread in and break an egg into the center, frying the whole thing. He made potato pancakes, too, my other favorite. It was the weekend of my birthday, and my dad had prepared a special breakfast for me, making me feel important and loved.

"John, you make such a mess in the kitchen," my mother noted. He had left mixing bowls on the counter and dishes in the sink.

"No complaints to the chef," he said cheerily and sat down.

We had glasses filled with orange juice already at out plates and my mom picked hers up. "Happy Birthday, Judith," she said.

With Kevin sitting at the same table with my parents and me, sipping coffee and eating my favorite foods, it was one of my most special birthdays, ever.

We ate the delicious meal and talked about Kevin's classes and my classes.

"Do you want some more coffee?" my mom asked.

"Actually," I said, looking at the clock, "we have to get going if we're going to get to the game on time."

We'd already missed Mass before the game. We cleared our plates, thanked my parents, kissed them and left. Out on the front porch, I remembered my camera and ran back inside for it.

Kevin snapped a picture of me standing on the front walkway. I had my hair curled neatly, my crisp uniform on, and a sweet smile on my face.

"You look pretty, birthday girl," he said. It felt so good to have Kevin home, loving me, and I gave him a kiss before we got in the car.

When we got to the game, it felt wonderful walking in front of everyone with Kevin by my side. The other cheerleaders were already there and the stands were filling up. While we were standing there, the O'Briens arrived. I shouldn't have been surprised. Randy played for the Wildcats and his parents often came to his games. But this was a major O'Brien outing. They were all there.

Kevin told them he had just come down for the day. I wasn't happy that he didn't tell them the truth: that he'd stayed with my family the night before. It was a strange, small betrayal, but it hurt.

The Wildcats won, and even though it was a Sunday, there was sure to be a party that night. But I wouldn't be there. Instead, I planned to take Kevin back to school. We said goodbye to his family after the game, and I was glad he got in the car with me instead of them. We went back to my house for dinner, but we couldn't stay long. His school was far away.

"I wish you could stay longer," Mom said as we were putting on our coats.

"Mommy, they've got to get going. It would be good if Judith were back before midnight!" My dad always called my mother Mom, or Mommy, when I was around. I thought it was cute, like once you were a parent that was always your title. Pretty soon I'd have that name too, I thought.

"I'll make sure she leaves soon after we get back," Kevin said.

"Make sure you do, and take good care of her," Dad said.

Mom added, "Have her call home before she leaves too. She can call collect."

It was like they were putting all of the responsibility on Kevin. He seemed to have some new status in their eyes, one that elevated him to a position of superiority over me, one that rendered me more fragile, like the Lenox plates my mother kept safe in the dining room hutch with soft cloth liners around each one. They were trusting Kevin to take care of their daughter, to hold me gently in his hands like a piece of fine china.

I didn't really mind. It meant they had faith in him. I already did, but now with my parents trusting him too, everything felt solid and real. I kissed my parents, and Kevin kissed Mom and shook my dad's hand. We went down the brick walkway. I grazed my hand over the evergreen bushes that lined our path. Kevin held the door for me while I got into the passenger side.

"Aren't you the gentleman?" I said.

"Well, your parents are watching," he said. And they were, both of them in the doorway behind the storm door. It was already dark out, and the light from the hallway bathed my parents as they stood together, waving. Kevin drove because I would have the long ride home alone.

We stopped at a rest area halfway to the school. When we got ready to leave, the car wouldn't start. Kevin asked some people at the rest area to give us a jumpstart.

When we got back to his school, we found a secluded spot on campus and went parking. I didn't dare turn the car off for fear it would stall out again, so we made love with the engine running at the end of a dark road.

I drove him back to his dorm, and we left the car running while I went inside to call my mother. I didn't want to leave, but it was getting late. Kevin walked me to the car, and we stood there. I started to cry.

"Hey, what's the matter," he asked, his voice soft.

"Oh I don't know," I said a little sarcastically. "I hate goodbyes. I never know when I'm going to see you again."

"Yes, you do," he said. "I'll be back for Thanksgiving break. It's just a couple weeks away."

"But that feels like forever."

"It's not. And I'll write. I'll write you every day. You'll get sick of hearing from me."

That made me smile. I'd never get sick of hearing from him.

"You have to go," he said. "You already called home, and they're going to be watching the clock." He was right.

"I don't want to leave," I wrapped my arms around him and buried my head in his shoulder.

"I know," he said and pushed me gently away. "But you have to."

We kissed goodbye, and I got in the car and left. When I pulled away, my headlights swept over Kevin, lighting him up for a moment, and he stood there in the beams waving.

I had a lot of time to think on the way home. I thought about my parents and how much they seemed to love and accept Kevin. I thought about Kevin's family and how much they seemed to hate me. How were they ever going to accept me? How would I fit in? I thought about the life growing inside and how every day the baby was changing me. Then I thought about Kevin, beautiful Kevin, standing there waving. In some ways, it felt like we were always saying goodbye. He was always leaving. He'd come back for a little bit and then have to leave again. Coming and going, coming and going. I was afraid one day he'd just stay gone.

Promised Kept
Three months and two weeks

He kept his promise. Every day a new letter appeared in the mailbox. The first one was on lined notebook paper with the writing done in black laundry marker because he kept losing pens. He could only write on one side of the paper since the marker bled through to the other side. The letter was full of little details: how long it took him to do his laundry, how he got his name in the weekly bulletin for playing a good game of football, and how he couldn't wait for the snow to fall. He shared so many bits and pieces of his day-to-day life that I felt like I was still a part it.

In the next letter, he was missing me and making plans. He counted down the days until Thanksgiving break when he'd be home to see me. Winter would be coming soon, and he wanted me to go away with him on a ski trip. Maybe we could stay at a quaint lodge where we could snuggle and be alone.

He wanted to wake up beside me, to have me there to give him a good morning kiss like when he was at my house for my birthday. I wanted that too.

Scrawled at the bottom was his signature line, *Believe in Me!* And I did. With a letter in the mail each day like a promise spoken, I believed in him with all my heart. The snow hadn't even come yet, and he was already making plans to take me skiing. That meant he was thinking about the future—a future that included me. I'd had my first prenatal visit, and the doctor said I could still ski. I was surprised, but he said since I was already a skier, I could still do it. I just needed to be careful.

I had sent Kevin a picture in my last letter, and he wanted me to send more, and every time I sent a letter I put my perfume on it. He really liked that. Even though it made him miss me more, it also made it seem like I was there.

I knew what he meant. When I pressed his envelopes to my nose, read his letters, and looked at the pictures I had of him, I felt like he was beside me, solid and read.

The letters we sent to each other might have mundane details about school, about our friends, or about how we might be feeling that day—*My room is cold. I miss you. Believe in me. I finished a paper. I got an A on a quiz! I'm so tired.* Sometimes a short letter was just as good as a long letter. It gave those tiny details that we'd otherwise never know.

We were still sharing our lives in ways that no one else could. And if some of the short letters made me feel like I was still special, then the long letters made me burst with pride and feel sure I was the most important person in Kevin's life.

I got a five-page letter that was so full of love, it made my eyes tear up, my heart swell. He asked me to send him a letter telling him why I loved him, and I chuckled to myself, thinking how that letter might run over fifteen pages. The ending to his long letter was one of the reasons I loved him so much—he wasn't afraid to put into words how much he felt for me:

> You are always on my mind. Even in class when I should be
> listening to the teacher! I even think about you when I sleep. Then
> I get to dream some good dreams with both of us in it kissing and
> stuff. I want to hold you again like I did on your birthday. You
> give the best kisses in my dreams, but they are nothing like the real
> ones. You don't know how much I miss you, Judith!
>
> It's almost 1 a.m. and I can't believe it! I've been writing this let-
> ter instead of studying. But I think I should get some sleep.
>
> I know that it's hard that we're apart. Sometimes it's like we
> have an ocean between us. But don't forget, we can always swim
> to each other. We can get in a boat, or your parents' car—ha, ha—
> and be together. We are not really that far away. I wish I could be
> with you right now. I would give you a kiss that would make you
> understand just how much I do love you.
>
> Love,
> Kevin
> Believe in me!

He was the master of fine endings. Sometimes the words were familiar, a mantra repeated over and over again … Believe in me! Other times, he would mix it up with something new, but it was the same overall message: we were going to stay together, for always, a team.

Still, words on the page were not enough for either of us, so we continued our long phone conversations. I called him a lot. At first, he didn't call me because he didn't have money for phone calls. Then he figured out a way.

The phone rang one Sunday at 12:15 a.m. My parents were already in bed, and I sat in the kitchen in my mother's chair, with my legs pulled up under my nightgown.

"It's you!" I said. "I thought you couldn't call."

"That's true, that's true," he said, slurring his words. I knew he'd been partying.

"So how is it that I'm getting this wonderful phone call?" I practically purred into the phone.

"Ah, the magic of it all," he said, a bit elusively.

"No, seriously, where'd you get the money?"

"Don't you worry your pretty little red head about that," Kevin said. "It's a trick Brian taught me."

Brian was his roommate.

"Trick?"

"Yes, my dear." He was struggling with his speech. "I charged it to someone else's number."

I didn't understand how he managed this, and even though my father worked for the phone company, I didn't press for details. Instead, I let myself sink into a long conversation with my drunk Kevin. We talked for nearly three hours. I didn't get off the phone until 3 a.m., and during the call I talked with Brian and some other guys who lived in the dorm. When I got off the phone, they were talking about filling barrels with water, leaning them against some kid's door, knocking until the kid opened the door and then running away. Kevin was having a good time, and it was great to hear his voice.

I slept late on Sunday, missed church, and woke up tired. I wondered how Kevin was feeling. Probably hung over. I wanted to talk with him about our wedding plans but hadn't bothered while he was drunk. He'd be home for Thanksgiving soon, and that would be a perfect time to meet with the priest.

According to the church bulletin, you had to make plans for a wedding at least six months in advance. If our baby was due in May, and Kevin wanted to wait until after he finished school, then it was time for us to meet with a priest.

I called him later that day. "Hi, how are you feeling today?" I asked and giggled a little.

"That's not funny."

"I'm sorry. I'm not really joking, I do want to know."

"Okay, I guess. My head was hurting this morning. But nothing some aspirin couldn't help. You can't stop this O'Brien machine."

"That's my man," I said. "So, are you up for a serious conversation?"

"Shoot," he said.

"Well, I was thinking we should meet with a priest when you're home over break."

"What for?"

"The wedding," I said, an edge creeping into my voice. It irritated me that he didn't seem to know what I was talking about, as if he'd forgotten we were trying to plan a wedding.

"If we're going to get married when your school year ends and after I graduate, then we're talking early June and we have to make our plans now. Have you talked with your parents yet?"

"You know how they are. Any time I bring something up about us or the baby, they freak. I think they think if we don't talk about it, it'll all go away."

"Nice," I said. Then I was quiet, the silence on the line a void between us.

"Judith?"

"Yeah?"

"Are you all right?"

It was hard to talk because my throat hurt and my eyes were stinging.

"Yeah," I choked out. But I didn't know what to think. If Kevin couldn't bring himself to talk to his parents about the wedding, the baby, or me, how could they ever learn to live with the idea of my being in their family?

"Hold on a minute," I said and put the phone down. I went over to the counter, grabbed some paper towels, and dabbed at my eyes. "I'm back," I said.

"Set up the appointment," Kevin said. "We'll set a date."

I wanted to feel happy, but I couldn't quite get there yet. I was excited about planning our wedding, but I knew he'd need to get his parents on board.

"You have to tell them, you know."

"I know, I know," he said. "But they're not going to like it."

"True, but we can't exactly plan a wedding without your family knowing."

He promised to call them later, and then we talked about other things: the finals he had to study for, the computer program he had to write, one more term paper, and a couple of other tests coming up. He felt overwhelmed by everything and wanted to know when I was going to send him the letter outlining my love like I'd promised.

"It's already in the mail," I said.

"How long is it?"

"That, my dear, is a surprise." We finally had to hang up so he could study.

After school the next day, I scheduled an appointment with Father Fred. He wasn't my favorite priest, but he was the one available on Thanksgiving weekend. We set the meeting for Friday at two o'clock. I felt giddy with excitement.

Tuesday at school I thought I would burst with my wedding-plan news, like I had the biggest, best secret welling up inside me. I couldn't wipe the smile off my face, and at lunch I had to tell someone.

I sat with Karen and Betty in the cafeteria. We opened up our brown sacks and plastic sandwich bags. "I've got big news!" I burst out.

They looked at me as they chewed their sandwiches. What further news could I possibly have? Being the only pregnant girl at this all-girls' Catholic school had been big news all right, but they already knew that.

Karen pushed her glasses back on her nose. "Don't keep us waiting," she said. "What is it?"

"Kevin's coming home over Thanksgiving."

"We know that, it's all you've been talking about since he left," Betty said.

"Yes, but we have an appointment with Father Fred. We're going to set the date!"

They both started talking at once, wanting details about when and where, formal or informal, big or small. Some of the details were things I hadn't really thought of yet.

"We're planning an early June wedding after the baby is born in May," I said, and saying the words made it so real. "I guess we'll keep it small, but his family is pretty big, and, of course, I want my friends to come."

"Will you have bridesmaids?" Karen asked.

"I'm not sure about that stuff yet. But you know I'll want you two in it if I do."

That got me thinking. I'd have Sandy as my maid of honor. After all, she was the first person I'd told at school. And I'd want Sally in the wedding too. The more I thought about it, the bigger the wedding seemed to get.

I couldn't wait to see Kevin, to hold him, to tell him the beautiful plans I was making.

The letter I got from him that afternoon started out in a funny formal way, thanking me for the phone call the other night. It sounded almost like a business letter, but then he opened up.

Sometimes we're gonna feel sad, and that's hard. But this being apart is new and we're still learning how to make all this work. We won't always know how to handle it. But we will figure it out. I think you were upset because I didn't tell my family about our wedding, but I just get angry and blow up when they don't listen. But you and me, we listen, and that's real important. Especially now when things can get confusing. I love how we pay attention and hear what the other person is saying. I can share my true feelings with you but only you. No one else cares like you do. We should talk on the phone more so we can practice sharing all of our thoughts. Can you call some night this week?

Hey, guess what? I put your letters in a box under my bed. I save them all, and I hope you keep my letters too. Wow, I am getting so tired. I can hardly keep my eyes open! I better hit the sack soon.

But listen, before I go, I want you to know something. I'm in this with you. Like I said earlier … we've got an ocean to cross. But we can get there in one boat. I'll use one oar and you can use the other. When you get tired, I can pull the oars for both of us.

Sleep tight and keep my little one safe.

Love,
Kevin
Believe in me.

Of course I kept his letters! I re-read them all the time. I loved how his thoughts flowed from one thing to the next. One minute he was serious and the next he was telling me some funny story. This letter, though, was practically poetic with the oceans we were going to cross together. His words were beautiful, and I treasured each letter he wrote. I was glad to hear that he treasured my words too, that he kept my letters in a box beneath his bed.

But the part about his parents bothered me as usual. If all they ever did was argue when I came up in conversation, how could Kevin get across his feelings for me? How could he convince them that he and I were meant to be together? That our worlds were melding together into one? How would he ever get them to understand? And if he couldn't get them to understand, where would we be then?

Thanksgiving Blessings
Four months

*F*inally, Kevin's Thanksgiving break arrived. On Thanksgiving Day, he called to wish my whole family and me a happy holiday. He was going to come visit if his parents would let him use the car.

I wished he could share Thanksgiving with my family, where we would both be welcome and loved. My mother's turkey and all the fixings were perfect, and my brother joined us for the meal—he even shaved and put on a clean shirt. I picked at everything, moving the food around the plate.

"Honey, why aren't you eating?" my mom asked.

"I guess I'm too excited. Kevin might come down tonight."

Paul rolled his eyes and took another bite of turkey. With his mouth full, he said, "Don't hold your breath."

"What's that supposed to mean?" I shot back.

"Nothing," he said. "Just don't be surprised when he's history."

"Paul!" my mother said. "That's enough." Dad kept eating, ignoring the rude comments.

"We're meeting with the priest tomorrow," I announced.

"Right," Paul said sarcastically.

It didn't take much to make me cry, and sure enough, tears started rolling down my cheeks. I got up to leave the table.

"Judith, you've hardly touched your food. And what about dessert?" Mom asked as I left the room.

"I'm going upstairs," I said. Up in my room, I cried into the pillow. I felt silly letting Paul's snide remarks get to me.

My mother knocked at the door and came in. "Come back down," she said, "You know squash pie is your favorite." It was. And we didn't have it very often.

"Paul's not going to say anything else," she promised. Mom had on a floral skirt with a silk white blouse and a pearl necklace around her slender throat. She looked so pretty.

I was being too sensitive, and I knew it. Plus, I wanted some of that pie.

After she went downstairs, I went in the bathroom to blow my nose and splash cold water on my face.

I'd just sat back down at the dinner table when the phone rang. I jumped up to answer it.

"Good news." It was Kevin. "My brother's going to let me take his car. He's staying in for the night."

"That's great. I'll wait to have my dessert with you."

"All right. I'll see you in a half hour or so."

It was closer to an hour before he got there. Paul had already left to meet up with his friends, and I'd helped Mom clear the table and start on the dishes. I was drying and putting away the china, thinking Kevin might not make it after all, when the doorbell rang. My dad, who had stayed at the table to smoke his pipe, got up to answer the door. Kevin came into the kitchen, swept me into his arms, and kissed me right there in the middle of the room. For a moment it was as if everything disappeared, everything but Kevin and me holding each other.

My father cleared his throat. I giggled, put my head on Kevin's shoulder for a moment, and then disentangled myself from his arms.

"It's so good to see you," I said with a huge smile.

He had a grin on his face too. Then the doorbell rang again.

I went and opened the door and there was Mrs. Zuastamachio, our neighbor from two doors down, the one who gave up desserts for me while I was on retreat, the one we called Mrs. Z. She bustled past me and into the kitchen.

"Any more of that apple pie left?" she asked. Mom made two apple pies and one squash pie for the holidays.

"Of course," she said. "You know I always make two." She put another pot of coffee on, and we all sat around the kitchen table.

Mrs. Z turned to Kevin. "How is school going?" she asked. "I hear you've got some big plans after that."

The Z's were neighbors who had always been in my life. They were a second family to me. In fact, when Kevin and I went to his senior prom, we went to Mrs. Z's house to take pictures.

"It's going to be a busy spring," Kevin said. "First, we'll have Judith's prom, her graduation, and mine. And then, of course, there'll be the wedding."

He said it almost casually, like it was on the same order as proms and graduations!

My mother was getting the apple pie ready, and I was scooping ice cream on top of each slice. I cut a piece of squash pie for myself and brought the plates to the table.

We ate our dessert, sipped coffee, and discussed the wedding plans. It was lovely sitting there with my parents, Mrs. Z and Kevin, and talking about a June wedding and the life we'd share after that.

When we finished eating, Kevin helped me with the dishes. He washed and I dried, and it felt good having him there on Thanksgiving. Every once in a while, he flicked the dishtowel at me, and we laughed.

Afterwards, we decided to go roller-skating. There were kisses to go around for everyone, and then we left.

"Do you really feel like roller-skating?" I asked as we got into his brother's Mercury Cougar.

"What do you think?" he said and laughed. He grabbed me once we were both in the car and started kissing me.

I pulled away and said, "Ah, excuse me, I don't think we need to do this right here in front of my house."

We started driving to an industrial park not very far away, but I couldn't leave Kevin alone and sat real close, running my fingernails down his neck.

"If you don't cut that out, I might just pull over on the side of the road, you know."

"Okay, okay." I scooted away from him.

We pulled behind one of the buildings, so the police who cruised the park wouldn't see us.

"There," he said, shutting the car off. "Now, come here." I fell into his arms, and we started kissing. "Hey," he said all of a sudden, "I got your letter before I left, the one saying why you loved me. Thirteen pages! It took me twenty minutes to read it all."

"Did you like it?"

"Oh, yeah," he said. "Now let me show you how much I love you." He started kissing me again and then made love to me.

Afterwards, he said, "I'm going to make love to you every day I'm here. In fact, maybe even more than once a day." He laughed and started kissing my neck. Then he loved me all over again.

Later, he brought me home. I didn't like lying to my mom about roller-skating, but I wasn't about to tell her where we'd been for the past few hours.

"Hey, tomorrow's our big day," I said at the door as he prepared to leave.

"That's right. What time is our appointment?"

"Two o'clock," I said. "We're going to see Father Fred. Do you remember him? He was one of the priests at the retreat we went to last summer."

"Yeah, I remember him. He's the guy who found us kissing in the hallway one night, right?"

"That's the one! I don't like him as much as Father Jim, but Father Jim went home to spend the holidays with his family."

"That's too bad."

"It'll be all right. We have to meet with a priest six months before we get married. But I'm sure there'll be more to discuss when the date gets closer. We'll have plenty of time to talk to Father Jim."

"Maybe Father Jim can do the service?"

"That's an idea," I said. "Or maybe my cousin who's a deacon? Hey, we can talk more later. You really have to go!" I didn't want him getting grounded when we had such an important appointment to keep the next day.

"Pushy, pushy," he said. Then he pulled me into a hug and nuzzled my neck.

"Come on. Enough of that."

He laughed. "I'll come early tomorrow morning so we can have the whole day together."

"I'll be ready."

"Sweet dreams." He gave me a kiss, flashed a big grin, and left.

I watched until he and his brother's car had disappeared up the street.

When I went to bed that night I was so happy and excited I couldn't sleep, just like on Christmas Eve when I was a child. When I finally fell asleep, though, I didn't dream of sugar plum fairies dancing around. Instead, I dreamed of wearing a wedding gown with flowers in my hair and Kevin by my side. We stood in front of an altar with God and our families watching.

The Edge of Darkness
Four months and one day

I was up early the next day and ready by 9:15. But by ten o'clock, Kevin still wasn't there and I was worried. When I called his house, the phone rang and rang. There was nothing I could do but wait for him.

Finally, at 11:30, he showed up. "I was so worried!" I said as I ushered him inside.

"Couldn't be helped." Somehow, he was a different Kevin from the one I'd seen the night before. Cool and distant, he barely kissed me when he came in.

"I need some ski boots for the coming season, so I thought we could go to Springfield," he said.

"Do you think we have time?"

"No problem," he said. "Let's go."

He had his mom's car and we headed south on I-91 toward Springfield. Kevin was speeding down the highway.

"Did you ask your Mom if we could have Julie's old crib?"

"Naw, I forgot."

He'd told me his mother still had his little sister's crib in the attic. Forgot? How could he forget? He knew we needed some furniture for our baby.

I started to say something else, but Kevin was cranking the radio, tapping his fingers on the steering wheel. He was singing along to a song about no stop signs, about not obeying speed limits, about doing whatever you felt like. He was singing loud, and it felt like he was closing me out of his world, a world where he could cruise along on a highway, the hell with everyone else.

I stared out the window at the Springfield skyline, the tall buildings stark against the gray sky. What the heck had happened between last night and this morning? I wanted to ask, but Kevin seemed almost angry, so I didn't say anything.

In the ski store, he knew just what he wanted. He went up to a sales clerk and told him about the boots he had in mind. He told me they were the best boots for racing—he'd seen them in an advertisement. He was going to join the ski team and there would be practices almost every day and then ski meets.

"I'm going to tear up the slopes," he said excitedly. When he tried on the ski boots, he was practically bouncing up and down. Normally, I would consider his exuberance cute. But the boots cost one hundred and fifty dollars. When he plunked the money down, I couldn't help but think it might've paid for our baby's things.

How could he be dishing out this much money for ski boots *and* telling me he wanted to be with me, marry me, and raise our baby together? Something wasn't right, and I started to feel sick.

I sulked on the way home, upset about the boots and hurt that he hadn't remembered to ask his mother about the crib.

We were atop the highest bridge in Springfield, going over the Connecticut River, heading North and out of the city, when Kevin told me his news. "I went to see a counselor this morning," he said. "My parents set up the appointment for me."

"Oh, you didn't say anything about it last night."

"I didn't know until this morning. The counselor thinks the best thing is for you to give the baby up for adoption. That way, the baby can have a better life. Some couple that really wants a baby can have one."

My head started to spin. *Some couple that really wants a baby?* I thought *we* were that couple.

"What are you talking about?" I whispered. "We have our own appointment today."

He didn't say anything.

"With the priest."

My words were barely audible because I was having a hard time getting my thoughts together and my words out. I didn't even have any tears in my eyes yet, just a growing hysteria rising in my chest like nothing I'd ever felt before.

I don't know if Kevin heard me because he just kept talking about what the counselor had said, like I hadn't even spoken.

"Some couple that has a good solid life, a nice home, somewhere the kid can grow up loved," he said.

The kid? It was more than I could take. I snapped.

I don't know remember what I said. It was all swimming in my head, around me and inside of me, welling up like a tidal wave I couldn't control. I only know I was screaming, and it wasn't enough to stop the pain, it wasn't enough to stop the crushing feeling in my chest, it wasn't enough. I wanted out of that car. I couldn't listen to his rambling anymore.

I wasn't thinking clearly, and I wasn't myself. Kevin wasn't himself, either. We weren't ourselves. I didn't know who we were anymore. I grabbed the handle and started to open the door. We must've been going seventy miles an hour down the highway, and I don't know how Kevin saw what I was doing. But he reached over and grabbed the door. The car swerved across the highway, and it's a wonder we didn't go careening over the edge of that bridge.

He got control of the car, and, miraculously, we didn't hit anyone or anything.

"What the fuck are you doing?" he yelled.

But I couldn't answer. I just sat there, numb.

"Fuck! What the fuck?" he said more to himself than me.

For the rest of the ride home, I sat in silence. I didn't know what to say. No one was home and I was glad. I didn't know what I was going to say to anyone.

Once inside, Kevin started up again. "What the hell were you trying to do? Kill yourself?"

I ignored him and went through the kitchen to a side door. On a shelf just inside the garage, my mother kept her wine. I poured myself a glass, sucked it back and poured another.

Kevin had followed me into the kitchen. "What are you doing now?" he asked, watching me suspiciously.

"What does it look like I'm doing?" I snapped. "I'm having a little drink. Care to join me?" I didn't wait for his answer and went into the living room to plop down on the couch.

"You're acting crazy," he said, following me. "You're not supposed to be drinking. You're going to hurt the baby."

"Your concern for the baby that you don't give a damn about is admirable," I said. "But fuck you." I took a big gulp.

I hadn't been drinking since finding out I was pregnant, and I couldn't hold my liquor much anyways. I didn't usually weigh more than a hundred and five—I was a little heavier with the pregnancy—but two drinks and I'd be buzzed. Three and I'd be cocked. The glass and a half of wine took the edge off my hysteria.

"Judith, be reasonable," he said. "I'm just trying to think of what's best for the baby."

"Reasonable? I think I *am* being reasonable. We have an appointment today in what, an hour?" I looked up at the clock on the living room wall, and it was already well after one. "Oops, less than an hour." I took another slug of the wine. "We're supposed to be setting our wedding date, but you're talking about giving our child away. I presume we're not scheduling our wedding date today?"

"Judith," he said, and his voice was soft for a minute, like the Kevin I knew from the night before, from the months before, from the beautiful letters he wrote.

But I wasn't really hearing that softness.

"Answer me!" I went right up to Kevin and screamed it in his face again. "Answer me!"

"No. There isn't going to be a wedding this spring," he said quietly.

"How can you do this to me, to us?" I yelled and pounded him on his chest.

He grabbed my hands to stop me from hitting him, and I started to cry.

Here I was with a baby coming in five months, and the man I loved was asking me to give our child away. He wanted me to give away the treasure we had made together. There wasn't anything I could do but cry.

Hold onto Me
Still four months and one day

We drove to my church in silence. Up West Street, left onto Woburn Street, and then right into the parking lot. Friday afternoon and the lot was nearly empty.

Father Fred answered our knocking. He led us into a waiting room outside his office. There seemed to be no one there but us.

"So, you're here to set a wedding date?" he asked uncertainly.

We must have looked young, and the slump to my shoulders hardly looked like the posture of a jubilant bride-to-be.

"No, I guess not," I said. "I'm not really sure why we're here. We were going to set the date, but now we're not, and it was too late to cancel the appointment." Saying it out loud made it all too real, and I started to cry.

Father Fred handed me some tissues.

"Well," he said and went no further.

We all stood there awkwardly for a few minutes. I was crying and Kevin just stood there with his hands shoved in his jean pockets.

"Why don't I speak with each of you individually," Father Fred suggested.

"Start with him," I said, heading to a chair.

Kevin went in with Father Fred into the priest's office. It was his second counseling session that day. For the half an hour they were inside, I zoned out. It was as if I went to a place of emptiness where I didn't have to think about what Kevin had said earlier, where I didn't have to think of anything.

When he came out, it was my turn. But I didn't have a thing to say. "Thank you," I said to Father Fred. "I'm sorry we wasted your time." And with that I headed to the door.

"Judith, don't you want to come in and talk?" Father asked, gesturing toward his open door. I shook my head no.

Kevin dropped me off at my house. He didn't bother to come in, and I didn't want him to.

"I'll call you tonight," he said. "Maybe I can come down later."

"Fine," I said. But my voice was flat, like it didn't matter one way or the other.

I was glad no one else was home yet. Exhausted and emotionally drained, I went up to my room and quickly fell asleep. Later, I woke to my mother's tapping on the door. She said Kevin was on the phone.

"Tell him I'm sleeping."

She came back to check on me and see if I wanted dinner. But I didn't feel like eating. I dug out some pictures of Kevin and me. I felt sure he was walking out on me, and it hurt to look at his smiling face.

In my diary I wrote about the day. Then I found my poetry journal and composed a poem:

My Child

I can feel you
growing in my womb,
a tiny infant
to be born so soon.

Sheltered now
from life and pain
another being
brought to earth again.
How will I love you,
and will you understand
that your father's absence
was never my plan?

I dreamed of love
and a happy home
but now it's you and me
without him, alone.

I'll try my best,
that's all I can do.
And I hope you'll know
it is all done for you.

Writing the poem didn't make me feel better. But it was honest and true. A man who wanted me to give away our baby didn't want me. I drew a picture at the bottom of the journal page of a very pregnant woman. I put a smile on her face even though I didn't feel like smiling. Like the way my mom was always saying *happy face in the morning,* I figured putting a smile on the face could only help.

I stayed in my room all night. Then at nine o'clock I heard the doorbell.

"Judith," my mother called up the stairs. "It's Kevin."

He'd said he might come back that night, but after the day we'd had, I wasn't counting on it.

"In a minute," I yelled and went into the bathroom to wash my face and brush my hair. My eyes were red from crying, but there wasn't anything I could do about that now.

"Bye, Mom," I said. I hadn't even had a chance to tell her how everything was changing so fast.

"Judith, come here," she called out as I was putting on a jacket. I found her in the kitchen. "Is everything okay?"

"No, it's not," I answered. "But I can't talk about it right now. I'll tell you more later." I gave her a kiss and left with Kevin.

We went and grabbed a bite to eat at McDonald's and then drove to our regular parking place in the industrial park. He was the one who said he couldn't marry me in the spring, and he was the one who was asking me to give our baby away. But that night, he was the one who started crying first.

"I love you so much," he said. "I don't know what to do."

Then we were both crying, and all the songs on the radio sounded so sad. We held each other and cried, rocking each other. And through the wetness of our tears, he started kissing me. He looked into my eyes as he was kissing me.

"I love you," he said.

"I love you too," I said. And although I knew we weren't getting married after our baby was born, and part of me doubted he would even be around, I let him make love to me.

The next day I baked Kevin some cookies. He didn't call all day, and I didn't know if I'd see him before he headed back to school. But he called later in the evening and said he'd be down sometime after nine.

We went bowling, and for part of the night it was almost as if nothing had changed. We laughed and had a great time. We didn't talk about the baby. We didn't talk about the broken marriage promise. We didn't talk about our future or lack of one. We just had fun. After bowling, we went to Friendly's for an ice cream. It almost felt like the good times we used to have in the summer.

Except I knew he was leaving for school the next day, and I didn't know when I'd see him again.

He took me parking, again. Like the night before, we were both crying.

"I'm scared," I told him. "I don't want to be alone."

"You're not going to be alone. It's not like I'm leaving you." But, of course, he was leaving, the very next day to go back to school. "I just can't marry you, yet."

And with that "yet," he was holding out a piece of hope.

He made love to me again, and later when I was writing in my diary, I realized he'd made love to me every day he'd seen me, just like he said he would the first night he was home. But what difference did those actions make if they didn't mean what they were supposed to mean? I felt love when he was making love to me, but I didn't know if I could trust myself to know what was real.

The next night, he called and said, "My parents want me to break it off with you, and maybe that's best. I'm not even sure how you feel about me."

Maybe he was having some trouble with reality himself because I was sure I'd made it abundantly clear that I loved him.

"What in the world are you talking about now?" I asked. "How can you say you don't know how I feel about you?"

"Well, I'm just not sure," he said, and that hurt.

"I love you. I would think you would know that, especially after this weekend." I was referring to the many times we'd made love, but he didn't seem to get it.

By the time we hung up the phone, it was clear to me that he wasn't sure of anything. He was going back to school, and I was left with a sort-of sometimes boyfriend who wanted to be my lover when it was convenient for him.

I said my prayers and went to bed feeling utterly confused.

When You Know What You Want
Four months and three days

The next night my mother wanted to find out what happened with Father Fred, with Kevin, with all our plans. It was painful when she brought it up at the dinner table with Dad sitting there, and I asked if we could talk later.

"Of course, dear," she said. And I saw her give one of her looks to my father, one that meant, *Leave her alone.*

I'm sure he wanted to ask questions too. I'd been with Kevin most of the weekend, but I hadn't told him or Mom anything.

She changed the subject. "How was school today?"

"Fine," I lied. Nothing was fine. My friends wanted to know about my wedding plans, and I didn't want to talk. They were full of questions at lunch, and I was full of silence.

I wanted to sink into that silence and stay there, not saying anything to anyone. Mom sensed my desire for privacy and didn't ask me any more questions during dinner, and we ate the rest of the meal in an awkward silence.

"John, why don't you go up and watch some TV?" my mom suggested when dinner was over. "Judith and I will do the dishes."

I had been planning on skulking away to my room and hiding out there for the rest of the night—the rest of my life if I could get away with it.

"I think I'll just go to my room," I said as I took my dish to the counter.

"Oh no, you don't. You're going to dry," my mother said and handed me a dishtowel.

She ran the water scalding hot, the way she liked it, and put the soap in the dishpan while I cleared the table. Dad had gone up to the den.

"Tell me what's going on, Judith," Mom said as she put the wet dishes into the drying rack. I let them sit for a few minutes before picking them up and wiping them.

"It's really hard to talk about, Mom."

She waited for me to go on.

"He doesn't want to marry me," I said. Then I added, "Well, not yet." It hurt to say the words out loud. If I kept them inside, unspoken, it was as if they weren't real. I still had a diamond on my left hand and a baby growing inside me. I could almost pretend it wasn't true if I didn't say it.

"Oh, Judith," my mother said, wrapping her arms around my neck. She pulled me to her in a hug, and there was nothing I could do but cry.

"I thought he loved me," I said through sobs.

"He does, Judith, he does," she said. "It's just you're both so young." She gave me a big bear hug and said, "Let's have some tea."

Sometimes I think my mother thought strong black tea would cure almost anything. It was what she prescribed when anyone in the family had a cold, a cough, or now, a broken heart. I sat down at the table while she made her magic tea.

When the water had boiled, and the tea had steeped, Mom put the two steaming cups on the table and sat down. And there was something magical about sitting in my own kitchen with my mother there to comfort me. But it was only enough magic to break my silence and get me talking. It couldn't take away the pain.

I told my mom about the trip to Springfield, the ski boots Kevin bought, how he forgot to ask his mother about the crib. I left out the details about trying to jump out of the car on Route 91, which would have killed me and my baby. I knew that would upset her, the way it had made Kevin mad, and I didn't think I could deal with any anger right then. I was feeling fragile, like it wouldn't take very much to break me.

Every so often as I told the story, Mom would say, "oh, no" or "dear, that's awful"—little interjections that let me know she was listening.

"You must be crushed," she said when I finished.

Sitting with my shoulders slumped, I did feel crushed.

"If you had to do it over, would you still keep the baby?" she asked.

I sat up a little straighter in my chair. She was talking about abortion, but we were way beyond that now.

"You know I wouldn't abort my baby. You know how wrong that is," I said, though I'd clearly forgotten my baby's safety when I was hysterical on the highway.

I didn't have to tell my mother what the Church said. After all, she was the one who was bringing us up in the Catholic faith. Besides, I didn't need the Church to tell me that killing my baby was wrong. I already knew that in the depths of my heart.

"If my own birth mother had done that, I wouldn't be here," I reminded her.

"Well, there wasn't much of a choice in the early sixties," she said.

"People still found a way," I said. "But that's besides my point. What's wrong is wrong. My baby is already alive inside of me and has been since I conceived."

I wasn't sounding like a crushed young teen anymore, but someone strong in her own convictions. Maybe my mother's tea and talk held more magic than I knew.

I wrote in my diary that Monday night, November 26, that I would have my baby, no second thoughts. My final note on that evening was: *Life goes on and grows within. An interesting thought and scary. Bye.* I said *bye* when I finished writing a day's events, but this time I meant it for more than a day. I didn't write again for eighteen days. It was as if writing a chronicle of the pain was more than I could bear.

I received only two letters from Kevin during that time. The first one was his written goodbye, sort of. The postmark was dated November 27, just a day after he left.

Hi Judith,

I love you and I want to stay, but other people say I should leave you alone for now. It's hard and I want to do what my parents say. Maybe we need space. Sometimes I can't think straight? Maybe we need to give each other space.

Thank you for inviting me to the winter prom. We've been to a couple proms already and they were fun. We got to dance to songs we loved and laugh. We should do that again.

Maybe we should give ourselves space. Call me before the prom. We can talk then. Send me a letter soon.

Love,

Kevin

So, he wanted space away from me. *Just great,* I thought. And he hadn't bothered to write *Believe in me!* at the bottom of the page. Well, at least that was honest. He certainly wasn't asking me to believe in him anymore. He was suggesting I question almost everything. Still, he might come down for my winter prom, and he did say I should call.

The next letter I received was postmarked December 10, five days before the winter prom. From his responses to things I'd written, I knew he'd received my letters telling him about going to the doctor and hearing the baby's heartbeat. I had a yeast infection, and I'd told him about that. In his letter, he sounded concerned but cool. He told me about his Christmas break but also mentioned he'd be busy with tons of homework over break. But he also mentioned my winter prom and said he wanted to come.

Part of his letter sounded so sad. He said he hadn't been feeling very good and was losing weight. I hoped he wasn't depressed. At the bottom of his letter, after signing *Love, Kevin,* he once again scrawled *Believe in Me.*

Those words on the page made me cry. More than anything I wanted to believe in him. But I didn't know what to think anymore.

He called me the Thursday before my winter prom and said he was coming. I could hardly believe it. Then on Saturday the fifteenth, the evening of the prom, he was late and I thought he wasn't going to make it after all.

But he did. I changed into my dress. It wasn't the one I'd originally planned on wearing because that one didn't fit right anymore. Instead, I wore a long lavender silky dress with spaghetti straps with a little jacket over it. My breasts had grown and my face was rounder than before. I was over four months pregnant and still didn't have much of a belly yet, which was good, because plenty of people at school still didn't know I was pregnant. I guess a lot of them just thought I was getting fat.

My mother took pictures of us. Kevin had on a suit coat and nice pants. He wasn't all that dressed up, but he still looked beautiful to me. I took a picture of Mom and Kevin together. Kevin had his arm draped over my mother's shoulder and he held her hand. He smiled a broad grin and she went to kiss him on the cheek. That's when I snapped the picture.

We were too late to make it to any of the pre-prom parties, so we went parking instead. It felt so good to hold Kevin again. The prom took place in the school cafeteria, and we had decorated the place on Friday with streamers and balloons. It was more a winter dance than a prom, not as formal as the spring proms. I hoped I'd still be able to go to my senior prom.

We arrived at the dance, and Barbara—my old boyfriend's girlfriend— had on almost the same dress as mine. I went to the bathroom and saw her at the sink crying.

"You've ruined my prom," she said to me. "You copied my dress. I told you I was wearing light purple, and you said you were wearing a tan floral dress." Her voice was rising.

She was right. I'd said I was wearing that other dress, but it didn't fit anymore. So I had to improvise. I didn't want to tell her this because she didn't know about the pregnancy.

"I didn't copy your dress," I said. "You are so far from the truth."

She stayed at the row of sinks with her friends, reapplying make-up and trying to fix her tear-streaked face. I had bigger things to cry about. But right then, I just wanted to have some fun.

Kevin and I danced and laughed and went to a party after the prom. He played pool with some guys, and I chatted with the girls. Most people were drinking, but I didn't. When the party was winding down, we left.

We drove to our usual deserted parking lot so we could talk in private. His voice full of hesitation, Kevin told me he couldn't see me anymore. It was too much for him to be sneaking around behind his parents' backs. I didn't even cry when he told me. Instead, I held him while he cried. Maybe I was getting numb to his stories. First he wanted to be with me—forever by my side. Next he wanted to follow his parents' rules and leave me as fast as he could. He was here for my winter prom, seeing me, dating me, taking me out in public. But in private he was saying he couldn't do it anymore. I comforted him late into the night. Back at my house, we stayed up practically all night talking.

In the morning, he'd changed his mind again. When I came down to say good morning, he told me he wanted to keep seeing me.

"I'm confused," I said. "You want to be with me, you don't want to be with me. You want me to believe in you, you don't want me to believe in you. It's hard to follow." I was angry and my sarcastic tone was clear. "Why don't you keep this until you make up your mind?" I took the diamond off my hand and gave it to him.

"No, Judith, that's yours, ours."

"Yeah, well, until you know what you want, maybe you should have it." I went upstairs to get the little velvet ring box. I didn't want him to lose the ring. Secretly I was hoping he'd return it to me soon.

I drove him to the highway and dropped him off. He thumbed his way back to school because no one would lend us a car for the long trip. He was headed back for his final exams, with our diamond in his pocket and our future so unclear. Many hours later, he called to let me know he'd gotten back safely.

It all seemed so strange. He had come a long distance, hitchhiking the whole way, just to be with me and go with me to my dance, but also to tell me he didn't want to be with me anymore. I couldn't believe I'd actually given the diamond back. I wasn't sure who was more confused.

In less than a week he'd be back at his home for Christmas break. Christmas, one of the most joyous times in the Christian calendar, a time of rejoicing over the birth of Jesus, and here I was pregnant and desperately uncertain about the future. It was the time of year when people were supposed to feel joy in their hearts. But I had just broken off my engagement. I didn't even know for sure if Kevin would want to see me anymore. I felt like despairing rather than rejoicing.

A Christmas to Remember
Four months, three weeks and four days

The Saturday before Christmas when I came outside after my shift at Foster's, I saw Kevin sitting there in the red Comet. "Hi there," he said.

"Hi," I said and jumped in the car.

"I went by your house, but Paul said you were working. He said he was going to pick you up afterwards, but I told him I'd surprise you."

"It worked. I'm surprised," I said. "Pleasantly." The last time I'd seen him was when I dropped him off at the highway.

I knew he'd been home for winter break since the nineteenth, but I hadn't heard from him at all. Now here he was waiting for me to get off work like nothing was different. He leaned over and kissed me.

"Trevor's having a party at his house. His parents are away," he said.

I didn't feel like seeing Trevor, Kevin's football buddy from St. Joseph's. He partied pretty hard and there were rumors he was into drugs, more than just pot. And I didn't want to share Kevin with anyone just then.

"Do we really have to go to the party?"

"Hell, yeah!" he said. "It's a big party, and I haven't seen Trevor for a while."

You haven't seen me, either, I thought. "Well, how were your finals?" I asked, changing the subject. "Did you get everything done?"

"I have some stuff to do over break—a paper I wish I didn't have to write."

"I have a term paper due right after break," I said, sounding just as stiff as he did.

When we pulled up in front of Trevor's house there were cars everywhere, and we had to park down the street. Inside, the music was blaring and people were hanging out in the living room and the kitchen with beer cans in their hands. I didn't recognize anyone. I thought there'd be guys from St. Joseph's that I'd know. Trevor came over and slapped Kevin on the back, and then we went into the kitchen. It seemed like Kevin knew everyone or at least felt comfortable around them. Maybe they were Trevor's new friends from college. He'd gone to a state college and hadn't needed an extra year of high school like Kevin. I hadn't seen Trevor for a while, and he'd gained some weight, a new beer belly. I was glad Kevin still looked good.

I was feeling out of place when some girl lit a joint and offered it to me. She was just being nice, trying to include me, but I hadn't smoked since the summer and shook my head no. When Kevin took the joint and held it to his lips, inhaling deeply, I was upset.

I glared at him, but he didn't even notice. Before I could say something, he went down to the basement with Trevor and some guys I didn't know. A couple of the girls followed.

Those girls were probably Trevor's friends, but I'd been deserted in the kitchen while Kevin was downstairs with them getting stoned. I leaned against the counter and breathed. I was steaming but didn't know what to do.

The girls with me in the kitchen were all tiny. Thin, petite and pretty, they were probably cheerleaders themselves. I could have told them I was a cheerleader, but it really wasn't true anymore. And at that moment, next to them, I felt fat with my large breasts and round face. I was wearing a maternity shirt over jeans that I had to leave unbuttoned at the top. They probably thought I looked like a whale.

They were giggling and talking about people I didn't know, and I was pretty sure that as soon as they could, they'd be talking about me, laughing behind my back. I just stood there feeling lost. One of them offered me a beer, and I took it. I drank it fast and bummed a cigarette from someone. The girls kept talking about their school and people I knew nothing about.

Time was going by, and still Kevin hadn't come back. I decided to go down to the basement and tell him I wanted to go. I was starting to feel sick. Maybe it was the smoke. Maybe it was the beer or the strong smell of pot.

When I got to the basement, I found Kevin sitting on the couch real close to a girl. He moved over quickly when he saw me but not soon enough. So he left me upstairs to hang out with some other girl?

"Kevin, I want to go home," I said. "I'm not feeling very good."

"Come on, Judith. We just got here."

"Yeah," Trevor said. "Go out and get some fresh air if you're feeling sick."

"That's a good idea!" Kevin piped up. It wasn't funny. But they all started laughing with him, the way stoned people do.

Suddenly I got it in my head to leave. So while they kept laughing, that's what I did. No one even noticed when I slipped out. I went down to the end of the road, took a left, and kept walking. Trevor didn't live in the same town I did, and I didn't know any of the people who lived on these streets. As I walked, it felt like that time I'd taken off from my house and wandered up the highway. At least this time I knew where I was headed. Home.

But I had nearly a four-mile walk ahead of me. After a little while, I started thinking how dumb I was to leave the party. I kept hoping Kevin would drive by, see me, and then pick me up. I was cold and I had a long way to go. Then he did pass me, but to my dismay, he kept going. I figured he hadn't seen me walking along the dark sidewalk. Or if he had, he'd been too angry to stop.

Exhausted, I got home late and went straight to bed. The next day I woke up feeling like an idiot. What had I done? I felt like Kevin had deserted me at the party, but when I looked back on the night, I realized I'd deserted him too. I should've stayed. I should have just sat in a chair and waited. I should have told him how I felt when I saw him sitting so close to that girl. Should have, should have, should have.

Too late for that now. I had plenty of time that day to think about what I'd done. But I also had time to think about what Kevin had done. He was stoned and drunk. Would I really want to get into a car with him? And he went off with Trevor and those girls. I kept thinking about the night and my long walk home. What had I been thinking?

I knew Kevin had gone skiing that day with his brother. When I called him that evening, he said his family was just sitting down to eat dinner and he'd call me back later. But that call didn't come.

He didn't call me the next day, either. And that was Christmas Eve. I didn't go anywhere and kept hoping he would call. Every time the phone rang, I jumped.

I ran to the phone one time and it was Mrs. Z, our neighbor. "Hi, sweetie," she said cheerily, "Merry Christmas."

"Merry Christmas to you too," I managed to get out. But it didn't have her cheer and she noticed.

"What's the matter?"

"Oh, nothing much," I said. "Let me get my mother." I wanted to get off the line quickly.

I liked to attend midnight Mass on Christmas Eve, and I knew it would be wrong to miss church, but I couldn't bring myself to go. I didn't think Kevin would call me so late at night, but I didn't want to chance not being home if he did.

Even on Christmas, he still didn't call. I could have called him, but I was sinking into a depression. I cried all day.

"Come on, Judith," my mom said as she came into my bedroom. "It's Christmas. Come down and join us."

"I can't," I said and turned over, putting my face into the pillow. I couldn't stop crying.

"Honey, this isn't good for you or the baby. Please," she was pleading with me, her voice drawing out the eee in *please*.

But I couldn't. I stayed in my room all day. I didn't even have the strength to go downstairs for dinner. Christmas day, and my baby's father didn't bother to call me.

Mom came upstairs again to try and persuade me to come downstairs and eat. "The baby needs food too," she reminded me.

"I'm sorry, Mom," I whispered. I hated to see her upset. She brought dinner to my room, and I picked at the festive food.

Christmas was on Tuesday, and I didn't really leave my room until Thursday. My mom worked on Wednesday, and when she came home and found me still in my room, she was mad.

"Judith, this is enough!" she said and came right in without knocking. "You cannot just lie in bed for the rest of your life and mope."

I wasn't so sure. It sounded like a fine plan to me. What did I have to get up for? Again she brought me some food when I refused to get up.

"Seriously, Judith, if you don't get out of bed, I'm going to have to call the doctor," she said. She sat down on my bed and felt my forehead. "You're not hot."

"Mom, it's not that kind of sick. It's just that Christmas is over, and Kevin didn't come to see me. He didn't even call."

"Oh honey, I know," she said, and she sounded as sad as I felt. I started to cry, and she put her arms around me.

"We were supposed to be getting married. And then I left him at the party, and I gave my diamond back." I was talking through my tears and I wasn't even getting the order of things right.

"There, there," she said and rocked me back and forth like a baby.

"I can't go on without him."

"That's no way to talk." She sounded shocked.

"I'm not going to *do* anything," I said. "I just wish I could die in a car accident or something."

"Judith! Don't say such a thing!" She didn't understand, and it upset her to know that I was thinking like that. Later I wrote in my journal:

> I had the worst Christmas ever. Kevin never called, and I think
> that was pretty low of him. Sometimes I wish I could just die. It
> has a lot to do with the way people feel about me. I heard my mom
> say to my father, "I guess I just trusted her too much." And my dad
> says it was my choice to get pregnant. Then the O'Briens think I
> did this to Kevin, like he was an innocent victim and I'm a slut.
> I guess I've ruined everyone's lives. I wish I could go to sleep and
> never wake up. Then, no one would have to worry anymore. But I
> still wish Kevin had called. Bye.

I put my journal into my bureau drawer and went to sleep.

In Front of the Crowd
Five months and two days

The next night when my mom came home, I was still in my room. I heard the phone ringing, and then she was at my door.

"Judith? Telephone."

"Is it Kevin?"

But she didn't bother to answer and was already heading back downstairs.

I went into Paul's room to take the call. It was only Sally. My mother had tricked me into getting out of bed by not answering my question.

"How was your Christmas?" Sally asked.

"Okay." I didn't want to talk about everything that had gone down.

"Come to the basketball game tonight," she said. "I'm cheering."

"I don't know. I'm kind of tired."

"Come on, Judith. Oh yeah, bring your uniform too."

Ah, so maybe that was it. They just needed my uniform back. I could drop it off at her house.

"I'll pick you up in half an hour, okay?"

I wasn't sure I could manage it. "I haven't been feeling so hot."

"It'll be fun," she said. "Maybe you'll feel better if you get out."

What the heck, I thought. *I guess I can't sit around forever.*

We went into the high school with me carrying my uniform in a paper bag. Some of the cheerleaders ran up and hugged me in the hall. It was good to see them, to have them clamoring around me, wanting to know how I was feeling. They needed to practice, and I was going to watch.

"Hey, where's Tammy?" I asked.

Tammy was new this year, and she'd missed a couple of games during the football season for no real reason. She almost lost her spot on the squad.

Sally went to the pay phone to call and find out.

"Her mother said she went out," Sally said. "I asked if she had her uniform with her and her mom said no."

"Oooh, that's not a good sign," I said.

The cheerleaders stood around talking about Tammy and how this was just like her. I chimed in, reminding them about what happened during football season, how she didn't seem very committed to the team.

"We can't cheer with only five people," Amy said. "The rest of the girls are at the hockey game." During basketball and hockey season, we split the team in half if the games happened to fall on the same night.

I was leaning against the wall by the trophy case.

Sally looked over at me. "I have an idea," she said. "I know someone who knows all of the cheers."

Next thing I knew, I was in a bathroom stall putting on the uniform that I'd planned to return.

"Does it fit?" Sally asked. She was my friend from way back. I'd convinced her to try out for the team. And before that, she'd convinced me to go to St. Anne's because she didn't want to go alone. Just like that I'd said I'd go, deciding on the all-girls Catholic school because Sally wanted me there with her. Now, here we were in our senior year. She was waiting to hear back from colleges she'd applied to, and though I'd done well in school and on my SATs, I had to put college off. By September, I'd have a four-month old baby to take care of.

"Hey, does it fit?" she called again.

I stepped out of the stall. "It's a little tight. It's a good thing these basketball uniforms aren't made out of wool like the football skirts. These stretch. But I need some help with the zipper."

I turned around and Sally pulled the zipper up, and the green polyester stretched tighter across my belly. "What do you think?" I asked, twirling around to show her.

"Well, you sure fill it out now!" she said with a laugh.

"Yeah, okay, but do I look pregnant?"

"No. You look like someone with a big chest."

"My breasts have gotten huge, haven't they?"

Sally hated the word *breasts*, and she screwed her face up in a funny, pinched way.

126

"Whatever," she said. "You look built like never before." She laughed and added, "But you don't notice the belly, really."

My belly was still small with just a slight baby-bulge. The tight uniform functioned like a girdle.

We joined the others in the hallway, and they bustled around me joking about my new voluptuous figure. A couple of them touched my stomach.

"Okay," I said, taking control. "Let's practice the halftime cheer. I haven't done this for a while." But that wasn't quite true. I still practiced in my room sometimes where no one would see me, and I could still do a split right down to the floor.

While we were practicing, Mr. O'Brien and Kevin's brother Richard walked in. They were there to watch Randy play. I don't know if they saw me, but they didn't acknowledge me if they did. They went straight into the gym.

When it was game time, we went and sat on the lowest bleachers, right at the sidelines. Our basketball team sat nearby. Everyone cheered when the players took the court.

The referee tossed the basketball in the air, and the two centers jumped. The ball went toward our basket, and we immediately broke into a defense cheer, clapping as we yelled, "Take that ball away, hey! Take it away!"

Our cheering advisor, Mr. King, came in just after the game started. He knew I was pregnant because I had to tell him when I quit the team. He looked pretty surprised when he saw me cheering with the other girls.

The boys' sneakers squeaked on the floor when they stopped short or turned fast to chase the ball. The game moved quickly, the boys taking the ball up and down the court, and the crowd cheered. We stood and screamed when our guys shot the ball into the net.

At halftime, we took the court, threw our bodies into the air, and shouted out our cheers to support the team. I loved the excitement of performing in front of a crowd.

I'd started cheering in fourth grade for Pop Warner football. And I'd cheered three football seasons for the Wildcats, plus two basketball and two hockey seasons. That was nine years of cheerleading.

This one time at halftime was different from all the rest, though. Mr. O'Brien and Richard were in the stands watching. Mr. King, too, and they knew I had a child growing inside. So did all the girls jumping and shouting alongside me.

I knew this would be my last time cheering, so I tried to make each jump perfect. I moved my arms precisely and stayed in sync with the other cheerleaders. My booming voice blended with theirs, and when I kicked my legs into a Russian split, my body high off the ground, I wanted it to be the best Russian split I'd ever done, this last time I'd cheer, this last time I'd feel myself soaring in front of a crowd, free.

New Year Surprises
Five months and three days

I called Kevin the Friday after Christmas when I still hadn't heard from him. I'd bought him a sweater and filled a stocking for him. He told me he was driving down my way to see Trevor and he'd come by for the presents then.

Around ten that night the phone rang. "Hi, Judith, listen, my brother never came home with the car, so I couldn't get down there. Sorry."

"That's all right," I said. "It's not like you could help that. When do you think you might be able to come down?" I didn't want to sound pushy.

"I'm not sure. Maybe we can go out on New Year's Eve."

"That sounds good." It sounded really good. But I didn't want to act too excited. New Year's Eve was on Monday night, only a weekend away.

I hung up the phone feeling sad and glad all at once. Sad that he hadn't come for a visit but glad that maybe I'd get to spend New Year's with him. I went up into the den with my mother after making tea for both of us.

"Don't get your hopes up too high," she said after I'd told her what he'd said about New Year's. "I mean, you waited all night for him tonight."

What she said was true, but I wasn't ready to give up on him yet. We watched a show and the eleven o'clock news and then I gave her a kiss goodnight.

"Happy face in the morning," she said to me, just like she and Dad always did when I was going to bed. *Wake up and greet the day with a smile.* No matter how hard things might be, welcome each new day. I liked hearing these words from her because it reminded me I still had some stability in my life, even when it felt otherwise.

"Happy face in the morning to you too." I started upstairs and then the doorbell rang. It was after 11:30.

"Who could that be so late?" my mom asked.

I went down and opened the door, thinking it might be one of my brother's friends. Kevin stood there with Trevor and another kid they used to play football with.

"Hey," Kevin said. "Surprise!"

"Hi, guys." I led them into the living room where they all sat down. "Can I get you a soda or something?"

"No, thanks," Trevor said. "We're just passing through."

"Yeah," Kevin added. "Can't stay long, but we were in the neighborhood, so I thought we'd come over."

"I'm glad you did." He came over to give me a hug, and I felt a little funny, especially in front of Trevor. But I was glad to have Kevin wrap his arms around me even though he smelled like beer.

"Let me grab your presents," I said and got them from underneath the tree. My mom came downstairs to say hello. I spotted my camera on a table and handed it to her so she could take a picture of us. Kevin was holding his stuffed stocking and the present from me, his arm draped around my shoulder, and we were both smiling.

Mom went up to bed and then they all left. Trevor and Joe were getting into the car as Kevin and I said goodbye at the door.

"I'll see you on New Year's," he said and gave me a wet sloppy kiss. He tasted like beer, and I didn't much like the taste or the smell.

"Okay," I said. And then he went down the walk, jumped in the car and drove away. He was here and gone in such a short time that it was like I'd imagined it.

I was shocked that he'd shown up—especially after he told me his brother never came home with the car. I guess that was a lie. What else was he lying about? Maybe the plans for New Year's Eve were a lie too.

But on Monday evening, he called me from Trevor's house. One of his brothers had dropped him off there. But why there and not at my house?

"Can you come pick me up?" he asked.

I had already arranged to have the car so we could go out. "Yeah, I'll be there in about twenty minutes."

It was pretty weird going back to Trevor's house, considering that's where the whole party fiasco happened. I still regretted walking out on Kevin that night. He was waiting at the door when I pulled up. "Hey," he said. "Happy New Year!"

"Happy New Year to you too," I said. And I was happy already because I was spending the evening with him. "So what do you want to do?" I asked. We didn't have any plans.

"Well, Trevor's friend George is having a party," he said. "Let's try to find that."

Oh, God, no, I thought. *Not another party*. Instead, I said, "Sure. Just tell me where to go."

We drove around trying to find the party. It was supposed to be on the other side of town somewhere. Kevin had the address on a piece of paper and some scribbled directions. But we couldn't find the house, and I was relieved.

"How about some Chinese food?" he suggested.

That sounded about right to me. Dinner alone with Kevin on New Year's Eve was just what I needed. We went to the Hu Lau Lau and ordered a pu-pu platter so we could have a bit of everything and some coconut frozen drinks with silly umbrellas in them.

"I'm not supposed to be out with you," Kevin said as we sipped on virgin pina coladas.

"What do you mean?" I asked. "Isn't that what we'd planned?"

"Yeah, but I mean my parents. They think I'm at Trevor's."

"Oh," I said, my voice growing cool.

"They don't listen to me, Judith. No matter what I say, they tell me I can't keep seeing you. That it just can't work. They don't understand."

"Oh," I said again. I didn't know what else to say. We'd had this conversation before. He wanted to see me. He didn't want to see me. His parents didn't want him to see me. It didn't matter to him what his parents thought. It did matter. His indecision made me dizzy, and I didn't know what to expect next.

"I don't care what they think," he said. "They can't stop me from seeing you. I love you."

Those were the words I was longing to hear. Ever since I'd left him at that stupid party, I hadn't heard them. And since I'd given back the diamond and we'd put off any wedding plans, I wasn't sure what he felt. He'd been home nearly two weeks and this was only my third time seeing him.

"I love you too," I said.

After dinner we went parking. He put his hand on my belly and said, "This is our baby growing, you know." I did know. He kissed my belly, kissed my neck. We made love to celebrate the New Year, to welcome the year that would bring us our own baby, and to celebrate the fact that we still loved each other.

Later we drove back to my house. There was a party going on, and all my brother's friends were there. My parents had been out with the Z's. But now they were back and already in bed. It was close to two in the morning, and I still had to drive Kevin home. I wished he could sleep over because I was tired and didn't want to drive for an hour. And it would be nice to keep him a little longer.

I dropped him off at his house after two-thirty. I hoped he wouldn't get in trouble for being out so late. Maybe his parents would look out the window and see that it was me, not Trevor, dropping Kevin off. Maybe then they'd know that they couldn't tell Kevin what to do.

Two days later, on the second day of January, I went back to school. A lot of my close friends already knew I was pregnant. But plenty of others didn't know. My school uniform didn't fit anymore, and I couldn't even fit into the blue chinos pants I'd been wearing before Christmas break. Now, I was officially in maternity clothes, and still some kids weren't getting it.

"How come you're out of uniform?" Madeline asked in the cafeteria. She was a senior but not someone I was close to.

Well, I was going to have to get used to answering this question. A lot had changed recently—1979 had turned into 1980, and I would have my baby in the spring.

"I'm pregnant," I said. "My uniform doesn't fit."

She looked shocked and walked away. It was kind of funny. I'd known about my own pregnancy pretty much from the beginning and had lived with that knowledge for five months. The teachers had known for a while, and they wanted me to keep things secret as long as I could. But I couldn't hide the pregnancy anymore. Here we were in January, and I was going to have a baby in four months. But to many of the girls in the school, my pregnancy was news—real big news.

It was the main topic of conversations for the whole day. I'd walk by a group of girls huddled together whispering, and suddenly they'd stop when I went by. I figured they were talking about me. I kept my head up and walked past.

Our school was small. My senior class had about sixty students, and each of the three other classes was about the same size. So, with fewer than two hundred and fifty girls, the news of my pregnancy spread like wildfire. By the end of the day, everyone knew.

I felt strange being the one person everyone was talking about. It was as if I were suddenly an outsider who didn't fit in where before I got along with every group. All day everyone was looking at me and then looking quickly away. But I was going to be in school for the rest of the year, so I couldn't let the whispering and sidelong glances get to me. But that first day was real hard.

After school, I went straight to the library because I had a term paper due the next day. I'd procrastinated over break. Well, I didn't just put it off—I couldn't get myself to do any work. There'd been so many days lost to depression.

But now it was due, and I had to buckle down. I'd chosen abortion as my topic. It was interesting to me to research what happened during an abortion and the various ways one could abort a baby. When I read scientific articles that stated only facts, the gruesome aspect of abortion was clear. I didn't need the Church to tell me what to think about abortion because I'd come to that conclusion on my own already. The photos of tiny infants floating in amniotic fluid at those points in a pregnancy where abortion was legal only underscored what I already knew.

I photocopied a lot of material so I could write the term paper at home. At dinnertime when we were just sitting down to eat, the doorbell rang. It was Kevin.

"I brought the diamond," he announced as he came into the living room.

"Kevin!" I practically pounced on him I was so happy to see him.

He told me he had to leave by eight o'clock because he was going out with Trevor. I didn't care. He was here—with our diamond. We sat on the couch and he slipped the ring back on my finger where it belonged.

"I do love you, Judith," he said to me softly. "And I am going to marry you someday."

Right then it didn't matter to me when. Just the fact that he was here was enough.

"Why don't you have some dinner with us?" I asked. We were just sitting down.

Kevin joined my mom and dad and me in the kitchen. I got a plate for him and we shared one of my mom's meals. It was a simple meatloaf with potatoes, gravy, and corn on the side. But having Kevin with me made even a simple meal special.

When it got close to eight o'clock, I reminded him about his plans with Trevor. I didn't want to, but I was afraid he'd get mad otherwise.

"Do you want to go see a movie or something?"

"What about Trevor?"

"Tough!" he said, surprising me.

He had his mother's car, a new Mercury, and he asked how I liked it.

"Nice," I said. "Not as nice as your dad's Cadillac, but it's nice!" We went

133

shopping because I needed composition paper for my term paper and cigarettes. I still hadn't kicked that habit, though I'd cut down some.

We didn't go to the movies, though. Instead, we went to our usual parking lot. We both cried when we talked about his parents. It was hard on him, having his parents so set against us. He wanted to feel the baby kick, but when he held his hand on my stomach the baby didn't move.

"She must be sleeping," I said.

"He must be sleeping," Kevin corrected.

"You never know. Could be a Jessica."

"Yeah, or my little Kevin," he said. If I had a girl, we'd name her Jessica, and if I had a boy, we'd name him Kevin. We loved each other and held each other for a long time.

Later we went to Friendly's for ice cream sundaes, and it felt like things were all right for us again. When he dropped me off, he said we should go skiing on Saturday and then kissed me goodbye.

Afterwards I wanted to think about our night together, remember how good it was to hold him, but I had to concentrate on my term paper and stayed up until 3:30 in the morning. I was exhausted but happy. I was engaged again, and just like the first time he put the ring on my finger, we'd gone to Friendly's on this occasion too. I was smiling when I finally dropped off to sleep.

Rugged Terrain
Five months and one week

*F*riday after school, I put my new ski boots on and walked around the house to break them in. They were part of my Christmas present from my parents along with skis and poles. I couldn't wait to go skiing with Kevin.

Just as I was getting ready for bed, though, the phone rang.

"Hi," Kevin said. "We can't go."

"What do you mean?"

"I had a huge fight with my parents. There's no way they're letting me go skiing with you. I couldn't even get the car."

"That sucks," I said. "Maybe I can try to get my parents' car?"

"No, I'm at Trevor's now. My brother dropped me off."

"Will I see you before you go back to school?"

"I don't see how," he said. "I'm leaving Sunday."

"Oh, all right, so I guess this is goodbye. Over the phone," I said. I didn't understand. He was only a few miles away. I didn't see why we couldn't find a way to see each other before he left.

"I'll try to call before I leave. If not, I'll write from school. I love you."

I told him I loved him too, and hung up. But I was feeling awful. Before I'd even hung up, I had already started to cry.

Sometimes, it felt like I was at some horrible amusement park, riding on rides I couldn't get off—up and down, up and down, round and round, round and round. It was like I was on a rollercoaster that never stopped or a merry-go-round that wouldn't let me off.

I hoped I'd cry myself to sleep because I didn't want to keep thinking about everything. Instead, I ended up in the bathroom throwing up.

The next morning, when I wanted to stay in bed all day, there was a knock at my door. Dad was standing there in jeans and a blue sweatshirt.

"Judith, Mommy and I want to talk with you down in the living room. Can you come down?"

"So what's this all about?" I asked when I joined them in the living room.

My mother started. "Well, we're a little concerned. Kevin hasn't been very attentive to you this break, and we don't like to see you so upset."

"I don't like being upset, either," I said.

"Mommy and I have been talking, and we think that it might be time to consult a lawyer." Dad sat in one of the wing chairs and I distractedly noticed that his shirt matched the fabric.

"A lawyer?" I asked. "What for?"

"There will be matters regarding the birth certificate and support," he said a little stiffly.

They knew I wanted the baby to have Kevin's name, especially since I was adopted. They were the only mother and father I knew, and I loved them dearly, but I knew very little about my biological parents—certainly not their names. But I didn't think it was going to be an issue with my own baby.

I had told my mom I was worried now that Kevin kept changing his mind about everything. She, no doubt, had been talking to my dad.

"But he gave me the diamond back, and he says he still wants to marry me," I said showing them my hand.

"We know, Judith," my mom said. "This is a hard step to take. Kevin might still prove himself. But it does seem unclear what he plans to do."

They were right, but I didn't want to admit it. I wanted to tell them something that would make them believe, and in the telling maybe I could convince myself too. But I couldn't think of anything to say.

"I'm going to talk with a lawyer to get some questions answered. But that's all for now," Dad said.

"Kevin loves me," I insisted.

"Honey, that won't change," my mother said. She moved closer and put her arm around my shoulder.

"Right, and it shouldn't be a problem for him to acknowledge this child as his," my father said, emphasizing the word his and raising his voice a bit.

Acknowledge his child? It sounded ludicrous to imagine he would ever act as if this baby inside me wasn't his. I mean, we'd dreamed about the baby even before the conception. But sitting with my parents and having this conversation made me realize that anything might be possible.

I wished I could believe in Kevin. He kept asking me to believe, even though he was so unsure about everything. It was nice to wear the diamond again, but all the uncertainty was still there.

What if he wasn't around when I had my baby? What if my baby was left without Kevin's name on the birth certificate? What if my baby was left wondering about whether or not his father even cared about him? I loved Kevin, but I needed security for my baby.

"Go ahead," I said quietly, "call the lawyer."

I was mad at Kevin for blowing off the ski trip. I'd begun to think he'd lied to me about not being able to meet me that day. After all, he was able to get a ride to Trevor's house and hang out there. And I was still upset that I'd seen so little of him during his Christmas break.

I wrote letters and told him I was angry, but I guess I didn't say why, because in his next letter he sounded confused.

> Dear Judith,
>
> I asked you to come skiing this weekend, and I want to see you. But your letters to me are all sad and angry. I don't understand. Are you sure you want to come see me? Maybe you'll want to hurt me when you see me! If I call you, can you explain to me what's happening? I feel like I don't know what's going on.
>
> Last night you came to me while I was lying in bed. I wasn't even asleep yet, but your voice was clear, telling me that you loved me. I told you that I loved you too. I wanted to hold you. But I just had this dream—you talking in my head and nobody in my room but me.
>
> Come skiing this weekend, so I can see the real you.

He went on to tell me about the fresh snow and how the ski team was heading to Killington to practice racing. He loved to ski, and I wanted to go see him and spend the day sharing some fun.

It was good to know he missed me so much that he was hearing my voice, and his emotions seemed heartfelt. But how could he miss me like that when he was away at school, yet not want to see me when he was back home? Something didn't seem right, didn't add up, but his words still called out to me.

He ended his letter by signing *Love, Kevin* and adding *Believe* at the bottom of the page. Even though I was having doubts, I knew I would go see him. I would go anytime he called. That is, if I could borrow the car.

Sometimes it seemed like rules governed my whole life: I couldn't go see Kevin unless I got my parents' permission, if I played by their rules—and Kevin couldn't see me at all, if he played by his parents' rules. There were rules everywhere, and at school on Thursday, I learned how arbitrary those rules could be.

"Did you hear the news?" Sandy whispered to me in homeroom. "Mrs. Doherty has to leave school."

"What do you mean?" I whispered so Sister Catherine wouldn't hear us.

"She's pregnant and they're firing her," Sandy said.

"But she's married," I whispered back.

"Ladies," Sister Catherine's voice boomed from the front of the room. "Is there something you'd like to share with the rest of us?"

"No, Sister," I said. "Sorry."

"It's not fair!" I said during lunch with Sally and Sandy. "How can they make her leave and not me? I mean I'm glad I can stay, don't get me wrong, but why does Mrs. Doherty have to go?"

"I don't know," Sally said. "Maybe there's some rule that says you can't be pregnant and teach here."

"They might think it would have a bad influence on us," Sandy said.

"Yeah, right, like we'd all go out and suddenly get pregnant," I said, sarcastically. "Oops, too late for me." I was pissed. "I'm going to go see her after school."

"You better do it today, then," Sandy said. "Tomorrow is her last day."

I went by the biology room right at the end of classes. Mrs. Doherty was packing up some of her things.

"Can I talk with you?"

"Sure, Judith, what's up?"

"I heard you're leaving."

"True, but I don't have a choice," Mrs. Doherty said.

"But why? I'm staying and I'm pregnant. And you're married."

"Yes, but I just got married," she said. "They know I was pregnant before."

"So what? That's not fair," I said. "They're letting me stay."

"It's just different. You're a student, and they're helping you. You need to graduate."

"I feel terrible, almost guilty. It's not right that I'm here and they're making you go."

"Listen, Judith, life isn't fair. But what you're doing is courageous. I admire you. And don't you worry about me. I'll be fine. You have enough things of your own to worry about. But you'll be fine too. You're very strong."

But I wasn't feeling very strong, and my eyes were like fountains these days. She gave me a tissue and a hug.

"I'm sorry," I said.

"Don't be. It's okay. And don't cry. You're going to make me cry. Now skedaddle."

I left feeling like all the rules were crazy and useless.

But if I wanted the car this weekend, I had to follow my parents' rules and get their permission.

I asked them that night at dinner, and they said that they'd think about it. I felt like screaming at them, *Do you want to keep me away from Kevin?* It was bad enough that his family didn't want us together. Did my parents have to get in on the action too? But I held it in. I knew I had to be sweet to get my way.

"All right," I said. "If you could let me know by the end of the week, that'd be great. Then I can let Kevin know. So, Dad, did you talk with that lawyer yet?"

I was curious. But more, I wanted to show my interest in a subject that interested him and my mom. I was kissing up to them in hopes of getting that car.

He hadn't talked with the lawyer yet, only left a message, and part of me was glad. When I thought about working with a lawyer, I felt like I was stepping in the wrong direction, away from Kevin while we were still trying to make things work, still trying to be together.

Later in the week, I got permission to visit him, and I arranged to be there bright and early Sunday morning.

By 5:30 a.m. I was on the road. By 8:45 I was in Kevin's dorm. He was in bed and I got to wake him with a kiss. I wished I could do that every morning of our lives. He showered and then got dressed right in front of me. It felt like I could step into his life at any moment and still be part of it. We were comfortable together, and I loved the way that felt.

After breakfast, we went to Sugarbush Valley. Kevin skied better and faster than I did, and I had to remind him to slow down and remember I was five months pregnant, after all.

I guess I thought he'd take me on some easy slopes—the ones whose signs had round green circles on them—or at least intermediate ones with the blue squares. Instead, he took me down a difficult trail, the black diamond marker indicating how challenging it was. The trail was covered in moguls, and I found these mounds of snow hard to maneuver around. Kevin moved easily through the run and had to keep waiting for me.

"Let's not do that run again," I said to him when we got to the bottom.

"But that was a blast!"

"Maybe for you. I found it really difficult." Sometimes he didn't notice my needs, and I didn't like his selfish side.

After lunch in the lodge, we bumped right into Kevin's older brother Richard.

"What are *you two* doing here?" he asked Kevin after acknowledging me with a quick hello.

"Skiing," Kevin said.

It was an obvious answer to a dumb question, but I don't think that's what Richard was getting at. He seemed shocked to see the two of us together. Again, the thought ran through my mind that something wasn't right. How long had his family thought we weren't seeing each other? I know Kevin kept telling me they didn't want him to see me, but now I was beginning to think he'd been lying to both them and me for a while.

We went back to his room after a full day of skiing. His roommate was away, and we had the place to ourselves. Maybe Kevin wasn't supposed to be with me, but when he was alone with me, he wanted to be with me completely. And on those occasions, I wanted to share myself completely too.

Like a Love Story
Five months, two weeks and one day

At lunch the next day at school, I went out to smoke a cigarette. Amy, the cheerleading co-captain, was in the smoking area with Laura, a girl we both knew.

"So when's the baby due, exactly?" Amy asked.

"The doctor thinks the beginning of May. He said the fifth."

"That's before the prom," she said. "What will you do?"

"I'll still go. I just hope I'm not too fat," I said and took a drag.

"Who are *you* going to go with?" Laura asked. She said it like there was no way I'd be at my senior prom.

"Kevin, of course."

"Yeah, right," Laura said and tossed her head, shaking her blond curls.

"What's that supposed to mean?" I asked. "We're engaged."

"That's not what I heard."

I wanted to know what she was talking about, and she was eager to spill the details. I smoked my cigarette while she told me what her boyfriend Neil had heard from Trevor: Kevin said there was no way he was marrying *that girl.* Trevor wasn't even sure Kevin liked me.

I crushed the cigarette under my foot. "So how come I have a diamond?" I asked angrily. "That Kevin gave me?"

"Beats me," Laura said. "I'm just telling you what I heard from Neil."

That night I called Kevin to get his side. He said what I'd heard wasn't true, but he didn't seem very angry or upset about the lies. Then he told me he was going skiing with Trevor over the weekend. I thought it was odd he hadn't told me about those plans sooner.

A couple of days later, I got a letter from him that tried to explain what he'd said to Trevor:

> Hi Judith,
>
> I'm not sure what to say. No matter how much I tell you that you should have faith in me, you don't. You keep thinking I am telling you lies. And you believe other people instead of me. I wish that you could hear me and no one else.
>
> During the Thanksgiving break, I said that we were getting married. But then when you left me at Trevor's party, I told Trevor I was thinking about not marrying you. I felt like you were leaving me. What was I supposed to think? But that was because of all the craziness with the party and all the stuff with my parents. You need to stop worrying, and you need to have faith in me like I keep telling you.
>
> We made part of our wildflower dream come true by making our baby together, and now we just have to make the rest of it come true by getting married when I'm done with school.
>
> Love,
> Kevin

Scribbled at the bottom was his classic *Believe in me*. Trouble was, I didn't. But I still *wanted* to. I really did.

I had a doctor's appointment at the end of the month. It would've been nice if Kevin had come with me, but it was my mother who took the time to drive me and stay in the waiting room during my checkup.

The doctor took a tape measure and placed it above my belly button and then measured down to my private parts.

"The baby seems to be growing fine," Dr. Sprague said. With his warm brown eyes and soothing voice, he seemed like a kind man. "Does he kick a lot now?"

"Yes, he kicks me all the time." And it was true. When I went to bed, that's when the baby was especially active. It was hard to fall asleep. I liked to put my hand on my stomach and feel the movement beneath. It was amazing to me that this little life had such power.

Dr. Sprague looked at my weight that the nurse had written on my chart.

"I see you've gained eight pounds. That's a lot for one month. Do you eat a lot of junk food?"

I thought about the ice cream and chips I ate before bed. I craved salty and sweet things at the same time, and I'd been giving in to those cravings. It was like I thought I could chase away my loneliness with food.

"I do like ice cream. And cookies and chips."

"Well, you should eat those only in moderation, now," he said gently.

I made a mental note to start a diet.

"Everything okay?" Mom said when I came out.

I smiled and said, "Fine. But I'm getting fat."

She took me to lunch, but I skipped dessert. Afterwards we went shopping, but I didn't find anything that fit me right and felt even fatter. I was quiet on the drive home because even though I didn't like that I was getting fat, I knew I had much bigger problems weighing me down.

Later, at home, I got all of Kevin's letters out of my bureau drawer and read them one by one. I sat on my bed with my pillow propped against the headboard. It was like reading a love story, each letter a new chapter. But the problem with the love story that these letters represented was that the chapters, and even the pages within chapters, didn't add up right.

Kevin's words were often beautiful, at least to me. But sometimes they were just plain confusing. When I looked at the letters all together, it was as if I could finally see a pattern emerging. He'd tell me one thing, then tell me another. Make a promise, then break it. Apologize and then insist that I *really* believe. Tell me his parents would never understand and he just couldn't be with me. Tell me he couldn't live without me.

I'd been so happy to get his letters that I'd missed his growing doubts, even when they were staring me right in my face. I still wished I could ignore the inconsistencies in his story and believe in the world we created together, where we loved each other and everything would work out. But maybe it was time for me to take his uncertainties as the reality. I had to think about how his unpredictable behavior and instability could affect the course of my life and my baby's.

That evening, I took a huge step and got the lawyer's phone number from my dad. After school the next day, I took a deep breath and placed the call. The lawyer said he thought Kevin and I would end up in court. He said we couldn't do anything until I was over six months pregnant and that he was booked until the beginning of March. We went ahead and set a meeting for March third. By then I'd be seven months along.

I went to a Wildcats basketball game that night, and Mr. O'Brien was there as usual. He rarely acknowledged me when I saw him, and it was hard to talk to him when he wouldn't even look at me. But with my new resolve, I decided to tell him I'd talked with a lawyer and expected Kevin to admit paternity.

I think he was surprised when I spoke to him, but he let me finish. "The normal procedure," he responded, sounding cool and aloof, "would be to have your lawyer contact me. Then I'd give him my lawyer's name and they'd handle things. You shouldn't have to talk with me about this." After that he turned and walked away.

I tried calling Kevin that night but couldn't reach him. The guys didn't have phones in their own rooms, just a pay phone in each hall. When I called, the phone just rang and rang. Finally I wrote him a letter about my conversation with the lawyer so he would understand my desire to protect our baby.

> Dear Kevin,
>   This is a hard letter for me to write, but I want you to hear this from me. I called a lawyer today to find out what I should do about the baby. I want to make sure that your name is on the birth certificate. That's so important to me, and I think you'll understand. It has a lot to do with my being adopted. I never knew who my birth parents were, and I don't want that for our baby.
>   The lawyer said that we'll probably end up in court and that I might have to use your letters to prove that you're the father. That sounds so scary to me. I don't want to go to court, but I want to make sure everything is done right for this baby. I know you tell me to have faith in you, and I want to. But it seems like every time I turn around you're changing your mind. I'm not sure what to believe anymore.
>   I love you, Kevin, more than you'll ever know. I hope we can still be together—I've never wanted anything more in my life. Please, try not to be too angry with me.
>
>   Love,
>   Judith
>   P.S. Please write back soon.

After that conversation with his father and the letter I wrote, his letters stopped. The last one, postmarked January 17, said he still wanted to marry me. But then, no more.

When I came home from school each day, the first thing I did was open the black mailbox by the front door. I'd sort through bills and the junk mail. Nothing. If the box were empty, I'd go inside and look on the counter. Paul sometimes tossed the mail there if he got home before I did. I'd look for an envelope with Kevin's return address. Nothing.

This went on for days. Then days turned into weeks. I couldn't believe it. I had a stack of more than forty letters bound with elastic in my bureau drawer. There had been a week when I received a letter every day. Other weeks, I got two or three letters. But was this *it*? Was this the end? One mention of a lawyer and our relationship was over? I tried calling and still got no answer. One time I did get through, but the kid who answered said Kevin wasn't around. I didn't know what to do. I thought he'd understand I was looking out for our baby.

I was miserable, but I made myself go through the motions of normal activities. I went to school and did my work. I came home and did my homework at night. When there was a basketball game, I'd go and sit with friends. Perched in the stands, the O'Briens ignored me, as if I were invisible. It seemed like Kevin and his family thought I really was. At night, I cried myself to sleep or just lay in bed staring at the ceiling. Sometimes I'd feel the baby kick, and a momentary rush of amazement would fill my heart. Then my sorrows would take over again. Without Kevin, I felt afraid and completely alone.

The Saturday before Valentine's Day, I baked cookies for Kevin. I couldn't reach him by phone, and he wasn't answering my letters, so I decided to send him a care package for that day honoring lovers. I had to let him know I still loved him, that my love could endure even this hard time without contact.

Maybe the way to a man's heart really is through the stomach, as the saying goes, because on February 14, when I was prepared to feel desolate and deserted, I finally got a letter in the mail. The envelope had the crest and name of Kevin's school stamped on it. Inside, there was a letter and a handmade card decorated with hearts and arrows. He wanted me to be his valentine and told me how much he loved me.

The card was great, but the four-page love letter was even better. He told me how much he missed me and apologized for not writing sooner. He was afraid and didn't want to get himself in trouble. What I'd written about the lawyer had shocked him, and he couldn't believe I'd actually use his letters to prove he was the baby's father. But even with all that weighing on his mind, he insisted he wasn't going to leave me. He knew, of course, the child was his. He wrote "I love you" in big letters and circled the message in case I wasn't paying attention. But of course I was. He told me how often he thought about me and tried to explain how that made him feel. That part was hard for him to put into words.

I completely understood. Sometimes, I felt happy when I thought about him, but other times I felt sad. He told me he talked with his friends at school and they tried to tell him everything would work out fine. I was glad to hear that. He needed people who could help him see that we could make it.

Along with the cookies, I'd sent him a picture of us because I wanted him to see how happy we were when we were together. He complimented me on the way I looked in the picture, and I liked hearing that he still found me attractive.

But the best part of the letter was that he wanted me to come and see him. He had a present for me, a teacup with my name on it that he'd made in his ceramics class. I thought that was sweet. He told me he loved me—always had and always would.

I'd been so depressed for the past month, but now I started to feel like my old self again. His letter cheered me and made me feel warm and loved. I wrote him back a long letter and tried to explain all about the lawyer. I told him how I wanted to make sure my child had his name. I told him, again, about my own feelings about being adopted. He knew these things already, but I wanted to get them down in writing, again, to try and say them in just the right way. Mostly, I wanted Kevin to know I loved him as much as ever, and I didn't want our relationship to end.

One part of his letter disturbed me. He wanted to see me, but he didn't want anyone to know. Instead, he wanted us to find some private place to meet up. On the one hand that sounded romantic, like we were running to each other, finally. But on the other, he wanted to keep me hidden like a dirty little secret. And I didn't like that at all. I wanted to be loved in a big way, with a wide-open abandon that shouted it to the world.

My family didn't trust Kevin anymore, and I told him how my parents thought I should let the lawyer continue, if only to protect myself and their grandchild. I didn't want to hurt Kevin, but I wanted him to understand how my family felt about the way he'd been treating me.

His next letter was postmarked February 22, more than a week later. This one was short. He seemed upset that my parents didn't think so highly of him anymore. Kevin loved them and wanted them to believe in him, but they had good reason for their doubts. He asked if I'd come up to his school that next weekend.

I didn't think I'd be allowed to go, but when I asked, my parents said yes. I think they were tired of seeing me so utterly depressed. But after receiving the Valentine's letter, I'd been much happier, and now I'd get to see Kevin. I could hardly wait.

All Business
Seven months

*A*ll week long I was excited about going to visit Kevin. I hadn't seen him in over a month. It was all I could think of during class, after school, at night. I was hoping we'd be able to straighten out our misunderstandings. I thought if we could hold each other while we talked, everything would make sense.

His family still ignored me anytime they saw me. And here I was carrying their grandchild. How could they not want to know their grandchild? I didn't get it.

On Friday I got a letter from him. It was short and to the point. I couldn't come see him on Sunday because he wouldn't be there. He was coming home for the weekend, but he said nothing about getting together with me. The letter didn't fill even one notebook page, and though he signed it *Love, Kevin* and told me not to forget his love, he didn't ask me to believe in him. And though I held the envelope close to my nose, there was no scent of his Coast soap.

My appointment with the lawyer was the following Monday, and Mom took a day off from work to join me because I was so nervous. The office building was in the center of town, across the street from Miss Ashington's Dance Studio and two blocks up from Pizza World where Kevin and I used to go. The one-story brick building looked like a post office, except for the fancy sign on the building that said Law Offices of Mosley and Mosley. I wondered if they were brothers, or a father and a son.

Inside, a secretary greeted us from behind her large wooden desk. There were rows of file cabinets behind her. We sat down to wait, and I looked around the room at the walls lined with floor-to-ceiling bookcases. We'd been seated only a few minutes when the secretary's phone rang and she told us we could go in. She got up and opened the door to one of the offices.

Mr. Moseley—one of the Mr. Moseleys—was seated behind a wooden desk even larger than his secretary's. When we came in, he walked around to shake my hand and my mother's. His massive furniture looked like it was made from cherry wood, like my parents' dining room set. We joined him at a big table with heavy chairs around it.

"There's a clear procedure if you decide to file a paternity suit," he said to us after a few moments of small talk. Reading aloud from a file folder, he said, "Under the Massachusetts General Laws, Chapter 273, Section 12, proceedings to determine whether a man is the father of a child born to an unmarried woman shall be brought in either the Superior Court where the alleged father or mother of the illegitimate child lives or in the district court."

I hated the sound of the word *illegitimate*, like somehow our child wasn't real.

He went on. "If the father pleads guilty or nolo contendere or is found guilty, the Court enters a judgment adjudging him as father of the child."

As he read, I frowned in concentration. *Found guilty?* I hadn't known the court could find Kevin guilty. We were both guilty of having had sex before marriage, and I knew it was a sin, but this confused me.

"I just want his name on the birth certificate," I said when he stopped reading.

"I understand, Judith," he said kindly. "But your father said we couldn't be sure the young man would cooperate."

I hated to think of my father describing Kevin as someone who might deny he was the father of our baby. It didn't seem right. But I knew my dad was watching out for his own baby, me.

Mr. Mosley went on to talk about the possibility of a blood test should the alleged father order one.

"We were planning to get married after he finished school," I said, wishing he wouldn't call Kevin the *alleged father*.

"Really?" He sounded surprised. "Your father didn't tell me that."

My mom jumped into the conversation, "Well, yes, Kevin did give Judith an engagement ring, and there was talk of marriage. But John and I are concerned that Kevin has been, shall we say, less than responsible. It's hard to predict what he might do. And his family is completely unsupportive." She put her hand on my shoulder.

"I see," Mr. Mosley said.

Did he? Was it all clear to him from a phone conversation with my dad and a brief meeting with my mom and me? How was it, then, that I was so blind?

"Well," he continued, "now that you mention the family's unsupportive nature, I should bring up the issue of support. It's against the law not to support an illegitimate child in Massachusetts. This would be a criminal case."

Illegitimate. There was that word again. It sounded dirty and made me feel dirty because I'd be called illegitimate too, having been born to an unwed mother, and I was going to have an illegitimate child. A baby was a baby. Why did we use such an ugly, demoralizing word? I hated it. Just hearing the word made me feel sick.

And then there was this issue of the courts. I'd actually have to bring a criminal case against the man I loved?

"Isn't there some other way?" I asked.

"I could draw up an affidavit for Mr. O'Brien, attesting to his paternity," Mr. Mosley said. "But do you think he'd sign it?"

I felt so depressed that I couldn't answer.

After a moment Mom spoke for me. "Why don't you draw up the affidavit, Mr. Mosley? I'm sure Kevin will sign."

I was glad for her confidence because I wasn't feeling that way anymore.

The lawyer got the paperwork ready and sent it off. Dated March 4, it wasn't exactly what I wanted. But I had to trust that he knew what he was doing. He wrote a very stiff, formal letter to Kevin—"Mr. O'Brien"—"concerning the anticipated birth of your child." He said he understood "that it was your intention to get married in June of this year. In the event that the marriage does not take place, you must still concern yourself with the child that is going to be born." He went on to say that because I wanted Kevin's name on the birth record, "we are requesting that you acknowledge the child as yours by signing the enclosed affidavit. If you are in agreement as to the affidavit, I would request that you have it notarized before a Notary Public in Vermont."

The second page was the affidavit, which stated that Kevin was engaged to me and planned to marry me on or about June 1, 1980. It also said he was the father of the child I was expecting and the child could carry his surname.

The letter seemed fine, but I was worried about the affidavit. I'd told the lawyer about our plans to get marred in June, but I didn't like seeing it written up in the affidavit, as if I were trying to force Kevin to marry me. I didn't see why that part needed to be there.

I called the lawyer, but he'd already put the letter and affidavit in the mail. He said we'd have to wait and see what happened. So I waited. But I didn't hear from Kevin—no letters and no calls. I tried calling him at his school but rarely got through. When I did, he was, mysteriously, never available.

I started prenatal classes at Baystate Hospital, even though I wouldn't be delivering my baby there. Because of my age, I was considered a high-risk pregnancy and would have to go to Springfield. When I walked into the room for prenatal classes, I was the only woman without a partner.

All the other women were older and had their husbands with them. I stood in the doorway for a few minutes, unsure whether to go in. I felt alone and scared. I considered leaving, but I wanted to learn how to breathe, wanted to learn what to expect when the baby came. We had been instructed to bring a pillow, and I took mine and sat down on the floor surrounded by all the couples.

The following day I had another appointment with Dr. Sprague. I was still gaining a good amount of weight, but he said he expected that now. He wanted to see me every other week and then after mid April, every week.

My pregnancy was progressing fast, and I felt like a cow—a deserted cow.

I finally reached Kevin the next night.

When he came to the phone, I asked him, "How come you haven't gotten back to me?"

"I've been busy with school."

"Oh yeah, me too. How are your classes going?" I wanted to talk with him. I wanted to know when he was going to return the affidavit, but even more than that, I wanted to hear his voice and find out how he was.

"Like I said, busy," he said. All his answers were short.

"Hey, I'm really big now. I've gained almost twenty-eight pounds, and I still have six weeks to go."

"Listen, I got to get going to study," he said.

"Wait, are you going to mail back the papers that the lawyer sent?"

"Yeah, you'll get them. Bye." And he hung up. I didn't even get to say goodbye. I didn't get to tell him I loved him. It was as if we'd never been lovers or friends, like we were suddenly strangers talking about someone else's life.

A week went by, and still there was no signed affidavit from Kevin. My lawyer called and suggested I try to find out what was going on. I'd been trying. But I called again.

If I thought Kevin was cool the week before, he was much worse this week.

"I'm not signing anything," he said.

I felt like I'd been hit in the face. The man I'd been loving all this time wouldn't sign a piece of paper acknowledging he was the father of our child?

"What are you talking about? I just—"

"Look, my father got a lawyer, and they won't let me sign anything."

He got off the phone right after that. So that was it. We'd go to court to establish that my fiancé was the father of my child? Ridiculous. I took the diamond from my left hand and moved it to my right. It was a pretty ring—that was all.

A few days later, my Business Law class took a field trip to the local courthouse. We walked up the granite steps and into the stately building with its pillars and brick walls. I hadn't told anyone at school about these latest developments involving Kevin and now a lawyer—I was too embarrassed. We sat quietly in the back while one trial after another took place.

The judge talked to us afterwards. He actually spoke about paternity suits, and I couldn't help but wonder if my teacher had suggested the topic. It seemed surreal to me, sitting there nearly eight months pregnant and listening to a judge talk about bringing a paternity suit in Massachusetts.

He was saying the same things the lawyer had discussed with my mom and me. It was like déjà vu and a premonition all at the same time. I'd heard the words before, but now I imagined myself in court with Kevin, our lawyers beside us, and the judge up front listening. The thought of it was terrible, and I left the court feeling dejected and depressed.

Before I went to bed that night, I took out my journal and wrote a poem. I was trying to express my pain, to take it from my insides where it was smothering me and spill it onto the page. I wrote:

Wildflowers don't smile anymore,
clowns seem to cry,
trees are lifeless,
and sunsets lonely.
A full moon is painful
on a quiet spring night,
the stars are shining
but nothing is bright.

It took me a long time to write the poem, and when I finished, I put the pen on my bureau and the journal in a drawer. I didn't feel much better, but at least I had pushed away the darkness enough that I felt able to pray. Whispering the words from my bed, I called out to the Holy Mother, *Oh Mary, conceived without sin, pray for us who have recourse to thee.* She knew I needed her consolation, and after saying the sweet prayer, I was able to close my eyes and sleep.

The Main Event
Nearly nine months

I spent a lot of time with my friends who took me shopping for baby things. We went to the movies. We went to the mall and got ice cream. School and friends, homework and naps, prenatal classes and doctor's visits—they filled my days and kept me busy. But I still felt lonely.

Sometimes a deep darkness fell over me, and I didn't want to do anything. The idea of death crept in again. It was a seductive presence cooing to me, asking me to disappear, asking me to forget my faith. But my baby was coming soon. Life and hope were so close on the horizon. I tried to concentrate on good things and push the pain and despair away.

During a visit with my doctor, I found out the baby's head had dropped down and was locked into position. Dr. Sprague said I might carry the baby for another month or give birth at any time before then. I'd gained thirty-five pounds, so I was rooting for any time.

While I waited for my baby, everyone else at St. Anne's was preparing for the annual play. *Oliver* was going to be a big production, and the whole school was buzzing with excitement. On show nights, I helped out in the back room, fixing makeup and hair. At the final performance, parents and boyfriends came to the door with flowers for their girls, and I felt sad and sorry for myself. But when Sandy's mom came, she gave me a hug and a pretty white carnation that lifted my spirits. I was glad someone had remembered me.

The last weeks of the school year were difficult. With no word from Kevin, I felt lost. No one at school understood what I was going through. I walked around in a daze. My belly barely fit in the space between my desk and chair. If I felt like a cow before, now I was more like a whale. I was glad when April vacation came.

When vacation ended, I didn't go back. The doctor said the baby could come anytime, and the school didn't want me going into labor in one of the classrooms. I was exhausted anyways and tired of being the pregnant girl everybody stared at. I was happy to stay home.

I was also glad to leave the drama behind. Out in the smoking area one day, a girl told me she thought she was pregnant and that she'd probably have an abortion. I don't know why she told me. Maybe she thought I'd understand how scared she was, and I did understand that. But I was also angry because she got to stay in National Honor Society, and I'd been kicked out for being pregnant, even though my grades were good. It didn't seem fair, and I said as much to one of the teachers who was out on maternity leave, someone I'd gone to visit. That was a big mistake.

Apparently, she told the administrators, and, suddenly, they all felt an obligation to find that pregnant girl and stop her from having an abortion. But she wasn't even sure she was pregnant! The school didn't know that and started calling my friends one by one into the office and interrogating them, drilling them for information. I was at home and didn't know what was going on until the call came from the school.

Then the principal—who had been so supportive of me—called, saying I wouldn't be able to graduate unless I told her the girl's name. I wouldn't. But they said they knew anyways, that one of my friends had told them. I didn't know what to do, so I asked if I could at least talk to the girl who thought she was pregnant.

I got off the phone and started crying, and once I started, it was like I couldn't stop. The sobs came in waves that wracked my body. No one was home at my house, so when the phone rang again, I picked it up. It was that girl, a student who still had another year of school left.

She said she was going to deny everything, and that gave me an idea. Having a plan—a kind of denial of my own—helped calm me down. When Sister got back on the phone I told her my story.

"I made it up," I said. "It was never true." Sister didn't believe me at first. But I insisted. In a matter-of-fact way, I claimed I'd made the whole thing up because I didn't want to feel all alone. In fact, there was no other pregnant girl at St. Anne's, at least as far as I knew.

I sounded believable even to myself. My convoluted, made-up story had a ring of truth to it. I *didn't* want to be alone, and when I said those words, I could say them with enough conviction to make Sister believe me.

"You still might not graduate," Sister hissed in my ear. "What you've done is despicable. You don't deserve to graduate," she said and then hung up the phone.

If I thought I'd been sobbing before, I really let loose now. In addition to thinking I was a slut, the teachers would now think I was a liar and a mean, base person who wanted to bring another girl down. I was afraid my friends and everyone else at school would think that too.

I sat down in the corner of our upstairs hallway, pulled my knees towards my chest and rocked, wailing. How could they stop me from graduating? I was home alone, and there was no one to talk to, so I prayed a simple prayer: *Dear God, help me!*

That night I cried myself to sleep. After midnight, I heard Paul coming into the house. He slammed the front door and tripped on the stairs. I tried to go back to sleep after he closed his door, but my stomach hurt. I rubbed it until the pain stopped.

I started to doze off, but then the tightening in my stomach returned, and when I touched it, it was rock hard. It felt like cramps but stronger. I wondered if I might be going into labor, but then I remembered something I'd learned at childbirth classes—if you had false labor, it would go away if you moved around.

So I got up and went downstairs. Mom and Dad had come home earlier, and they were sleeping now, so the whole house was quiet. I went and sat in the living room, and when the pain started again, I got up and walked around.

The rooms on the first floor were all connected like a big square, and I paced heavily from one to the next and hoped the pain would stop. It didn't, so I gave up walking and made myself a snack of hot cocoa and Oreo cookies. I leaned against the counter when the cramping started again and tried to think about something besides the pain. When it subsided, I finished my cocoa and cookies and went upstairs to draw a warm bath.

Getting into the tub wasn't easy. I'd gained forty pounds and my stomach and breasts were huge. When I lay in the water, my stomach and chest were like mountains jutting out. More pains came while I soaked, and I fervently wished they'd go away. Then I realized that I probably should start keeping track of the time between the pains. I didn't want to call them contractions yet because I still thought this was false labor. If I moved around and changed my position, maybe I could make it all go away.

At 1:45 a.m., I reached for my watch and discovered the pains were five minutes apart and coming on strong. I added hot water to the tub to keep the bath warm. But when the contractions hadn't stopped by 2:30, I got out and got dressed.

I knocked on my mom's bedroom door and then opened it. "Mom, I think I'm in labor," I whispered.

"Are you sure?"

"No. It could be false labor. I don't know."

My mom had never been in labor, so she didn't know what it would be like for me. She got up and dressed and came down to the kitchen with me. When my stomach got hard again, I let her feel how tight it was, and this pain seemed stronger than the others. I made a face and let out a groan. I was scared now and wished my mother had been with me during the prenatal classes. She hadn't been able to get the nights off from work.

"We better call the hospital," she said.

St. Margaret's was all the way over in Springfield, more than an hour away, so we didn't want to go unless I was really going to have the baby. When Mom told the nurse my contractions were about five minutes apart, the reply was that we should come in right away. Mom told Dad we were going.

I was glad there were so few cars on Route 91—this was one benefit of going into labor in the middle of the night. Still, the ride to the hospital seemed to take forever, and the contractions kept coming.

At the hospital front desk, I told them I thought I was in false labor, but that if this were fake then I was scared about the real thing. Mom stayed at the desk to fill out some papers while I was taken to an examining room.

The nurse had me take off my pants and put on a jonnie, and then a doctor came in. With a glove on, he put his hand inside me and felt my cervix. Another pain came while he was checking, and I wanted to cry.

"I want to go home," I said, whimpering a little.

"Well, you're not going anywhere tonight," the doctor said. "You're already five centimeters dilated. I expect you'll have a baby sometime this morning."

I was taken to a room for labor, and Mom joined me. Then a nurse came in and got me into bed. She didn't even smile or ask me how I was doing.

"I don't feel so good," I said. "I need to go to the bathroom."

"You're going to stay in bed now," the nurse said.

"But I don't feel well. I really feel like I'm going to be sick."

"You have to stay in bed," she said sternly. She came over to the bed with a pink plastic container, just in case. But when she went to give it to me, I threw up everywhere. Some went into the pink plastic, but plenty went on me, and some got her too. The hot chocolate and Oreos made a gross dark brown river on my jonnie and on her white uniform. She didn't look happy. Mom got a cloth and helped wash me up.

"It's okay, you couldn't help it," Mom said as she wiped my face.

The nurse brought me a fresh jonnie and clean sheets. She changed the bed around me by having me roll onto one side and then the other while she took off the sheets and put on the new ones. I couldn't see why she wouldn't just let me get out of bed.

"I need a phone," I said after Mom and the nurse had me all cleaned up. "I have to call Kevin."

"Judith, it's nearly five in the morning." Mom said. "I don't think you'll be able to reach him."

"I don't care what time it is. I need to call him."

Mom talked to the nurse, and they brought me the phone. I dialed the number for the pay phone on his hall, but no one answered. I wanted Kevin to know his baby was on the way—not that he'd be able to get down in time to be with me, but I wanted him to know. I tried calling a few more times. But now the contractions were coming closer, and I had to concentrate.

Mom held my hand when the pains came. She got a clean face cloth, wet it and put it on my forehead. The doctor checked on me once in a while to see how I was progressing. When I was almost eight centimeters dilated, he ordered an epidural.

"Lie on your side," the anesthesiologist said. "Now, bring your legs up close to your chest, and don't move."

I was uncomfortable curled in a ball with my fat belly in the way, and then he stuck a needle into my spine. He didn't get the needle into the right spot on the first try and had to do it again. I couldn't decide what was worse—the contraction pain or the needle in my back. The needle had a catheter—a small tube—threaded through it. When they took the needle out, the tube stayed inside. It was taped down to stay in place, and this was how I got periodic doses of pain medicine.

They moved me to a delivery room and asked if I'd allow medical residents to be there for the birth. St. Margaret's was a teaching hospital, and new doctors needed to learn. At that point, I didn't care who watched so long as I had my mother by my side.

"It hurts," I screamed as a strong pain hit me, the wave crashing over me like nothing I'd ever felt before. The epidural wasn't helping yet.

"Come on, it's not that bad," a young woman in scrubs said. "Toughen up."

"Have you ever had a baby?" I asked in a not-so-friendly tone.

She shook her head no.

"Then shut up," I said through clenched teeth.

My mom always said, *if you can't say anything nice, keep your mouth shut,* and normally, she wouldn't like the way I'd spoken to this young doctor. But Mom knew I was in pain and didn't say anything about my rudeness. In fact, she consoled me, holding my hand and telling me it would be all right. I tried to concentrate on the breathing I'd practiced in birthing classes. What was I supposed to do, the hee—hee—ha—ha breaths or the candle blowing? I couldn't remember.

I got a couple more doses of medicine through the epidural, and finally the unbearable pain subsided. I was able to look up at my mom. She was helping me give birth to her grandchild, and she was going to watch.

The pushing seemed to go on forever. I could feel the urge to push, despite the epidural, and I squeezed Mom's hand, clenched my teeth, and pushed with all my strength. But I wasn't making much progress, and after two hours of work on very little sleep, I was getting tired.

The irritating resident was now my personal cheerleader. "You can do it," she said. And I really wanted to do it, to push the baby out of my exhausted body.

"I can see the baby's hair!" my mother said.

They had mirrors down by my legs, so I could see too. There between my legs was a bulge, my baby's head jutting outward, stretching everything. It looked scary, like I had a grapefruit stuck there with a patch of dark wet hair. Dr. Sprague told me he needed to make an incision to help the baby come out.

"There's the baby," my mom gasped. And sure enough, the head was out, and a nurse suctioned mucous out of his nose.

"The baby passed meconium," the nurse said to the doctor and someone rushed out.

"We need to get the shoulders out," the doctor said. "This baby's big. Now don't push on this next contraction."

The nurse reminded me to blow, and my mother was blowing too, like she was helping me blow the candles out on a birthday cake.

"Okay, a little push now," the doctor said. I pushed and the baby slipped from my body. The doctor said, "It's a boy," and held him up for me to see, and then passed him off to another doctor standing by.

They put little Kevin into a warming bed and checked him from head to toe. I didn't know that meconium was his first bowel movement and that passing it in the uterus could prove toxic if a baby got it into his lungs. I just knew they weren't giving me my baby.

"Is he all right?" I asked.

Dr. Sprague was busy stitching me up down there, but he assured me the baby looked fine. They just needed to check out a few things. When I glanced at Mom, though, I could see the anxious look on her face.

Little Kevin was born at 9:04 a.m. on May 2, 1980, and when they finally brought him to me, all cleaned up and wrapped in a blue blanket, he was beautiful. My healthy little one weighed in at a solid eight pounds and ten ounces.

Both my mom and I cried, but they were happy tears for this child, a perfect gift welcomed into our world, and I sent up a prayer of thanks to God for my new son.

Baby's First Days

*A*fter I had a chance to visit with baby Kevin, the nurses moved me to a recovery room, and I went to sleep almost right away. While I slept, my mom went home to get Dad. The nurses came in to check on me, to check the bleeding and make sure I wasn't hemorrhaging. I was vaguely aware of their coming in and changing my pad, but mostly I just slept.

Later, I was moved to my own room, and a nurse brought the baby in for me to feed. But my milk hadn't come in yet.

"Will he get enough to eat?" I asked.

"What he gets now isn't milk. It's called colostrum," the nurse told me. She said it was full of vitamins and would help make him strong.

I held my baby to my breast, and he turned his head and sucked the nipple right way.

"He must be hungry," I said.

"Well, he's taking right to it!" the nurse said.

I didn't know that some babies had a hard time holding onto a nipple, and it never occurred to me my baby might have a difficult time breastfeeding. I only knew that my doctor had said breast milk was the best food for a baby, and I wanted mine to have the best of everything.

But the best of everything also included a father, and I still hadn't talked with Kevin. Away at school, he didn't even know I'd given birth.

"Can I use the phone?" I asked the nurse.

"Sure. Your phone should be working."

When she left, she took the baby with her, and I dialed Kevin's school. I was scared he wouldn't take my call. It was afternoon, so I wasn't surprised when someone picked up the phone pretty quickly, but I was surprised it was Kevin. I recognized his voice right away. It had been months since I'd heard that voice, but as soon as I did, I wanted to keep hearing it.

"Hi, Kevin, it's me, Judith. I had the baby this morning, just after nine," I said quickly. I wasn't sure how he'd take the news or how long he'd stay on the line.

"What did we have?" he asked.

"It's a boy."

"Did you name him after me?" he asked, and his voice was quiet. "Like we planned?"

"Yes, he has your name."

We talked for a while, and it felt good. Kevin said he wasn't sure when he'd be able to get down to see his new son. He asked me to make sure I got a football for him, to make sure I kissed the baby for him too.

I didn't want to get off of the phone, and we talked for a long time. He told me all about school and how he'd be heading into finals soon. I told him I still planned to graduate with my class and that I'd have to take finals too. It was hard saying goodbye and not knowing when we'd speak again.

In the evening, my parents came and brought flowers. My dad got to hold little Kevin who looked so tiny in his arms. They stayed until visiting hours ended, and I called Kevin again before going to bed. I wanted to hear his voice now that he was taking my calls. We talked, and the talking came easy again, like it had earlier in our relationship, before everything got so complicated. I wished it could always be this way.

The nurse brought the baby in for a feeding, and I told Kevin about his little boy, how he was taking right to the breast.

"Of course he is. He's my son!" We laughed, and finally I had to say good-night.

The day after Kevin was born I wrote in my diary:

> Today I was really tired! Having a baby takes a lot out of you and the stitches hurt, but you look at your baby and it's all worth it. I wish Kevin could see his baby. By the time Kevin (sr) gets to see little Kevin, little Kevin won't be little anymore! It's rather sad that I won't be seeing Kevin, but what can I do? He's going to college next year and he'll be away at summer school all summer!

I'm going to miss him. But it's been almost four months since I saw him last and we're still fighting (to stay together). He's so frightened and it's hard to accept the way he acted, but I have to realize how it's been for him too.

I still loved Kevin and figured that was all that mattered—our love for one another and the baby. It would take a lot, but possibly we could make it.

On my third and fourth day in the hospital—back then, it was normal to stay that long after having a baby—I had lots of visitors: friends from church, friends from school, a couple I'd met at childbirth classes, and of course, my parents. They all brought presents for the baby and flowers and cards for me. The room was filled with the love and warmth of my family and friends, but without big Kevin, it still felt empty at times.

Between visits, I shut my door and rested, but I guess this made the hospital staff nervous. "Is everything all right?" a nurse asked.

"Yes," I said. "Why?"

"Well, we've noticed that you keep the door closed all the time. We were getting worried that you might be depressed."

"No, I'm fine. I just like some privacy." This was part truth, part lie. I did like my privacy, but I also liked to sleep the day away when I didn't have to feed little Kevin because I didn't like to think too much. Thinking made me sad and gave me a headache.

The next time I spoke with Kevin, he said his parents didn't want him to see the baby or me. "But I'm coming down for your prom," he said, "and I'll finally get to hold my son." I'd mentioned the prom to him in an earlier conversation, though I didn't think he'd come. Even now when he said he would, I wasn't sure he'd make it.

I wanted him to meet his new baby and hold him, and I wanted him to feel his son's soft skin, so he'd know the miracle of this new life we created together. Plus, I couldn't wait for Kevin to arrive at my house so I could see him and hold him again. I went to sleep feeling better and hoping I would dream about Kevin, our baby and me—together as a family.

The First Week Home

My dad came to get me from the hospital and take me home. My mother was at work so he'd come by himself. It was the fifth day after little Kevin was born, and I felt odd leaving the maternity floor, saying goodbye to the nurses who had taught me how to hold my baby properly and how to change him. I was nervous about taking care of him all by myself, but at least I'd have my parents to help.

I held Kevin in my arms while I sat in a wheelchair and Dad took us outside and went to get the car. The half-circle driveway made it easy for cars to pull right up to the entrance. He parked and opened the back passenger door. He was smiling, happy to take his daughter and new grandson home.

I buckled Kevin into the car seat and had him facing the back of the car for safety. I checked the seat belt to make sure it was secure and then I got into the back seat.

"Aren't you sitting in the front?" my dad asked.

"I won't be able to see Kevin," I said, wondering how my father could think I'd leave him alone in the backseat.

Dad drove away from the hospital and said, "When you were a baby, Mommy used to hold you in her arms."

"I guess I'm lucky to still be alive," I said and thought about a driver stopping short and a baby flying from its mother's arms. I shook my head at the gruesome thought and looked over at Kevin who had quickly fallen asleep from the lull of the car's motor and the movement of the vehicle.

Dad merged onto Route 91 North, and the flow of cars passing us felt like a sea of disaster moving by. "Be careful," I said. "Don't go too fast."

It felt dangerous. Like at any moment a car from another lane could careen into ours and send us crashing off the highway. It was like I had suddenly acquired paranoia about dangers that had always been around. But now those dangers could cause my baby harm. It was one thing when the threats in the world endangered only me, when the hurts of the world hurt only me—it was another thing completely if the threat was to my child.

When we finally pulled up in front of the house safely, nearly an hour later, I was exhausted. Giving birth to my baby had made me tired, but worrying about him made me even more tired. My dad helped carry my things in, and I took little Kevin up to my room and put him in the bassinet next to my bed. I sang rock-a-bye baby to him, and he went right to sleep. I watched him sleeping. Then, I put myself down for a rest too.

But babies don't give you much resting time, and little Kevin was crying to be fed in what seemed like only minutes. Then the doorbell rang, and it was Sally.

"He's absolutely beautiful," she said when she was holding Kevin.

I smiled. "I know. Look at his dark hair," I said. "It's so funny that it's so dark what with my red hair and Kevin's dirty blond hair. But the nurses said this hair will probably fall out and then he'll get his own. What color do you think he'll have?"

"Hopefully, Kevin's," Sally said. "No offense, but I don't like red hair. Hey, are you going to the awards ceremony next week?" she asked.

The awards ceremony was an annual event up at the school we cheered for. The cheerleaders were invited, and we sat at our own table and watched the boys get awards for player of the year, player with the best sportsmanship, and things like that.

"Yes, I am. Mr. King sent me an invitation. I was so excited that he included me. He didn't have to," I said.

"I know, but he always liked you," she said. Little Kevin started fussing and crying, so I took him from Sally and put him up on my shoulder and rubbed his back. He stopped.

Mr. King had been the cheering advisor for the three years that I'd been on the team. During hockey season, he drove the cheerleaders to games in his own car. We'd pile into his station wagon feeling all excited about another game.

"The O'Briens might be there," I said.

"I would think so," Sally said. "Randy plays football and basketball, right?"

"Yeah, he does," I said. It made me feel sad to think about Randy. We used to be friends. After Kevin and I got engaged, when football season started, Randy and I would talk while we waited for our rides home after his practice and mine. But those days were gone. "Well," I continued, "whether they're there or not doesn't really matter. I'll have fun no matter what. But I've got bigger news than the awards ceremony."

"What?"

"Kevin is coming to my senior prom."

"No!" Sally said.

"Yes, he is," I said, and the thought made my sadness about Randy and the other O'Briens disappear while I imagined Kevin by my side at my senior prom. I told Sally about talking with Kevin while I was in the hospital and how he wanted to come to my prom, maybe even graduation too. She couldn't believe it.

I found it hard to believe myself. Four months without seeing him had made me feel empty, even though I'd been full with his baby. The last trimester had gone by one minute to the next, one hour to the next, one day to the next—time moving on. I got up each morning and moved through each day, putting one foot in front of the other, but I'd felt empty and alone with a hollowness that hurt down to the center of my being.

Now, with little Kevin's birth and the promise of big Kevin's love and presence, I felt full of life, with a renewed sense of hope. I prayed for good things to continue.

Sally left, but a parade of visitors came after her. That first day home, I had seven visitors. On the second day there were five. On the third, eight people came to see us! I wasn't getting much rest, but it was fun to see so many friends who wanted to share the joy of my son's birth.

On my mother's day off from work, she babysat so I could run some errands. I got my hair cut and picked out flowers for the prom. I even went shopping for Kevin's tuxedo since he couldn't be at my house until the day of the prom and wouldn't have time to get a tux beforehand. At the first store I went to, the salesclerk said Kevin would have to come in and get fitted. That wasn't going to happen, so I found another store that was willing to let me order a tux and shoes for him. He'd told me his sizes over the phone, and I hoped everything would fit.

Mother's Day fell on the weekend before the prom, and on Saturday, I received a funny card from Kevin. It showed a guy sitting in a comfortable chair in a living room, waving and talking. The caption on the front of the card read: *Happy Mother's Day from the guy who made you what you are today!* Inside, it said *A Mother! Happy Mother's Day!*

I chuckled when I read the card. It was my first Mother's Day card from the man I loved, and it felt good. My brother got flowers for both my mother and me, and I thought that was sweet. My parents gave me a pretty card and a cute little-boy card from little Kevin. I wished I'd been able to see Kevin on Mother's Day, but I knew he was coming next weekend for my prom. Just thinking about that brought a smile to my face. Everything was ready well in advance. I had my dress, Mom was going to babysit, and my new haircut looked good. The flowers were ordered, and a tuxedo and a pair of nice shoes were waiting for Kevin, the father of my beautiful baby boy.

The Awards Ceremony

Two days before the prom, I attended the awards ceremony at St. Joseph's Academy, Kevin's old school. My mom drove me to the school with little Kevin in his car seat. Most of the cheerleaders hadn't met the baby yet, and they'd asked me to bring him. We drove up the long driveway and parked in front. The girls were outside waiting for me.

I unbuckled Kevin from his seat and lifted him out. He was wearing a light green sweater over a white shirt, and I thought it was funny how he was dressed in the school colors the way we were when we cheered, the way the boys were in their football uniforms. My mom waited while I took him to meet the cheerleaders.

Sally was the only one in the group who had already met him at my house. "Let me hold him." She took Kevin right out of my hands, and the other cheerleaders passed him around from one girl to the next. I felt proud to have them all admiring my son.

"You know," Sally said when she was holding him, "he might just be the cutest baby I have ever seen. Look, he's smiling!" It did look like a little grin flashed across his lips.

"It might be gas," I said and laughed. "Here, let me take him," I said when little Kevin started getting irritable. I put him up over my shoulder and patted his back.

While we were standing there, Mr. O'Brien, Randy, and Kevin's older brother Richard drove into the parking lot. I noticed the Cadillac as soon as it pulled in. Right away, I felt nervous. This would be the first time they saw the baby.

"Here come the O'Briens," Sally said to me as they walked across the parking lot.

"I know," I said, sucking in air as I said the words.

I turned Kevin around so they could see him.

As they came to the entranceway, I called out, "Mr. O'Brien, would you like to meet your new grandson?" I hadn't planned on doing that, but I wanted them to meet our new baby. They walked right past us and into the building without saying hello. They didn't even look over in my direction. It was as if they didn't see me, as if I were a ghost, invisible to the naked eye.

Maybe they made a pact with each other in the car when they drove up and saw me standing there: *Oh God, there she is. Don't anyone talk to her. Don't even look.* I imagined what they might have said to each other. Maybe they were surprised to see me there with little Kevin, so surprised they didn't know what to do and rushed past me to avoid the whole situation.

"That's just rude!" Sally said once they were inside.

It felt more than rude, though. It felt like a slap in my face, but a true slap would still be a kind of acknowledgement. This was worse. It was as if I didn't exist, as if I were dead to them. But not just me—baby Kevin too—as if we were nothing.

It hurt real bad, like they were saying I was worthless. And worse than that, they were saying baby Kevin was worthless too. But to me he was everything. He was the living proof of the love I shared with their son. My baby was tangible, real, and solid, and they couldn't take him away from me.

I had been looking forward to this evening, glad Mr. King had wanted to include me. But now, before the awards ceremony even started, I was thinking maybe I should leave. It was supposed to be a fun night, but I felt like crying.

I walked back to the car, and by then I was crying.

"Mom, did you see that?" I asked through tears. She had the window down.

"What's wrong, dear?" she asked.

"The O'Briens. They acted like they didn't see me."

"Come here," she said, and I leaned down. She kissed my cheek.

"I think you should take me home," I said.

"Listen, honey, you need to keep your chin up," she said and touched my chin, tilting it up. "You have nothing to be ashamed of. You are a beautiful young woman and you have a beautiful son. Now go in there and have a good time with your friends."

"I don't know. What about the O'Briens?"

"What about them?" She looked at me, and her face turned from concerned to angry. "If they don't want to know their own grandson, what kind of people are they?"

Neither one of us answered the question, but Mom's words made me feel stronger. I decided to go in after all and buckled Kevin back into his car seat.

"Thanks, Mom." I bent down and kissed her. "I'll get a ride home with one of the girls." I waved as she drove away.

It didn't matter how much the O'Briens wanted me to go away. I wasn't going anywhere. I joined my friends at the door, and we went into the cafeteria. The tables had either green or white tablecloths, and in the center were vases filled with white and green carnations. There was a table set aside for the cheerleaders, and we all sat together.

The O'Briens were not near us, but I could see them across the room. They didn't look at me once that whole evening. But throughout the night I did see other parents who glanced over at me and then looked away—it was like being back at school and having people gawk at me.

By that point, everyone knew I was the cheerleader who'd gotten pregnant and had a baby. Many of the parents sitting there probably wished I'd stayed home. I imagined they thought of me the same way the O'Briens did—as evil incarnate, representing the awful fate that awaited boys who weren't careful. Right in front of them, I felt like a manifestation of their fears, and it made me uncomfortable. I tried to put these dark thoughts out of my mind so I could have some fun.

The coaches came to the podium and spoke into the microphone, calling out the names of the boys who'd won awards. Randy's name was called, and he walked up to get his prize. I could see Mr. O'Brien and Richard smiling and clapping.

I had been to these annual award ceremonies twice before, and at one of them, Mr. King had given us little silver megaphones to wear on chains around our necks. I wore my necklace that night, the megaphone dangling, reminding me of that earlier, carefree time. But back then, I was an actual cheerleader, not the odd one allowed to participate though no longer a member of the squad.

I felt out of place and a little awkward, but I tried to make the best of the evening. I smiled when I was supposed to. I clapped when I was supposed to. I didn't want the O'Briens to know they'd upset me, and I didn't want Mr. King to think I didn't appreciate being included in the night's festivities—because I did.

Whenever I started to feel really sad, I remembered that in two days I would see Kevin, and he would meet his new son for the first time. I remembered that he still loved me and wanted to be with me, and I thought how the O'Briens didn't know I was going to pick up Kevin at his school and drive him back to my house. I held that in my heart like a secret treasure no one could take away.

Reconnections: Prom Weekend

Two days later, on Friday, I packed little Kevin into the car and headed north. It was a long drive, but he didn't seem to mind and slept most of the way. When I arrived at the school, a guy was coming out of Kevin's dorm just as I was getting the baby out of the car.

"Hey, is that Kevin's kid?" he asked.

"Yes, this is little Kevin," I said, holding the baby up.

"Wow," he said, shaking his head. "That's crazy."

"Is Kevin around?" I asked, ignoring his last comment.

"I think he's still at lunch," he said and added, "I'll go find him."

I sat down on the steps with the baby in my arms. I'd been sitting there for about five minutes when the front door opened suddenly, and Kevin bounded out. He stood there looking at us, his eyes open wide. In a recent letter he'd told me he lost some weight. But he looked the same to me—tall and beautiful.

"Hey," I said. I couldn't believe I hadn't seen him for four months, and yet here he was, looking at me, and it was as if no time had gone by. He was still Kevin and I was still me. It's just now we had this new human being that we'd made. Our own flesh and blood. Our own love made real.

Kevin came and sat down beside me.

"Hi," he said. His voice was all soft. He draped his arm around my shoulders and looked at his son. Kevin touched a long finger to the baby's cheek, gently stroking the soft skin. I turned to look at Kevin and there were tears in his eyes. He kissed me on the lips gently, and I thought I might melt into his mouth. I wanted to stay in his arms forever.

But the dorm door swung open again, and a group of guys came out.

"Hey O'Brien, is this your kid?" one of them asked him.

"Yeah, this is my son Kevin." He stood up, and it seemed his chest swelled out a bit. I stood up too. "And this is my fiancée, Judith."

He seemed proud of the two of us.

One of the guys said, "The kid looks like you, O'Brien."

Kevin smiled and someone else said, "Nah, he's not that ugly!"

Someone else slapped Kevin on the shoulder and said, "Nice work."

It felt good to be acknowledged and accepted, even doted upon, by Kevin's friends, and Kevin stood there proud and strong, acknowledging me and the baby as his. It felt good to be standing there beside him, our sweet reunion after months apart.

"We have to get going soon if we're going to the prom," I reminded Kevin, and he went inside to grab his duffel bag.

Part way through the trip home, little Kevin started to cry, and we had to stop so I could feed him. We found a secluded spot by the side of a road. I lifted my shirt and unsnapped my nursing bra while Kevin got the baby from the car seat and handed him to me.

"Wow," Kevin said when he saw my exposed breast. I had been small before the pregnancy, an A or sometimes a B cup. When Kevin had seen me last, while I was pregnant, I was bigger than pre-pregnancy, but since giving birth and after my milk came in, I was huge—double D.

He reached over to touch my breast and some milk came out. The baby was screaming, so I brushed my nipple against his cheek and he turned and latched on. He sucked at my breast, and my milk let down. While the baby nursed, Kevin started to kiss my neck. It felt wonderful to have my baby suckling at my breast, and my love kissing me at the same time.

I had put nursing pads in my bra before I left Massachusetts, but now they were soaked, and my shirt was damp where the milk had leaked through. While Kevin was kissing me, he tried to touch my other breast, but I pulled away.

"What's the matter?" he asked.

"I don't know."

"Don't you want me to touch you?"

It had been a while, a lot had changed, and I was scared to open myself up to Kevin's love. I wanted him, but part of me was afraid.

"Of course I want you to touch me," I said, giving in. "It's just that I'm all wet with milk, and little Kevin's eating."

"Oh, I don't think he'll notice," Kevin said as he put his hand up under my shirt, "and I don't mind the wetness at all." He started kissing me again.

"Whoa, you better stop. I don't think I can take much more of that," I said, "and we can't do anything besides kissing. We have to get back."

"Do I have to stop?"

"Pleeeasse," I said, "we really have to go soon."

Kevin pulled away. I stuck my finger in the baby's mouth breaking the suction, and his little mouth was pursed and wet with milk. Kevin looked at him and laughed.

"Look, he's still sucking," he said.

It was true, little Kevin's lips moved up and down sucking in and out quickly. His eyes were closed, and it looked like he was dreaming of nursing.

I put the baby over my shoulder to burp him.

"I have to stop him from eating so I can burp him. Otherwise, he'll just keep eating and eating. Then when he does burp, he pukes everywhere," I said.

"Gross," Kevin said.

"Oh yeah, this little guy can create a lot of gross things, can't you, Kevin?"

After the baby had burped and gone to sleep, I got him secured in his car seat and we left. Little Kevin slept soundly, and Kevin and I had the time and space to reacquaint ourselves with each other. He told me about the last quarter of his school year, and I told him about mine, and it was as if the months apart had never been.

"Hey, I even have a present for you," he said.

"Do you?" I asked. "What for?"

"Because I love you, and I've been thinking about you all this time. Even when I wasn't staying in touch, I was still loving you and thinking about you."

"Aw," I said. "That's nice. I never stopped thinking about you, either. So what's my present?"

"You'll see."

We almost forgot to pick up the flowers for the prom, but at the last minute I remembered. Once in the house, I had to change Kevin and then feed him again. I'd only given him one side to tide him over for the trip home, so he was hungry again.

"He eats a lot, doesn't he?" Kevin asked while we were sitting on the couch.

"He does," I said. "Hey, where's my present?"

He went over to his duffel bag and took out a shirt that seemed to be rolled into a ball.

"A dirty shirt?"

"No, silly," he said and unrolled the shirt. Inside was a dark blue mug. He handed it to me. "I made this in ceramic class for you. Remember, I wrote and told you about it." On the mug, he'd put my name.

"Thank you." I said.

I did remember the letter then. It was the one he'd written around Valentine's Day when he sent me the handmade card and the long letter.

"The mug might be cracked, I'm not sure," he said. "I haven't used it since I made it."

"Go put some water in it," I suggested. He went into the kitchen and came back. The mug wasn't cracked and held water, so I drank from it while I finished feeding Kevin.

When little Kevin had fallen asleep, I put him in his bassinet. Kevin and I hung out on the couch kissing and holding each other. Then my mom and dad came home, and Kevin and I dressed for the prom. Before we left, I fed the baby one more time.

The tuxedo that I'd picked up for Kevin fit him well. He looked fine in his gray tux with the white shirt and a white carnation on his lapel. My dress was white like a bridal gown with a scoop neck and lace circling it in intervals down its length. My parents took pictures of us in front of the fireplace before we left, and the mantle still held congratulations cards from when baby Kevin was born and a bouquet of flowers my aunt had sent in a small blue bootie.

Kevin was quiet when we got to the country club, which was decked out for the prom. At each place setting there was either a glass goblet or a glass mug inscribed with Saint Anne's School, the date, and Senior Prom—goblets for the girls and mugs for the guys.

"What's the matter?" I asked Kevin. "You seem real quiet."

"Everyone's looking at me," he said.

Most of my friends knew Kevin and weren't acting weird, but some of the teachers came over and introduced themselves to Kevin. I didn't see them doing this with other girls' dates. But I guess they wanted to meet the father of my child.

"That's because you look so good," I said, trying to lighten his mood. Kevin smiled. "Let's get our picture taken before dinner," I suggested.

We went into the foyer and waited in line. When it was our turn, the photographer told us to smile and then snapped our picture. In my long white gown and with Kevin beside me in his formal gray tux, we looked as much like a bride and groom as we did prom dates for the night.

The evening went by quickly, and we ended up having a good time, dancing and laughing like any other couple in the room—except that when the night was over and other couples were going out to post-prom parties, we were going home to our newborn son.

Back at my house, we stayed up most of the night talking. It was in the early morning hours when Kevin finally went downstairs to the living room where my mother had made the couch into a bed with clean sheets, a blanket and pillow. I wished he could have stayed in my bed all night, but even though we had a baby, there was no way my Catholic mother would let us sleep in the same room, let alone the same bed.

On Saturday, we spent the whole day together. We returned the rented tux and then went to the hospital to visit my friends from childbirth classes. They had welcomed me and talked with me during those classes when I'd felt awkward and alone.

Kevin hadn't been around when I gave birth to his son, but here he was visiting some other newborn. I felt a little irritated and jealous, and we didn't stay long.

On the way home, he brought up the subject of babies.

"You know," he started, "we won't be able to have any more babies for a long time. I'm going to go to college. First, I have summer school, and then regular classes start up in the fall. College takes four years, so Kevin won't have a brother or a sister for more than four years."

Four years was a long time, and that made me sad to think of Kevin away at college, but I was excited that he was making plans for more babies with me.

"Yeah, I'm not ready for any more babies. This one is exhausting me!"

"Good, let's stop and buy something so you don't get pregnant," Kevin said.

He hadn't made love to me yet since he'd come back, but clearly he planned to. We stopped at a store and bought condoms and contraceptive cream. Birth control was against Church rules, but we couldn't chance making another baby.

When we got home, I fed little Kevin and put him down for a nap. My dad had been watching him and was going to be home for a while, so Kevin and I went for a walk around the neighborhood. We found a clump of our special wildflowers, the same kind that grew in Kevin's backyard, the same ones he'd picked last year—one for him, one for me, and one for the baby we dreamed of having. *Wildflowers*: our secret code word for getting married and making a baby. We had the order wrong, but we had our baby, now.

We went up to the park and played on the swings where I felt free, flying next to Kevin. We were acting pretty goofy afterwards—twirling around and practically dancing in the street on the way home, and it felt great to get outside and have fun.

Later, Dad had to go get Mom from work. Since the baby sometimes cried in the middle of the night, my brother frequently stayed over with a friend. Kevin and I had the house to ourselves.

The baby was fussy, and I walked around, bouncing him on my shoulder. When that didn't work, Kevin tried rocking him in the rocking chair. He fell asleep in Kevin's arms.

"Don't you have a magic touch!"

Kevin laughed. "Oh yes, I do," he said suggestively.

"That's not what I meant."

"No? I'd still like to show you." He got up and put Kevin down to sleep. Then he came to me and started to kiss me, his soft thick lips pressed against mine. We were all alone, except for our baby, and it had been so long since we'd been together intimately. We made love to each other, using the contraceptives we'd bought earlier so we wouldn't make another baby. But now that we had our own child, when we made love it felt like we were closer than we'd ever been before.

We were watching TV together when my parents came home, but I kept falling asleep. I was tired from being a new mom, but I was overtired because we'd stayed up practically the whole night before. Kevin was sleepy too.

When little Kevin woke for his night feeding, Kevin came into our room.

"I don't want to leave," he said when the baby had finished eating and burping.

"I don't want you to, either."

After I changed the baby and settled him into the bassinet, I got into bed. It was a small bed, and when Kevin crawled in beside me there wasn't a lot of room. But neither of us minded. I lay on my side, and Kevin lay on his. With his arms wrapped around me, I fell asleep feeling warm, wonderful, and safe.

Parting, Returning, and Graduating

On Sunday morning we both woke up when little Kevin started to cry. Big Kevin went downstairs while I fed the baby, so it would at least look like he'd slept on the couch. I felt content waking beside Kevin and then feeding our baby boy.

Over coffee, Kevin told me he had to get going early.

"But I thought you had tomorrow off!"

"I do. But there's this party tonight that I want to go to."

"You're kidding, right?"

"No."

"Just checking," I didn't want to start a fight so early in the morning after we'd had such a beautiful night. But I added, "I can't believe you're going to leave us for a party."

"Come on, Judith. I've been with you all weekend. And I'm coming back next weekend for your graduation. I'll be here on Friday."

So it was true. He really did plan to come to my graduation. For a moment I was afraid he'd leave and never come back, and the prom weekend would be like a dream I'd conjured to convince myself that Kevin still loved me. But here he was, flesh and blood, telling me he'd be back in five days.

When it was time for him to say goodbye, he held the baby in front of him and stared. It was as if he were studying every aspect of little Kevin so he could save that mental picture in his mind.

"I love you, kid," he said and brought the baby's face to his lips. He kissed his son, and I could see that he was crying.

I was crying too, watching him say goodbye. Why couldn't he stay? I didn't understand. We left the baby with my mom, and I took Kevin to meet his friends. We sat in the breakdown lane, waiting.

"Maybe they're not coming," I said, hopefully. "Are you sure you don't want to stay another day?"

"You know I'd love to stay another day," he said. "I'd like to stay for always. But they'll be here."

I hated goodbyes. It had been so long since I'd had him at my side, and I didn't want to let him go. He dried my eyes with the corner of his shirt. His eyes were wet too.

"I love you, you know," he said. "Always have, always will."

Hearing him say those words made me feel a deep happiness inside, but it didn't take away the sadness I was feeling right then. When Kevin's friends finally came for him, he got out of the car and came around to my side, and kissed me one last time.

The following week was hectic. I had final exams, and I was nervous I might flunk because I hadn't studied. We had graduation practice, and I had to shop for white shoes to go with the graduation gown. I also had an appointment at the lawyer's office.

I couldn't put Kevin's name on the birth certificate because he hadn't signed the papers the lawyer had sent. So now, the only way to have Kevin named as the father was to bring a non-support claim against him. I wished he would just admit he was the father, legally, on paper. Even though he was back by my side now that our baby had arrived, I couldn't forget what had happened before—one minute he was here and the next he wasn't.

On Thursday night we had a Baccalaureate Mass and awards ceremony at school.

I didn't receive any awards during the ceremony, and this didn't surprise me since I wasn't even allowed to be in the National Honor Society, but after the ceremony, my English teacher Ms. Maxwell took me aside.

"This is a special service award," she said, "for your service to unborn children and for being a mother when that wasn't the easiest choice to make. I'm proud of you, Judith." She gave me a pin with two tiny hands and a small card that explained that the hands were the same shape and size of a preborn baby ten to twelve weeks after conception.

"Thank you," I was touched by her gesture.

Kevin sent me an invitation to his graduation and a letter that asked me to bring little Kevin with me, so his family could meet the baby. I definitely wanted to go, but I was worried about how his family would treat us. They wouldn't acknowledge us at Randy's award ceremony, so why would Kevin's graduation be different?

I called him Thursday night to make sure he was really coming the next day.

"I'm thumbing down," he said when I asked how he was going to get here.

"It's so far," I said. "What if you don't get a ride?"

"I'll get a ride, don't worry."

"I wish I could come and get you," I said. "But I can't get the car." I hated that we had to rely so much on other people's cars.

"I told you not to worry your pretty little head about it. I'll be there," he said, and that reminded me of all the promises in his letters, how he'd told me I should have faith and he'd be here in the end. And here it was the end of my senior year, and he was still here. Our baby had arrived, and he was still here. I allowed myself to hope.

The next day, Kevin arrived right before lunch. It made me feel good to think of him out on the highway with his packed duffel bag and his thumb out, waiting on a ride so he could come down to see me and his new son. He loved us that much.

He was lucky and got a ride that took him the whole way. I was feeding baby Kevin, and we sat on the couch together. Kevin told me about his finals and how he thought he'd done well. He told me he'd studied and tried really hard for me and for little Kevin. He said he wanted to make me proud.

I was proud of both of them, and I was proud of myself too. I was graduating from high school when some people thought I'd drop out. Kevin was here supporting me, showing the world how much he loved me when there were people who thought he'd leave. He was going to graduate in a week from his prep school, and he'd have his son and me there by his side, showing everyone our love. Yeah, I was proud.

When little Kevin had finished nursing, we put him down for a nap in his bassinet.

"He's beautiful," Kevin whispered.

"Just like his daddy," I said.

"Or his mommy." He put his arms around my waist.

"I think he looks more like you."

"Maybe," he said, "but it's kind of hard to tell."

We gazed at our son sleeping. His hair was dark brown, and it stuck out from his head in spiky bits. The hair was fine and soft like mouse fur, and

Kevin reached down to touch his son.

"It's amazing that we did this," he said, and his voice caught in his throat.

I looked into Kevin's blue eyes, and they were filled with awe, and love and tears.

I put my arms around him and pulled him close. We kissed, and the salt from our tears fell into our mouths. But this time they were joyful tears.

It was one of the happiest days of my life having Kevin with me again, and he took me gently onto my bed, and we made love with our sleeping son beside us. Afterwards, we took a shower together and took turns lathering each other's bodies. Kevin was beautiful and I told him so.

"Not as beautiful as you," he said and kissed me on the forehead. My parents weren't home, but while we'd been in the shower my brother had come home with some friends. I could hear them.

"Shhh," I said to Kevin when he started talking as we dried each other off. "They'll hear us."

We'd left our clothes in my bedroom, so there was nothing to do but wrap towels around ourselves and dash across the hall. We had to go right past my brother's room, and I heard him and his friends laughing as we closed the door.

My face reddened.

"Now, that was embarrassing," I said when we were safe in my room.

"Don't worry about it." I giggled when he tickled me to make me laugh. "See, it's funny."

"Yeah, right!" I said.

We got dressed for graduation, and I wore a lightweight white dress so I wouldn't be hot underneath my graduation gown. By the time we were ready, my parents were home.

"Kevin," Mom said when we came downstairs. "You're here!" She sounded surprised and that aggravated me. The baby had awakened while we were dressing, and I had him in my arms. "Here, let me hold him," she said and took him from me. She loved her grandson, and she loved to scoop him up and nuzzle his neck. Kevin went over and kissed her.

Dad sat in his chair drinking a beer. "How was your trip down?" he asked Kevin.

"Not bad. I made good time."

"Well, I guess we should get ready too," my mom said.

We took the baby down the street to Mrs. Z, who was babysitting for us that evening. When we walked back, Kevin held my hand, and I loved the feel of his strong hand in mine.

"We're glad you could make it down for Judith's graduation," my mom said once we were all in the car and driving to my school. My brother didn't bother coming, and that hurt, but he said he had other plans.

"I wouldn't miss it," Kevin said and squeezed my hand.

"Does this mean we'll be seeing more of you, now?' my dad asked.

"Daaad!" I said. I hated the way he said it. I didn't like his tone, which seemed sarcastic, with the emphasis on the now, pointing out with just a word how Kevin hadn't been around much in the past few months. I felt embarrassed and angry.

Kevin just answered the question. "Of course I'm going to be around." He squeezed my hand again. "I do have to go up to college at the end of next month for some summer classes, but I'll come home on weekends."

My heart sank a little at the reminder of his leaving again, but the promise of his coming home to me on weekends kept me from getting too upset. Besides it was the night of my high school graduation, and he was here with me.

We walked into my school, and Kevin had his arm around my waist. My friends were gathering in the foyer, but we needed to go down to the choral room to get ready. I kissed Kevin and my parents and went down the hall.

We put on our white gowns and our matching caps with the blue tassels, checked our makeup, and made a few last-minute adjustments. Then, when it was time, the teachers led us down the hallway and to the auditorium where we filed down the aisles.

I saw Kevin sitting with my parents. The three of them were turned around in their seats watching for me, and my mom blew me a kiss while my dad waved. Kevin smiled—a broad I'm-proud-of-you smile across his whole face—and I smiled back.

My senior class had only sixty graduates, so the ceremony wasn't long. The class valedictorian gave a speech about reaching for your dreams, about college and all the challenges ahead. But for me, college would have to be a dream deferred. I wanted to go, but I'd have to wait.

The challenges that I'd already faced were nothing my friends could understand, and I couldn't understand their challenges about getting ready to go away to college. But when I watched my friends walk across the stage in their gowns, I did feel like a part of the group because we'd shared so many years together.

Suddenly, it was my turn to walk across the stage. I stood up and walked down the aisle. The lights on the stage were bright, shining on my accomplishment. I'd made it, and I shook Sister Claudia's hand. I looked her in the eye and thanked her, took my diploma, and walked off the stage with my head held high.

Afterwards, Kevin took some pictures of me with my parents. Mom stood on one side and Dad on the other. Mom and Dad had big smiles on their faces, and Dad had my elbow in his hand. He held on tight and then patted me on the head. I didn't mind. Then Kevin took a picture of me holding my diploma, and Dad took a photo of Kevin and me.

"Be careful, Dad," I reminded him. I was afraid the picture might not come out right because sometimes he put his finger in front of the lens.

Other people were snapping pictures in the foyer too, and I was happy to be there enjoying the crowd. I was especially happy my teachers and friends saw Kevin with us, being a part of my family. After all, he was the father of my baby, my love, my fiancé, and my best friend.

Later, we went for ice cream, just Kevin and me. My parents were going to pick up the baby from the neighbor's and bring him home. I think they gave us this gift of time alone because they understood our need to bond with each other and learn how to be together again.

At the Friendly's that we liked to go to, I ordered a Swiss chocolate almond sundae. Kevin had a banana split. The air conditioning in the restaurant was cooling, and over ice cream, I told Kevin what the lawyer wanted me to do.

"Since you wouldn't sign the letter saying you're the baby's father, I have to take you to court." I took a bite of my gooey sundae.

"Do we have to talk about this now?" he asked.

"No, I guess not. It's just I want you to understand."

"Yeah, well, I don't." He sounded mad.

"If you signed the papers I wouldn't have to do this," I said.

"My parents won't let me sign anything."

"Right," I said. But I didn't get it. Why wouldn't they let him admit he was the father of his baby? It didn't make sense. Here he was with me, seeing his son, and yet he couldn't admit legally that he was the father?

"Why do you have to take me to court?" he asked.

"I guess it's the only way now to make sure little Kevin has a father."

Kevin looked up from his banana split. His eyes narrowed.

"I'm here, aren't I?"

"I know. But you know how I don't know who my real parents are since I'm adopted. I don't want my baby to have that same problem."

It was hard to explain, especially with Kevin getting angry at me. I didn't want to tell him that sometimes I felt certain he would be by my side, but other times I wasn't sure what to expect. Sometimes I was afraid I would be all alone. We finished out ice cream in an awkward silence.

On Saturday, my dad and Kevin put the baby's crib together, but it wasn't the one Kevin had promised to get from his parents. He never asked them, so my older cousin gave me a crib she'd used for her children. I loved watching Kevin working with my dad. I'd always be able to tell little Kevin when I put him to bed, *your daddy and your papa built this for you.*

We went out for breakfast later and then picked up our prom pictures at CVS. "Look at that handsome devil," Kevin said as he held up a picture of himself. I looked over his shoulder. It was true—Kevin's six foot, one frame filled the gray tux well, and his blue eyes sparkled in the picture.

"Not bad, not bad," I said and gave him a playful shove.

"Not bad? Come on! We should've been the king and the queen, we looked so good," he said.

I giggled. It wasn't as if the teachers and nuns chaperoning the prom would have wanted us to be king and queen—the one couple with a child born out of wedlock, the one couple who had sinned so obviously. But even though we didn't get that recognition at the prom, we felt beautiful to each other.

We left the store, and the sun was high, the air warming a perfect spring day. The trees were filled with their bright green leaves, and flowers were decked with their tender petals. Adorned with fresh smiles and hope, we held hands as we walked through the parking lot. I skipped like a little girl who believed in the promise of the warm days ahead.

Goodbye, Again

The rest of the weekend went by quickly. Kevin and I played tennis on Saturday afternoon at the courts in front of Barrows, my old elementary school. The lessons I'd had a few summers before helped. I was winning in games 5-2.

"You're better than I thought," Kevin said, after I won another game.

"Surprised?" I asked, smiling.

"No, but I'm just warming up," he said and bounced the ball before hitting it across the net. His mouth was set in a firm line, and I thought it was funny that he seemed so serious.

I could have beaten him. But there was something in the way he'd stopped laughing, stopped having fun, that didn't make winning worth it. I let him have the next two games, though I didn't make it obvious and kept the games close. But then I started getting pains in my lower stomach and we had to stop.

"Are you all right?" he asked when he saw me bent over with cramps.

"Yeah, I'm okay. My stomach hurts, though. Maybe I'm overdoing it." Our son was just three weeks old, and my doctor had told me to take it easy for six weeks.

"Maybe we shouldn't play anymore," Kevin said.

After that, we spent the rest of the day inside, watching TV up in my room and putting pennies into rolls. I wanted to save coins and open a bank account for little Kevin. I figured it was never too soon to plan for his future.

When it was time for the baby to eat, Kevin fed him using the breast milk I'd been storing in the freezer.

"You need to burp him," I said when half the bottle was gone.

He took the nipple out of the baby's mouth, and little Kevin's bottom lip pushed out in a pout and Kevin laughed.

"I don't think he wants to stop," Kevin said.

"He'd drink the whole bottle if you let him. But then he'd throw it all back up," I reminded him. Baby Kevin's projectile vomit was disgusting.

I loved sharing all of these moments with Kevin: feeding our son, burping him, changing him, getting him ready for bed. It seemed natural and normal—a life I could get used to.

But Sunday came, and after a graduation party at a friend's house, Kevin had to go back to school. We sat in the living room before he left, and he held his son. He held the baby's arms so that little Kevin was standing in his lap.

"Look how strong he is," Kevin said in a whisper. "I wish I didn't have to go," he added, and his voice cracked a little. It was like his goodbye the week before.

He sat in an armchair, and I snapped a picture of him saying goodbye to his son. Kevin had tears in his eyes, and so did I.

My parents stayed with the baby while I drove Kevin part way back so he wouldn't have so far to hitchhike. I ended up taking him to Rutland, Vermont, which was further than I'd planned to go. When we pulled onto the side of the road, we had another sad goodbye.

"Hey, don't cry," Kevin lifted my chin and kissed me gently on the lips. "Remember, you'll see me again this Saturday at my graduation. It's not even a week away."

That did make me smile.

"There, now that's better. I want to remember your pretty smile, not these tears," and he brushed a tear off of my cheek.

We kissed some more and then he got out of the car. I drove up the road a bit looking for a place to turn around. When I passed Kevin, he waved to me, and I waved back. Then in my rear view mirror I could see him, still waving as I drove away.

Later that night, he called to let me know that he was safe.

"When you come up on Saturday, bring me the mug from your prom. I forgot it again."

"That's not all you forgot."

"I know," he said. "I left one of my shirts for you, so you can smell me even when I'm not there."

"Very thoughtful," I said. "I'll probably bring it to bed with me."

"Great, my shirt gets to go to bed with you but not me."

"Maybe some day soon you'll get to come to bed with me too."

"Yeah, like the weekend of your prom, remember?"

"Of course, I remember. How could I forget falling asleep with you right next to me, holding me," I said softly.

"That was real nice," he said.

"Mmm," I said and closed my eyes, remembering how it felt to have his arms around me.

We talked for a long time, but I was getting tired and got off of the phone when little Kevin started crying.

"I got to go," I said. "Your son wants to eat again."

"I can hear him," Kevin said, and his voice sounded funny, like he was crying. "Can you give him a kiss for me before you put him to bed?"

"Of course I can. See you Saturday, then."

"Wait, don't go yet," he said. "I love you."

"I love you too," I said. "You know that."

"Yeah, I do. But I want you to know that I love you guys. Don't ever forget that. Even if it doesn't always seem it. I do. I always will."

My throat was starting to hurt. "Hey, you're going to make me cry," I said.

"Sorry," he said. "Okay, until Saturday, then. Get here early, okay? Maybe you can drive up with my parents. Give them a call this week."

We said our goodbyes and hung up the phone. I couldn't imagine calling his parents and asking for a ride when his dad wouldn't even say hello to me. I'd told Kevin about that night at the awards ceremony, but he didn't seem to remember.

Before I went to bed, I looked at the invitation to Kevin's graduation. The ceremony started at 9:45 a.m. I would have to get on the road by 6:30 in the morning. I put the invitation on my bureau, laid little Kevin in his crib, and kneeled down next to my bed to pray. I asked God for blessings and then put myself to bed. I held Kevin's shirt in my arms and smelled his sweet scent as I drifted off to sleep.

On Tuesday, I wrote two letters to Kevin. One was a funny, long letter, talking about the good times we'd had over the past two weekends and the fun we would have in the summer ahead. But the other letter was the one the lawyer said I should write.

Dear Kevin,

As you know, raising our baby, Kevin, is expensive. I'm therefore requesting $25 a week. I need your help.

Love,
Judith

It seemed strange writing such a short, terse letter to Kevin with nothing but a cold request for money. But it also seemed funny asking for twenty-five dollars. It was such a small amount, but I didn't want to be unreasonable. Kevin had summer classes at college. Still, he could get a part-time job, something to help with his child.

Maybe he could ask his parents to help him. They could certainly afford to help with their grandson. After all, they drove around in a Cadillac, and they owned their own company. They had a beautiful house with an in-ground pool. Why should all of the costs fall to my parents and me?

I felt uncomfortable mailing the two different letters. It was as if there were two versions of me. There was the carefree me who thought only of her heart and the love she had for her fiancé, and believed everything would work out. And then there was the other me, the rational one who doubted Kevin and saw the need for legal action.

This second me was the one that agreed to see a lawyer, the me that sensed that not everything Kevin said was true. I tried to hide from this second me, tried to push her away, shut her up when she started in with the doubt and confusion. I preferred the first one, who wanted to believe Kevin when he said that he would always be around.

But it had become harder to believe in him by the end of the pregnancy— all those months without a call or a letter, all those months when I felt like my heart was breaking. I had even wished myself dead, and if it hadn't been for my baby moving inside, I might have done something awful. Thankfully, I'd never gotten beyond hoping that some morning I wouldn't wake up.

With our baby's birth and Kevin's loving return to my life, I wanted to believe in him again. But I couldn't stop the doubts from resurfacing when he was away, so I did as the lawyer instructed and sent the letter off.

When I came home from my walk to the mailbox, the phone was ringing, and I ran to get it.

"Hey," I said when I heard Kevin's voice. "I just mailed you a couple of letters."

"You can't come on Saturday," he said, and his voice was hard.

"What do you mean, I can't come?" I wanted to think he was kidding, but his tone let me know he was serious.

"You just can't come. My parents said you can't come."

"But it's your graduation, and we had it all planned!"

"I'll call you when I get home, Saturday," he said and hung up the phone. He didn't tell me goodbye. He didn't tell me to kiss his son for him. He didn't tell me he loved me. I stood there with the phone in my hand, stunned.

Just like there were two mes—the one who believed in him and the one who doubted him—apparently there were two Kevins. There was the one who loved me and meant to be by my side with our son, and there was the one who did whatever his parents told him.

I went up into my room and cried. I couldn't believe he'd uninvited me. I cried for a long, long time. When I just couldn't cry anymore, I sat up on my bed. Little Kevin was asleep in his crib. It didn't bother him that we were uninvited. He was too young to understand any of it.

I wrote Kevin another letter and tried to explain my confusion:

Dear Kevin,

It seems like you're trying to live in two worlds. In one of those worlds you have Kevin and me, and you love us and hold us and tell us you'll always be there. But then, in the other world you are a little boy who only listens to his parents.

I wanted to believe in you, to trust that you would be there in the end. It's what you've always said in your letters and whenever you saw me. But then because I asked you to acknowledge that you are the father of my baby, suddenly I didn't hear from you for almost three months. It was like you had dropped off the face of the earth. I had to go through the end of my pregnancy alone.

But then you came back to me, and your love seemed stronger than ever. You were there for my senior prom, my graduation, and you were proud to be by my side, proud to hold your son in your arms.

Now, you've uninvited us to your graduation, cutting us off like we mean nothing to you. I don't understand what could have changed from the time I dropped you off on Sunday night to today, Tuesday. Did you suddenly stop loving us in two days?

I'm so confused. You're going to receive three letters: one so full of fun, one the lawyer asked me to send, and this one. I just feel so sad, and I wonder what you're feeling? You sounded cold on the phone, today. It was like it wasn't even you. I don't know who it was. Who are you?

You know it was one thing when it was just me that you were hurting. I guess I could take the on again, off again relationship that seemed to be us. So long as you kept coming back, I could wait. I love you so much it hurts when you're not around. But I could take that hurt, knowing you would come back.

Now, it's different. I have your son, and he's just a tiny baby. You can't hurt him now with your coming and going, but what about as he gets older? Are you going to keep coming in and out of his life? I don't understand how you can just cave in to your parents' demands. Don't you love us enough to stand up for us?

I'll be waiting for your phone call on Saturday—that is, if you really plan to call me.

Love,

Judith

There, I'd said it. I put the letter in an envelope, mailed it, and waited.

I didn't have to wait long. On Friday, I received a short note back from Kevin. Inside, on a small slip of paper he'd written that he didn't have a job so he wouldn't be sending me money. He signed it *Love, Kevin.*

That's it. That's all he had to say? I was surprised that he'd signed it Love, Kevin, and part of me still wanted to hope. If he could sign his letter with love, maybe that meant something. Maybe he really did love us. I wanted to believe he always would.

Saturday came, and I felt so depressed. All day long, I kept looking at the clock. I even woke up early, as if I needed to get little Kevin ready, as if we were going to hop in the car and drive to graduation. When it was the time that Kevin was graduating, I went to my room and cried. Then, I tried to figure out what time he'd get home.

I figured there would be a celebration for the graduates and their families, so they'd probably get home by late afternoon or early evening. I made some coffee and sat at the kitchen table watching the clock and waiting. But the phone never rang.

After supper, I took little Kevin out for a stroll. We walked up past Kevin's old school, and while I was out, I saw Kevin's cousin. He waved, and it all seemed so surreal. The baby I was walking was related to him, so in a way Kevin's cousin was my relative too. But no one in Kevin's family thought of us that way. In fact, I was pretty sure they were trying not to think of us at all.

Gone

After Kevin's graduation day, I filled my days with activity to try and keep my mind off what had happened. I went to the beach with friends, welcomed more visitors to meet my baby, and stayed busy taking care of little Kevin. But it was nearly impossible to fill every minute of the day, and in the quiet moments, I thought of Kevin.

I knew he was home with his family and close enough to visit us. But my phone wasn't ringing, and I hadn't called him, either. It made me sad that he didn't want to see us, but I had to focus on my son. Alone, I took baby Kevin to his first doctor's appointment.

He was a month old. The doctor was pleased with his growth and told me to keep doing what I was doing. Little Kevin was healthy in every way and weighed a hardy twelve pounds. I was happy to learn I was doing a good job with him.

When I left the doctor's office, I buckled the baby in his car seat and got into the car. I decided I'd write to Kevin when I got home and tell him how much his son was growing. I wanted to share every detail about our son, and I wanted to share time together as a family again. I wished I knew how to make those daydreams come true. I was thinking about how special it was when the three of us were together when I put the car in reverse and backed up.

The sound of metal on metal surprised me. I thought I'd checked in the rearview mirror, but maybe I only glanced at Kevin's car seat, making sure he was okay. I looked in the mirror and saw that I had backed into another car. I put my car in park and sat there with my heart racing, and suddenly my whole life felt like a car crash.

My car's bumper had a small dent, but the other car had a good-sized one. I went up to the nearest house and knocked. No one answered, and I'd left Kevin in his car seat. I couldn't desert him while I went up and down the street trying to figure out who the car belonged to, so I wrote a short note: *I'm sorry that I hit your car. Please call me.* I put my phone number on the note and stuck it under the windshield wiper. Then I got back in my car. Shaking, I looked carefully many times before I finally put it in reverse.

That Wednesday, my mom, the baby, and I went to Greenfield District Court. I remembered being there with my business law class and felt nervous coming for my own real problem this time. We met our lawyer there, and he helped us file the complaint against Kevin, who would get a summons to court in the mail. After we filed the complaint with a court clerk, the lawyer sat down with us to discuss what would happen next. He told me he wouldn't be in court with us. The district attorney would take over the case because non-support of a child was a criminal offense. He told me to bring the baby and to be ready to talk in front of the judge.

I sat quietly on the bench as Mr. Moseley explained everything. "Judith, does this make sense to you?" he asked.

I wanted to scream, *No, none of this makes sense!* Instead, I just nodded my head.

"All right, I'll go over the details with the D.A. He'll want to meet with you before court, so plan on arriving an hour early."

On the drive home, my mom said, "You're awfully quiet, honey."

"I can't believe it's come to this," I said.

"Well, if he'd just sign the paperwork, we wouldn't have to go through this."

I didn't feel like talking about it, so I put my head back on the seat.

"That's a good idea. You should rest," my mom said.

On Saturday, a week after Kevin's graduation, I spent the whole day inside. He said he'd call as soon as he got home from graduation, and here it was a week later and still no word. Not a call. Not a letter.

I stayed up in my room with baby Kevin. I didn't even get dressed. I took out all the letters Kevin had written to me and read them one by one. While I read them, it was as if I could hear his voice. I brought them to my nose so that I could smell the soap he'd rubbed on them, and it was almost like being with him—smelling him, hearing him—but that just made me even sadder. I smiled when I read some of his sweet words but cried when I finished and remembered that I was alone.

Another week went by, and then at 11:59 p.m. on Saturday June 14, the phone rang.

"Hello?" I said into the receiver. I had just gotten baby Kevin to sleep and was in the kitchen getting a drink of water.

"So can a man come down and see his son on Father's Day, or what?"

"Kevin," I said softly. I was so glad to hear his voice, I didn't care that he sounded drunk.

"I'll be there in ten minutes," he said.

"Where are you?"

He told me he was at Trevor's and that he'd see me soon. I looked at the clock on the stove. 12:02 a.m. Father's Day.

I waited in the living room, and when I heard a car pull up, I went to the door. But it was my brother, so I sat back down on the couch.

"What are you doing?" he asked.

"Kevin's coming over," I said and smiled.

"Judith, when are you going to realize he's not worth it?" He didn't say it cruelly but like he was just trying to warn me.

I didn't answer. He was saying something I didn't want to hear.

"You'll see," he said and walked upstairs shaking his head.

Fifteen minutes had gone by, and I started to doubt Kevin would show. Maybe this was his idea of a joke. But then I heard a car, and suddenly the doorbell was ringing, and he and Trevor were standing in the doorway. Kevin picked me up in a bear hug and nuzzled my hair.

"I missed you," he said. I could smell beer on his breath.

"Missed you more," I murmured. It was strange holding him as if two very hard weeks hadn't passed, as if he hadn't uninvited me to his graduation.

"Come on in," I said, breaking away from our hug.

We sat in the living room, and I lit a cigarette.

"I thought you quit," Kevin said, sounding irritated.

"I cut back," I fibbed. "Things have been stressful. Hey, did you get my letters?" I'd refrained from calling him when he hadn't called me, but I'd sent him short letters every couple of days. I'd even put in some pictures for him.

"What letters?" he asked. He said he hadn't received any. Not one. He thought his mother must have been taking them. That made me angry. Did she read the letters? Look at the pictures? Or did she just toss them into the trash when she saw my handwriting and return address?

"Where's my son?" Kevin asked.

"Upstairs sleeping," I said.

"Can we go see him?"

My parents were already in bed. I didn't think it would be a good idea for us to go traipsing up the stairs and wake them. "I'll go get him and bring him down."

Kevin took him from me when I came back. He showed him off to Trevor, holding the baby high up in the air and saying, "Look at my boy!"

The baby was crying, and though Kevin looked proud and happy, I didn't like what I was seeing. He wasn't supporting the baby's head properly, and it was wobbling back and forth, flopping forward.

"You're going to hurt him! Here, let me take him." I lifted the baby out of his hands. Kevin's breath smelled so strong. I didn't know how drunk he was, but I knew I didn't want him dropping our son.

"Hey, wait a minute," he protested. "You always get to hold him!"

"Okay, okay, let me get him settled first. I'll just nurse him for a minute." The baby was really fussy by now. Trevor said he'd wait outside in the car. I gave the baby my breast and he quieted right down.

Kevin sat down next to me on the couch and touched his son's cheek. He gazed at his baby and then me.

"I love you guys," he said, and his words slurred a bit.

"We love you too," I said.

I wanted to ask him why he hadn't bothered to call, but I didn't feel like getting in an argument with him. He was drunk. Besides, what reason could there be? What reason would I find acceptable? There wasn't one.

He stayed until 1:30 in the morning. I brought up the baby's christening, and he said he wanted his baby baptized as soon as possible. So we talked about some tentative dates. Then, he said he had to go and was gone.

After he left, I couldn't go to bed until I'd changed the baby's diaper, nursed him, and put him down for the night. Once I'd done those things, though, I lay awake. I kept seeing Kevin and reliving the past hour in my mind. It felt good to be in his arms, but I kept thinking about how he'd held our son, how he could have really hurt him.

I also thought about how Kevin told me he'd be there for the baptism, and I imagined us in church together with a priest pouring water over our son's forehead. I imagined the conversations we'd have with family at the party, how everyone would wish us blessings and love. It was almost like a dream, a beautiful dream.

192

The Courtroom

The next time I saw Kevin was in court.

"All rise," the court clerk said when the judge entered the room.

Everyone stood until the judge had seated himself. When our case was called, Kevin and his lawyer walked to the front of the room. I went forward with the baby in my arms and stood beside the district attorney. Before court started, I'd given him my letters from Kevin. They would be used as evidence. The judge called the two lawyers to the bench and they conferred briefly. Kevin glanced over at me and the baby, and I smiled, but he didn't smile back.

"Is this the child?" the judge asked, addressing me.

"Yes, your Honor," I answered clearly and calmly, but I was shaking.

"Is there any chance that the two of you will get back together?" he asked.

"I hope so," I said. "I still love the baby's father very much."

It felt crazy standing in the courtroom, telling this man in black robes that I loved Kevin and hoped we could still be together. But it was true, and standing there, I felt like the truth was necessary.

His lawyer was old with thinning white hair and a large belly. He interjected, "No, there's no chance of that."

How could he know that? What did he know about the love Kevin had for me and our baby?

"He's been ordered not to have any contact with the girl or the baby," he added, and I assumed he meant by Kevin's parents.

"Is there a reason you can't support your child?" the judge asked, addressing Kevin this time. Peering over metal rim glasses, he looked stern but spoke in a calm, nice manner.

"He's going to be a student next year," the lawyer said. "Actually, he's part of the summer program—"

"Excuse me, Mr. Farn," the judge said, interrupting. "Is there any reason you keep answering my questions when I am directing them to your client, Mr. O'Brien?"

"I represent Mr. O'Brien's parents," he said.

"Approach the bench, please," the judge said in a different, sharper tone.

"You may sit down," the judge said to Kevin and me, and his voice softened when he spoke to us.

Kevin's lawyer and the D.A. talked with the judge. His calm manner seemed to change with them, and from where I sat, it looked like he was angry with Kevin's lawyer, Mr. Farn. I couldn't hear what they were saying, but the judge pointed a finger at him and raised his voice.

"Stop wasting this court's time!" he said loudly. I wondered what he meant by that.

The court adjourned for a short recess, and I went with the D.A. to his office.

"Apparently, Kevin's lawyer is representing Kevin's parents," the D.A. told me.

"Yeah, I heard Mr. Farn say that," I replied. "But what does that mean?"

"Well, for one thing, it means the judge is angry." The D.A. laughed when he said this, and his smile was nice. I was confused and it must have showed because he continued. "Kevin's eighteen, and the judge thinks he should have his own lawyer. This isn't his parents' case. It's about Kevin paying support."

"Oh," I said. But I still wasn't sure how this would impact our case. "I only wanted Kevin to admit that he's our baby's father."

"Right, I know that. So when I told the judge that and then told him I had all those letters and cards from Kevin where he talks about his baby and says the two of you were engaged, the judge blew up at Mr. Farn."

Now I understood why the judge thought this was all a waste of the court's time. I thought so too.

The recess ended, and we went back into the courtroom.

Again the court clerk said, "All rise" when the judge entered the room.

He called the lawyers back to the bench, and then everything was over in a few short minutes.

"That's it," the D.A. said as he came over to me. "Kevin's going to sign. Apparently, he never wanted to deny that he's the father of your baby. He was only going along with what the lawyer had advised his parents."

Relief washed over me when I realized that it wasn't Kevin's decision to refuse signing papers for his son. "That's wonderful news," I said.

"Yes, but the bad news is that Kevin's parents have forbidden him to have any contact with you. Not by phone, not by letter, not at all. They made it a condition if he wanted to go to college."

We were walking down a hall when he told me this, and then Kevin went by with his lawyer. As they passed by, Kevin looked at me, and I searched his eyes, trying to figure out if I could see any love there. I thought I did, like his eyes were showing me what he really felt inside.

I waved, but he didn't wave back. He left the courthouse without looking back at me or his son, and I stood there holding baby Kevin feeling lost and broken. Kevin was leaving, and though he'd finally signed the papers, it was clear that what we had was gone.

I waited to cry until I was in the car. I got little Kevin fastened into his car seat, and then I got into the driver's seat. I let the tears come, then, and they streamed down my face. Once I started, I couldn't stop. There was so much to cry for.

I cried for the lost dreams of a life with Kevin. I cried for my lost youth. I cried for the emptiness I felt inside. And I cried because I felt utterly alone. I cried and I cried.

Then I heard baby Kevin fussing in the back seat. I'd been sitting in the court parking lot for many long minutes. I wasn't sure how long I'd sat there, but besides the wetness from my tears, there was also the wetness of perspiration. The car was hot and little Kevin was hot too.

It's not just about you anymore, a little voice inside my head reminded me. It might have been my own voice, a kind of internal lecture, or it might have been a gentle whisper from God, His spirit sent to help me, nudging me and saying: *Sitting here in this parking lot crying isn't going to change anything. You've been crying long enough.*

I had been crying for a long time, and not just in the parking lot but also at home when I didn't hear from Kevin, when his letters didn't appear in my mailbox, when the phone didn't ring.

It was as if I thought my happiness depended on Kevin and what he did. But that wasn't going to help me or my son. It was one thing to wallow in sadness when it was only me. Things were different now that I had Kevin's baby. It was time I started acting differently.

Sitting outside the courthouse, I began to realize I was going to have to rely on myself and my family. I wouldn't be able to rely on Kevin or his family. I should have seen it sooner, but I had wanted to believe in him. I'd wanted to believe in all his promises.

But the promise for my future and my baby's future rested in the palms of my own hands. I was going to need to put those palms together in prayer and try to begin figuring out some things. I started the car and drove home, and on the way, I thought, *I need to make a new plan.*

Moving On

My action plan: 1. Get a job. 2. Go to college. The two items on my to-do list were short and to the point. I needed money, and I needed an education. I didn't want to depend totally on my parents' help, so it was time to find a job.

That part of my action plan was easy. I went back to the grocery store where I'd worked part-time for several years and asked to speak to the manager. Mr. Dionne took me to his office above the courtesy booth.

"What can I do for you, today, Judith?" he asked.

From that vantage point, you could see the whole store, the customers taking products from the shelves and putting them into their shopping carriages, and the workers taking grocery items from pallets and putting them onto the shelf.

"I was wondering if I could come back to work for you," I said.

"Well, you were always a good worker," he said. "We were disappointed to lose you when you left before."

I told him I had a son now, and that I planned to work for them for a long time. He hired me back on the spot, and I was assigned to the registers that Saturday. I'd always done well there, moving customers through quickly, smiling and thanking them for shopping with us. He told me that if I worked hard there might be a spot for me in the courtesy booth. He'd been considering me for that position before I left.

I was flattered. Cashing checks for customers at the courtesy booth, counting money during a work shift as the cashiers' drawers came in, and balancing their drawers at the end of the night was an important job. It was good to be hired back, and it was even better to know that Mr. Dionne valued me and already had plans for me.

But working in a grocery store for the rest of my life was not what I'd dreamed of doing. I had always dreamed about being a writer. I'd written poetry since I was in grade school and some stories too. All through school, I'd planned to major in English at college, go to graduate school, and then teach at the college level. I figured I would have time to write my own stories and poems during the summer months.

But becoming a professor seemed too big a dream for my life right now. It was hard enough just caring for my infant son by myself. How would I handle caring for him, plus working and going to college? I didn't know the answer to that question, and I didn't know how I would juggle the various roles— mother, worker, student—but I knew I had to find a way.

Making plans gave me a new path to concentrate on. But if I thought that having a plan of action would make being alone any easier, I was wrong.

The summer went by, and most of my time was filled with caring for little Kevin. I found some time for fun and visited with friends before they went off to college. It was hard to see them preparing to leave when I was staying behind. I had to remind myself I would go to college too, just not this fall.

At night, when my son was asleep, I still thought about big Kevin. I spent a lot of time remembering the things we'd done together. Sometimes I enjoyed turning these memories over in my mind, soft pages of a book I carried inside my heart. Other times, though, the memories played over and over again in my head, and I couldn't make them stop. I didn't want to forget any of the memories, but I wanted to touch them when I wanted to, and sometimes it seemed like they possessed me.

I would replay the story of Kevin and me—young lovers torn apart by his family—and our lovely baby who might mend the tear. But when I came to the last part, I wanted to rewrite the story, make a better ending, different from the reality of being alone.

Kevin had told me over and over again he would be there for us in the end. But what end did he mean? He was going off to college, and I was left alone with my son, working a part-time job at a grocery store.

Sometimes I wondered if I had done the right thing. Maybe if I hadn't gone to the lawyer, Kevin and I would have found a way to stay together. Maybe his parents would have learned to accept the fact that we loved each other. Maybe Kevin and I would have been making plans for our wedding. Maybe, maybe, maybe.

But I couldn't change the past, couldn't turn the clock back to change what I had done. I lived at home, so my parents helped a lot, and when I worked nights and weekends, they watched little Kevin for me.

The best part of my job was that I got out of the house. After spending all day alone with the baby, I needed a break, and working was my break. The store had many employees around my age. I was only seventeen, but during the day when I was watching my son, I didn't feel like a teenager anymore. It was only at work that I could almost feel young again.

On Friday and Saturday nights, the kids I worked with would grab a bite to eat or go to a party. Most of the time, I had to go home. But sometimes I'd go along, and for a few hours I was free from the responsibilities of motherhood. I loved my baby, but I needed some time for myself.

When I looked at my son, I saw the gift of love I'd shared with Kevin, and the love he shared with me. Here was something solid, something tangible, to hold up as a testimony to our love, real living proof of our time together. Our child was something that wasn't going to go away.

Yet the months went by and I never heard from Kevin. It seemed he was able to forget us, but I knew I would never forget him. I had the diamond he had given me tucked away in a drawer. I had the stacks of letters he'd written. And I had his living child.

The cool days of autumn gave way to the snowy days of winter, and my old cheerleading friends came home for winter break. We got together for coffee or lunch, and it was good to hear their stories about dorms and roommates, and the new young men they were meeting in their classes.

In comparison, my stories about taking care of baby Kevin and working at the local grocery store seemed boring. But I had a secret. I had sent away for a packet from the University of Massachusetts, and inside it was an application form. A booklet described campus living and the courses offered. I wouldn't be able to live on campus and would have to commute from home. But I could go.

I had held onto my dream of going to college, and now my dreams of getting an education and a secure life for my son and me were beginning to take shape. I filled out the application, wrote the required essay, and got my sealed transcripts from St. Anne's.

When I put all the material in the envelope, it was like I'd compiled all my hopes, all my dreams, all the little pieces of myself. I bundled baby Kevin up in his snowsuit and secured him in his car seat. We drove downtown to the post office, and I was nervous, thinking about how much my future, and my son's, depended on what I'd placed in that envelope.

I handed the packet over, and even though it was winter, my palms were sweating. I paid for the stamps that would take my package to the admissions office, then turned and walked out the door.

When I mailed my application, I had faith I was stepping into my dreams and embarking on a journey that would move my life and my son's life forward. This new direction would require a continued belief in myself and all the gifts that God had given me.

Now that the package was on its way, I felt better, and feelings of anticipation swelled inside me. I walked down the steps, knowing that the essay I'd written was solid and true, a piece of myself, a part of my story told. In it I told about being a young mother alone, about struggling to survive and trying to hold onto my hope of getting an education.

I held that dream, and in my mind I saw myself walking onto campus. I saw the rolling lawns and the large buildings with pillars—all there waiting for me—and I saw myself walking up the granite steps and opening those doors to my future.

EPILOGUE
The Next Year

Some of my friends went to the same college that Kevin attended, and when I visited them, I always looked for him. One time when I was there, I called him, and we arranged to meet at his dorm. I wanted to find out what it would be like to see him after long months apart.

When he opened the door, he looked the same but thinner. He let me in, and right away he wanted to know about our baby. I told him how little Kevin had started to walk and babble—in May he would turn one year old—and Kevin listened. At one point, we were sitting close on his bed, and he kissed me and said he still loved us. But it had been so long without any letters or calls from him that I wasn't sure how to take those words.

He showed me a dream-catcher his sister Julie had made for him. The small wooden hoop had a web of crisscrossed strings with a hole in the center. It was supposed to keep out evil spirits while you slept but let good dreams come through. I thought about the good dreams Kevin and I had. Maybe we should've had a dream catcher of our own—or some other lucky charm. Maybe then we could've made things work.

Going to see him at his college was like a big adventure, a quest where I went searching to find out how Kevin could live his life as if his baby and I didn't exist. But the trip only made me realize that perhaps there weren't any answers. We were each living out our lives separately now.

I went home and continued to raise our son alone. Then, late on baby Kevin's birthday, the phone rang. It was Kevin calling from college, singing.

In a boisterous voice, he sang the birthday song. I held the phone away from my ear, he was so loud. "Do you know who this is?" he asked when he finished.

"Of course I know who it is."

We talked for a while, and from his slurred speech, I knew he was drunk. I could hear his friends calling out to him in the background, and there was loud laughter and music. He told me they were having a bash in honor of his son, but it sounded like a college party to me. We didn't stay on the line long because he was drunk, and I didn't have much to say. But before we hung up, he asked me to call him when he came home for his summer break. I said I would.

When I called him at his house a few weeks later, we talked for just a few minutes. He kept his comments short and clipped, like someone else was in the room and he couldn't talk. It had been nearly a year since our day in court, and I told him I could use a little help supporting our baby. I figured he'd be working for his father that summer, and I thought it was time he contributed something.

He said he understood and would be in touch with me soon.

But that didn't happen, and then the phone company called my house to ask questions about the call Kevin made on the baby's birthday. Apparently, he'd charged it to someone else's number like he used to do back in prep school. It seemed to me that he was stuck in a place of immaturity. He didn't think he needed to take responsibility for anything.

After that when I tried calling his house, he wasn't home—or so his family members always said. But one time, he actually answered. When he heard my voice, he just hung up the phone. I couldn't believe it. I was so angry that I called right back, but his brother answered and said he wasn't home. I guess the whole gang wanted to play games.

His brother asked if he could take a message.

"Yes, you can," I said. "Tell Kevin if he wants to be so childish and hang up on me because I asked him to start helping with support, then I have no choice but to take him back to court. I need help with our son!"

I was steaming. I had let the non-support claim drop that first time in court because I was still thinking Kevin would help out, that he'd find a way to be there for us. But that clearly wasn't the case.

I started a new non-support claim, and since he'd already acknowledged paternity, we got a quick court date. At the end of July, I took baby Kevin to the courthouse once again.

I saw Kevin at the back of the courtroom when we went inside, and he asked us to sit with him. We did, and Kevin watched his baby, smiled at him, and even played with him for a little bit. But when the baby started crying, the court clerk asked me to take him outside until our case got called.

When our time came, we stood together in front of the judge, the same judge we'd had the year before. I held the baby in my arms. Kevin pled guilty to non-support and said he'd pay twenty dollars a week. The court said twenty-five dollars and put him on probation for six years.

While we were standing there, the judge asked if I had married someone else.

I said, "No. Actually I still care very much about the baby's father." And it was true, I did. But it was also true that I had started to date a man from work who didn't mind that I was a single mom and who treated me and my son kindly.

We left the courtroom, and Kevin held the door for us like a gentleman.

We had to go to the probation office to sign some papers, and while I was in there I said, "You have to realize I didn't want to go to court. I tried my best to settle out of court. I really did."

Kevin didn't say anything.

So I said again, "Kevin, you have to realize that. You gave me no choice."

He nodded his head, and I was glad that he seemed to understand.

Outside, as I walked across the parking lot, I saw Kevin standing by his lawyer's car. When he saw me, he waved.

I waved back and said, "Kevin, take care of yourself." He didn't answer, and then I left.

In September, while I was getting ready to go to college, I wrote in my journal:

> I'm writing this as quickly as I can since there are many other
> things I should be doing. I start school next week, and I am nervous
> and excited. Kevin has been sending $25 every week, so that's good.
> He goes back to school this week also, so this would have been the
> last weekend he could've gotten in touch with me. I didn't expect to
> hear from him. His birthday is coming up at the end of the month,
> and I plan to send a card and a letter—nothing serious, just a casual
> letter saying hi. I don't want to put any pressure on him at all. It's
> odd after all that we've been through—I still love him. I guess I
> always will. I wonder if he still cares about me.

My dreams of a life with Kevin were gone, but I'd grown during my time with him. And in my time without him, I'd learned to recognize the hard truth of loss. But along with loss, I recognized there'd been real love too.

The love I shared with Kevin gave me little Kevin, and when I carried the baby inside of me, I knew all along I would keep him. That made me think about my birth mother and try to understand her more. She carried me inside too, and during those nine months, I'm sure she learned to love me the way I'd learned to love baby Kevin.

I don't know how she was able to give me up for adoption, but perhaps that was her great gift of love to me. By giving me away, she was choosing a sacrifice I found difficult to comprehend, but one she found necessary. Love requires much, and sometimes that includes sacrifice as well as faith.

She had to believe that what she was choosing was the best she could do for me, and I had to believe that what I was choosing for little Kevin was the best I could do for him. We each had found our way through pregnancy without the benefit of marriage, though we had come to different decisions. But I believe we both made our choices out of love.

I even believe that Kevin *did* love me and our son, and that perhaps some of his hard choices grew out of that love. Perhaps he just didn't think he could be a good enough father for our son. By stepping aside, he would allow us to find other, lasting love.

The thing about love is that it lasts beyond boundaries of time and space— when it exists, it doesn't die. Love remains true and pure somewhere in the particles of air floating about, in the spaces between breaths and molecules, in the places we can't see. The turning of the earth, with its tragedies and crises may make it seem otherwise, but love endures beyond years, beyond death. When I look back on my time with Kevin and my life since then, I know this belief is true. Faith, hope, and love sustained me, but the greatest was love—is always love.

ACKNOWLEDGEMENTS

So many people have encouraged me over the years that it is hard to know where to begin in thanking those folks. I have been well blessed with family, friends, and teachers, and I am grateful for their support.

I thank God daily for everything, and I thank my parents, who have passed from this world, for teaching me faith, hope, and love. Thank you to my husband Bill for loving me and understanding how difficult and necessary it was for me to write this book. Thank you to my sons Matt and Tim for continuing to bring joy into my life, and thank you to my brother Paul and my sister Ellen whom I love, and to all my extended family.

To Hilary Holladay and Jefferson Park Press, thank you for believing in me and my story—your support and encouragement inspired me to revise and revise. Thanks to Joshua Logsdon at Jefferson Park Press for his careful reading and suggestions that strengthened the book and to Lisa Wayand for her inspired design of the book. My heartfelt thanks go out to my friends who were readers or who listened to my plans and dreams: Carolyn Alessi, Beth Brassell, Jeanne Coleman, Rebecca Dakin-Quinn, Liza Crowley, Rita Rouvalis-Chapman, Paula Haines, Tammy Ryan, Jessica Banks, Mary Banks, Katie Baldwin, Terry Farish, Gina Moscato-Fucci, Bethany Phrakonekham, Maureen Dumont, the Keo family, Alison Gervais, and the young parents at the Cambodian Mutual Assistance Association—your thoughts, comments, and friendship were invaluable.

Thank you to the Dorset Writers' Colony, Wellspring House, and the Vermont Studio Center for providing wonderful spaces in which to think and create. Thank you to the Bread Loaf Writer's Conference, Emerson College, UMass Lowell, and the Institute of Children's Literature for the writing workshops and the many fine writing teachers who helped sharpen my skills.

Thank you to the West River Valley Poetry Group, the South Newfane Writers' Group, my friends at Our Lady of the Valley, my Circle of Friends, Cursillo, my friends at the Cambodian Mutual Assistance Association, and my friends at Lowell Adult Education—your good energy and friendships have supported me in many ways.

Thanks go out to the writers who offered constructive criticism, encouragement, and inspiration in the early years: Peggy Rambach, Karen Propp, Paul Marion, Jane Brox, Kathleen Aponick, Richard Farrell, Jay Atkinson, Ellen Bryant Voigt, Nancy Butts, and Ed Cyzewski. Thanks to writers I've shared workshop time with, and thanks also to the students I've had over the years—through teaching there is learning.

There are many others who have touched my life, including those from my childhood, high school, and college years. Thank you to those who have helped me stretch and grow. Please forgive me if I have forgotten anyone. My heart is full of gratitude and thanks.

AUTHOR'S NOTE

Judith Dickerman-Nelson became a mother at age seventeen. She later earned her B.A. in English from the University of Massachusetts in Lowell and her MFA in writing from Emerson College. She has taught writing to both college students and high school students, and for fifteen years worked with young parents at the Cambodian Mutual Assistance Association in Lowell, Massachusetts. Her poetry and other writings have appeared in numerous journals, magazines, and anthologies. She has attended the Bread Loaf Writer's Conference, the Vermont Studio Center, the Dorset Writer's Colony, and Wellspring House. She lives in Vermont with her husband and has two sons who both earned degrees in chemical engineering.